PRAISE FOR
THE FALLING WOMAN

"I loved Pat Murphy's novel THE FALLING WOMAN. It's a good story with a beautiful realized background and strong characters. What more could anyone want?"

—Kate Wilhelm

"THE FALLING WOMAN is a wonderful, subtle and thoughtful book. Its understated yet precise prose, its nuances of structure and theme, exemplify what is best in the New Fantasy, and with this book, Pat Murphy establishes herself as one of the field's most accomplished practitioners."

—Lucius Shepard

"Murphy splendidly captures the atmosphere and spirit of the dig, and adds a well-realized backdrop ... Impressive archaeological fantasy in dramatic Yucatan setting."

—*Kirkus Reviews*

"Pat Murphy has mixed fantasy, horror and contemporary realism in a literate and absorbing tale."

—*Chicago Sun Times*

PAT MURPHY

THE Falling Woman

A TOM DOHERTY ASSOCIATES BOOK

THE FALLING WOMAN

Copyright © 1986 by Pat Murphy

All rights reserved, including the right to reproduce this book or portions thereof in any form.

First printing: November 1986
First mass market printing: September 1987

A TOR Book

Published by Tom Doherty Associates, Inc.
49 West 24 Street
New York, N.Y. 10010

Cover art by Peter Scanlon

ISBN: 0-812-54620-2
CAN. ED.: 0-812-54621-0

Library of Congress Catalog Card Number: 86-50322

Printed in the United States of America

0 9 8 7 6 5 4 3 2 1

For my mother,
a remarkable woman who taught me many things,

and

For Richard,
who swam with me in the sacred cenote at Dzibilchaltún

This is the true account, when all was vague, all was silence, without motion and the sky was still empty. This is the first account, the first narrative. There was neither man nor beast, no bird, fish nor crab, no trees, rocks, caves nor canyons, no plants and no shrubs. Only the sky was there.

—*Popol Vuh* of the Quiché Maya

Notes for City of Stones
by Elizabeth Butler

There are no rivers on Mexico's Yucatán peninsula. The land is flat and dry and dusty. The soil is only a few feet deep, a thin layer of arable land over a shelf of hard limestone. The jungle that covers the land is made up of thin-leafed trees and thorny bushes that turn yellow in the long summer.

There are no rivers, but there is water hidden deep beneath the limestone. Here and there, the stone has cracked and cool water from beneath the earth has reached the surface and formed a pool.

The Maya called such pools *ts'not*—an abrupt, angular sort of a word. The Spanish conquerors who came to the Yucatán softened the word. Cenotes, they called these ancient wells. Whatever the name, the water is cold; the pools are deep.

Hidden beneath the water are fragments of the old Mayan civilization: broken pieces of pottery, figurines, jade ornaments, and bits of bone—sometimes human bone. In the mythos of the Maya, the cenotes were places of power belonging to the Chaacob, the gods who come from the world's four corners to bring the rain.

Dzibilchaltún, the oldest city on the Yucatán peninsula, was built around a cenote known as Xlacah. By Mayan reckoning, people settled in this place in the ninth katun. By the Christian calendar, that is about one thousand years before the death of Christ. But Christian reckoning seems out of place here. Despite the efforts of Spanish friars, Christianity sits very lightly on the land.

The ruins of Dzibilchaltún cover over twenty square miles. Only the central area has been mapped. One structure, a box-shaped building on a high platform, has been rebuilt. Archaeologists call this building the Temple of the Seven Dolls because seven doll-sized ceramic figures were found buried in its floor. Archaeologists do not know what the ancient Maya called the building, nor what the Maya did in this temple.

The Temple of the Seven Dolls offers the best view of the surrounding area—a monotonous expanse of thirsty trees and scrubby bushes. Near the Temple of the Seven Dolls, the jungle has been cleared away, and mounds of rock rise from the flat land. Fragments of walls and sections of white limestone causeways are barely visible through the grass and soil. The view would be bleak were it not for the enormous sky, an unbroken expanse of relentless blue.

Do not look for revelations in the ancient ruins. You will find here only what you bring: bits of memory, wisps of the past as thin as clouds in the summer, fragments of stone that are carved with symbols that sometimes almost make sense.

—— Chapter One: Elizabeth Butler ——

"**I** dig through ancient trash," I told the elegantly groomed young woman who had been sent by a popular women's magazine to write a short article on my work. "I grub in the dirt, that's what I do. I dig up dead Indians. Archaeologists are really no better than scavengers, sifting through the garbage that people left behind when they died, moved on, built a new house, a new town, a new temple. We're garbage collectors really. Is that clear?" The sleek young woman's smile faltered, but she bravely continued the interview.

That was in Berkeley, just after the publication of my last book, but the memory of the interview lingered with me. I pitied the reporter and the photographer who accompanied her. It was so obvious that they did not know what to do with me.

I am an old woman. My hair is gray and brown—the color of the limestone monuments raised by the Maya one thousand years ago. My face has weathered through the years—the sun has etched wrinkles around the eyes, the wind has carved lines. At age fifty-one, I am a troublesome old woman.

My name is Elizabeth Butler; my friends and students call me Liz. The University of California at Berkeley lists me as a lecturer and field archaeologist, but in actuality I am a mole, a scavenger, a garbage collector. I find it somewhat surprising, though gratifying, that I have managed to make my living in such a strange occupation.

Often, I argue with other people who grub in the dirt. I have a reputation for asking too many embarrassing questions at conferences where everyone presents their findings. I have always enjoyed asking embarrassing questions.

Sometimes, much to the dismay of my fellow academics, I write books about my activities and the activities of my colleagues. In general, I believe that my fellow garbage collectors regard my work as suspect because it has become quite popular. Popularity is not the mark of a properly rigorous academic work. I believe that their distrust of my work reflects a distrust of me. My work smacks of speculation; I tell stories about the people who inhabited the ancient ruins—and my colleagues do not care for my tales. In academic circles, I linger on the fringes where the warmth of the fire never reaches, an irreverent outsider, a loner who prefers fieldwork to the university and general readership to academic journals.

But then, the popularizers don't like me either. I gave that reporter trouble, I know. I talked about dirt and potsherds when she wanted to hear about romance and adventure. And the photographer—a young man who was more accustomed to fashion-plate beauties than to weatherworn archaeologists—did not know how to picture the crags and fissures of my face. He kept positioning me in one place, then in another. In the end, he took photographs of my hands: pointing out the pattern on a potsherd, holding a jade earring, demonstrating how to use a mano and metate, the mortar and pestle with which the Maya grind corn.

My hands tell more of my history than my face. They are tanned and wrinkled and I can trace the paths of veins along their backs. The nails are short and hard, like the claws of some digging animal, and the wrists are marked with vertical white scars, a permanent record of my attempt to escape my former husband and the world in the most drastic way possible. The magazine photographer was careful to position my hands so that the scars did not show.

I believe that the reporter who interviewed me expected tales of tombs, gold, and glory. I told her about heat, disease, and insect bites. I described the time that my jeep broke an axle fifty miles from anywhere, the time that all my graduate students had diarrhea simultaneously, the time that the local municipality stole half my workmen to work on a local road. "Picture postcards never show the bugs," I told her. "Stinging ants, wasps, fleas, roaches the size of your hand. Postcards never show the heat."

I don't think that I told her what she wanted to hear, but I enjoyed myself. I don't think that she believed all my stories. I think she still believes that archaeologists wear white pith helmets and find treasure each day before breakfast. She asked me why, if conditions were as horrible as I described, why I would ever go on another dig. I remember that she smiled when she asked me, expecting me to talk about the excitement of discovery, the thrill of uncovering lost civilizations. Why do I do it?

"I'm crazy," I said. I don't think she believed me.

It was three weeks into the field season at Dzibilchaltún that Tony, Salvador, and I held a council of war. We sat at a folding table at one edge of the central plaza, an area of hard-packed dirt surrounded by mud-and-wattle huts. The plaza served as dining hall, classroom, meeting place, and, at that moment, conference room. Dinner was over and we lingered over coffee laced with aguardiente, a potent local brandy.

The situation was this. We had thirty men to do a job that would be difficult with twice that number. Our budget was tight; our time was limited. We had been at work for three weeks out of our allotted eight. So far our luck had been nonexistent. And the municipality had just commandeered ten of our workmen to patch potholes in the road between Mérida and Progreso. In the Yucatán, the season for road building coincides with the season for excavation, a brief period in the spring before the rains come. In five weeks— sooner if our luck was bad—the rains would come and our work would end.

"Shall I go talk to the commissioner of highways?" I said.

"I'll tell him that we need those men. I'm sure I could convince him."

Salvador took a drag on his cigarette, leaned back in his chair, and folded his arms. Salvador had been working on excavations since he was a teenager in Piste helping with the restoration of Chichén Itzá. He was a good foreman, an intelligent man who was respectful of his employers, and he did not like to tell me I was wrong. He stared past me.

I glanced at Tony. "I think that means no."

Tony grinned. Anthony Baker, my co-director on the excavation, was older than I was by just a few years. We had met nearly thirty years before at a Hopi dig in Arizona. He had been an affable, easygoing young man. He was still easygoing. His eyes were a startling shade of blue. His curly hair—once blond, now white—was sparse where it had been lush. His face was thin, grown thinner over the years, and sunburned as always. Each season he burned and peeled and burned again, despite all his efforts to block the sun. His voice was low and gravelly, a soft rough whiskey voice with a deep rumble in the throat, like the voice of a talking bear in a fairy tale.

"I'd guess you were right," he said to me.

"That's too bad," I said. "I was rather looking forward to barging into the commissioner's office. I can be rude to young men." I sipped my coffee. "It's one of the few compensations for growing old."

Salvador took another long drag on his cigarette. "I will talk to my cousin," he said at last. "My cousin will talk to the commissioner. He will reason with the commissioner." He glanced at me but did not unfold his arms. "It will cost some money."

I nodded. "We budgeted for that."

"Good."

"If it doesn't work, I can always go negotiate with the man," I said.

Salvador dropped the stub of his cigarette to the ground and crushed it out with a sandaled foot. No comment. Tony poured another shot of aguardiente into each cup.

The sun was setting. The hollow wailing of conch shell trumpets blown by Mayan priests rose over the trilling of the crickets and echoed across the plaza. I alone listened to the sweet mournful sound—neither Tony nor Salvador could hear the echoes of the past.

At a folding table on the far side of the plaza, three of the five graduate students who were working the dig this summer were playing cards. Occasionally, their laughter drifted across the plaza.

"The students are a good bunch this year," Tony commented.

I shrugged. "They're like every other bunch of students. Every year they seem to get younger. And they want to find a jade mask and a gold bracelet under every rock or else they want to have a mystical experience in the ruins when the full moon rises."

"Or both," Tony said.

"Right. Some hide it better than others, but they're all treasure hunters at heart."

"And we hide it better than any of them," he said. "We've been at it longer."

I glanced at his face, and could not continue pretending to be cynical when he was grinning like that. "I suppose you're right. Do you think this is the year that we'll find a tomb bigger than King Tut's and translate the hieroglyphics?"

"Why not?" he said. "I think it's a good idea."

We sat in the growing darkness and talked about the possibilities of the site. Tony, as always, was optimistic despite our limited success to date.

From 1960 to 1966 a research group from Tulane University surveyed just over half of the ceremonial center at Dzibilchaltún, completed extensive excavations in a number of structures, and dug test pits to sample some six hundred other structures. Unlike the Tulane group, we were concentrating on outlying areas rather than on the ceremonial center, expanding the surveyed and sampled area.

By the time the sun was completely down and the moon was rising, Tony and I were well into planning the third year of excavations. Salvador had wandered off, impatient with us for being more interested in next year's plans than tomorrow's work. We quit with the third year, and Tony wandered over to join the students for a time.

Tony always got along well with the students, drinking with them, sharing their troubles and laughing at their jokes. By the end of the summer, they would call him Tony and treat him with affection. Even at the end of the summer, I would be a stranger to them. I preferred it that way.

In the moonlight, I went for a stroll down to the sacred cenote, the ancient well that had once supplied water to the city. Along the way, I passed a woman returning from the well. She walked gracefully, one hand lifted to steady the water jug on her head. From the black and white pattern that decorated the rim of her jug, I guessed that she had lived during the Classic Period, around about A.D. 800.

I do not live entirely in the present. Sometimes, I think that the ghosts of the past haunt me. Sometimes, I think that I haunt them. We come together in the uncertain hours of dawn and dusk, when the world is on the edge between day and night.

When I wander through the Berkeley campus at dawn I smell the thin smoke of cooking fires that flared and died a thousand years ago. A shadow flits across the path before me—no, two shadows—little girls playing a game involving a ball, a hoop, a stick, and much laughter. For a moment, I hear them laughing, shrill as birds, and then the laughter fades.

A tall awkward young man in a dark green windbreaker, a student in my graduate seminar, hails me. We stand and talk—something about the coming midterm exam, something about the due date for a paper. I am distracted—an old Indian woman walks past, carrying a basket of herbs. The design of the basket is unfamiliar to me, and I study it as she trudges by.

"So, you think that would work?" the earnest young man is saying. He has been talking about the topic he has chosen for his final paper, but I have not been listening.

"Let's talk about it during my office hours this after-noon," I say. Students sometimes find me brusque, abrupt. I try to show interest in their concerns, but my attention is continually drawn away from them by apparitions of the past.

I have grown used to my ghosts. It's no worse, I suppose, than other disabilities: some people are nearsighted, some are hard-of-hearing. I see and hear too much and that distracts me from the business at hand.

Generally, the phantoms ignore me, busy with their own affairs. For these shadows, as for my students, the times are separate. The Indian village that I see is gone: past tense. The campus through which I walk is now: present tense. For others, there is no overlap between the two. I live on the border and see both sides.

The water of the cenote was cold and clear. The air beside the pool carried the scent of water lilies and wet mud. I stopped at the edge of the pool, sat down, and leaned back against a squared-off stone that had once been part of a structure.

Here and there, other stone temple blocks showed through the soil. Three thousand years ago, the Maya had built a temple here. One thousand years ago, they had abandoned the temple and retreated into the forest. No archaeologist knew why, and the ancient Maya were not saying. Not yet.

The heavy rains of a thousand springs had eroded the stones; the winds had blown dust over them. Grasses had grown in the dust, covering the rocks and hiding their se-crets. Trees had grown on the crest of the mound, and their twisted roots had tumbled and broken the stones. The jungle had reclaimed the land.

I liked this place. By day, I could watch the shadows of women draw water from the pool, slaves and peasants stoop-ing to fill rounded jars with clear water, hoisting the full vessels to their heads, and moving away with the stately grace required to balance the heavy jars. They talked and laughed and joked among themselves and I liked to listen.

The wind rippled the water, and the moonlight laid a pale

silver ribbon on the shining surface. Bats swooped low to
catch insects that hovered just above the pool. I saw a movement on the path that led to the cenote and waited. Perhaps
a slave sent to fetch water. Perhaps a young woman meeting
a lover.

I heard the soft slapping of sandals against rock as a
shadow crossed between me and the pool. The figure walked
with a slight limp. There was a bulkiness about the head that
suggested braided hair, a hint of feminine grace when the
figure stooped to touch the water. She turned, as if to continue along the path, then stopped, staring in my direction.

I waited. Crickets trilled all around me. A frog croaked,
but no frog answered. For a moment, I thought I had mistaken a woman of my own time for a shadow of the past. I
greeted her in Maya, a language I speak tolerably well after
ten long years of stammering and mispronunciation. My
accent is not good—I struggle with subtleties of tone and
miss the point of puns and jokes—but I can usually understand and make myself understood.

The person standing motionless by the edge of the pool did
not speak for a moment. Then she said, "I see a living
shadow. Why are you here?" By the sound of her voice, I
guessed her to be a woman about my age. She spoke Maya
with an ancient accent.

Shadows do not speak to me. For a moment, I sat silent.
Shadows come and go and I watch them, but they do not
speak, they do not watch me.

"Speak to me, shadow," said the woman. "I have been
alone so long. Why are you here?"

The crickets filled the silence with shrill cries. I did not
know what to say. Shadows do not talk to me.

"I stopped to rest," I said carefully. "It's peaceful here."

She was a shape in the darkness, no more than that. I
could make out no details. She laughed, a soft low sound like
water pouring from a jug. "Peace is not so easy to find. You
do not know this place if you find it peaceful."

"I know this place," I said sharply, resenting this shadow

for claiming I did not know a place that I considered my own. "For me, it is peaceful."

She stood motionless for a moment, her head cocked a little to one side. "So you think you belong here, shadow? Who are you?"

"They call me Ix Zacbeliz." When I was overseeing a dig at Ikil, the workmen had called me that; it meant "woman who walks the white road." The nickname was as close as I came to a Mayan name.

"You speak Maya," the woman said softly, "but do you speak the language of the Zuyua?" Her voice held a challenge.

The language of the Zuyua was an ancient riddling game. I had read the questions and answers in the *Books of Chilam Balam*, Mayan holy books that had been transcribed into European script and preserved when the original hieroglyphic books were destroyed. The text surrounding the questions suggested that the riddles were used to separate the true Maya from invaders, the nobility from the peasants. If I spoke the language of the Zuyua, I belonged. If not, I was an outsider.

The woman at the well spoke again, not waiting for my answer. "What holes does the sugarcane sing through?"

That was easy. "The holes in the flute."

"Who is the girl with many teeth? Her hair is twisted in a tuft and she smells sweet."

I leaned back against the temple stone, remembering the text from the ancient book. As I recalled, many of the riddles dealt with food. "The girl is an ear of corn, baked in a pit."

"If I tell you to bring me the flower of the night, what will you do?"

That one, I did not remember. I stared over her head and saw the first dim stars of evening. "There is the flower of the night. A star in the sky."

"And what if I ask you for the firefly of the night? Bring it to me with the beckoning tongue of a jaguar."

That one was not in the book. I considered the question, tapping a cigarette from my pack and lighting it with a match. The woman laughed. "Ah, yes—you speak the language of the Zuyua. The firefly is the smoking stick and the tongue of the jaguar is the flame. We shall be friends. I have been lonely too long.'' She cocked her head to one side but I could not see her expression in the darkness. ''You are looking for secrets and I will help you find them. Yes. The time has come.''

She turned away, stepping toward the path that led to the southeast, away from the cenote.

''Wait,'' I said. ''What's your name? Who are you?''

''They call me Zuhuy-kak,'' she said.

I had heard the name before, though it took me a moment to place it. Zuhuy-kak meant ''fire virgin.'' A few books referred to her; she was said to be the deified daughter of a Mayan nobleman. So they said. I have found books to be completely unreliable when it comes to identifying the shadows that I meet in the ruins.

With half-closed eyes, I leaned my head against the stone behind me and watched her go.

A modern psychiatrist—that shaman sans rattle and incense— would say that Zuhuy-kak was wish fulfillment and hallucination, brought on by stress, spicy food, aguardiente. If pressed, he might say, with waving of hands, that Zuhuy-kak— and the less talkative shadows that haunt me—are aspects of myself. My subconscious mind speaks to me through visions of dead Indians.

Or he might just say I'm mad.

In any case, I have never made the test. I have never mentioned my shadows to anyone. I prefer my shamans with all the window dressing. Give them rattles and incense and bones to throw; take away their books. Let the white-coated shamans of the modern world chase shadows in the darkness. I know my phantoms.

Generally. But my phantoms do not speak to me and call me friend. My phantoms keep their distance, going about their lives while I observe. This ancient Mayan woman named Zuhuy-kak did not follow the rules that I knew. I wondered, in the lily-scented night, if the rules were changing.

Back in the hut that served as my home for the field season, I lay in my hammock and listened to the steady beat of my own heart. The palm thatch rustled in the evening breeze.

The hammock rocked me to sleep and the sounds changed. The steady beat was a *tunkul*, a hollow wooden gong that was beaten with a stick. The cricket's song grew harsh and loud, like the buzzing of stones shaken in a gourd rattle. The whisper of the palm thatch became the murmuring of voices: a crowd surrounded me and pressed close on all sides. I felt the weight of braids on my head, a cumbersome robe around me. When a hand on my arm tugged me forward, I opened my eyes.

A precipice before me, jade-green water far below, a drumbeat that quickened with my heart, and suddenly I was falling.

I woke with a start, my hands clutching the cotton threads of the hammock. The rising wind stirred the palm thatch and sent a few thin leaves scurrying across the hard-packed dirt floor of my hut.

In my brief glance over the edge, I had recognized the steep limestone walls and green waters of the sacred cenote at Chichén Itzá. The scent, I thought, had been copal incense. The music—rattle and drum—was processional music.

I closed my eyes and slept again, but my dreams were of more modern pasts: I dreamed of the long ago time when I had been a wife and mother. I did not like such dreams and I woke at dawn.

Dawn and dusk are the best times for exploring ruins. When the sun is low, the shadows reveal the faint images of ancient carvings on temple stones; they betray irregularities that may hide the remains of stairways, plazas, walls, and roads. Shadows lend an air of mystery to the tumble of rocks that was once a city, and they reveal as many secrets as they hide.

I left my hut to go walking through the ruins. It was Saturday and breakfast would be late. Alone, I strolled through the sleeping camp. Chickens searched for insects among the weeds. A lizard, catching early-morning sunlight on a rock, glanced at me and ran for cover in the crack of a wall. In the monte, a bird called on two notes—one high, one low, one high, one low—as repetitive as a small boy who had only recently learned to whistle. The sun was just up and the air was still relatively cool.

As I walked, I fingered the lucky piece that I carried in my pocket, a silver coin that Tony had given me when we were both graduate students. The design was that of an ancient Roman coin. Tony cast the silver himself in a jewelry-making workshop, and gave the coin to me on the anniversary of the day my divorce was final. I always carried it with me, and I knew I was nervous when I caught myself running my finger along the milled edge.

I was nervous now, restless, bothered by my dreams and my memory of the old woman named Zuhuy-kak. I started when four small birds took flight from a nearby bush, jumped when a lizard ran across my path. My encounter with Zuhuy-kak had left me feeling more unsettled than I liked to admit, even to myself.

I followed the dirt track to the cenote. On the horizon, I could see the remains of the old Spanish church. In 1568, the Spanish had quarried stones from the old Mayan temples and used them in a new church, building for the new gods on the bones of the old. Their church had fared no better than the Mayan temples. All that remained of it now was a broad archway and the crumbling fragment of a wall.

Each time I left California and returned to the ruins, I found them more disconcerting. In Berkeley, buildings were set lightly on the land, a temporary addition—nothing more. Here, history built upon history. Conquering Spaniards had taken the land from the Toltec invaders who had taken the land from the Maya. With each conquest, the faces of old gods were transformed to become the faces of gods more acceptable to the new regime. Words of the Spanish Mass blended with the words of ancient ritual: in one and the same prayer, the peasants called upon the Virgin Mary and the Chaacob. Here, it was common to build structures upon structures, pyramids over pyramids. Layers upon layers, secrets hiding secrets.

I lingered for a time on the edge of camp. A stonecutter, working alone in the early hours, was tapping a series of glyphs into a limestone slab. The clacking of stone chisel on limestone beat a counterpoint to the monotonous call of the distant bird. I leaned close to see if I could identify the glyphs he carved, but a chicken chose that moment to wander through the space occupied by the limestone slab. The stoneworker and his tools faded into dust and sunlight, and I continued on my way.

I walked past the cenote, following the trail that the shadow called Zuhuy-kak had taken, winding through the brush to the southeast plaza, where we had begun excavating a mound designated as Structure 701, renamed Temple of the Moon by Tony. I strolled slowly along the side of the mound, studying the slope for any regularities that might betray what lay beneath the rubble.

About a thousand years ago—give or take a hundred years—the open area beside the mound had been a smooth plaza, coated with a layer of limestone plaster. Here and there, traces of the original plaster remained, but most had been washed away by the rains of the passing centuries.

Workmen had cleared the brush and trees from the open area, exposing the flat limestone slabs that had supported the plaster. Uprooted brush was heaped at the far end of the mound in the shade of a large tree. I reached the brush heap, began to turn away, then looked again.

A stone half covered by the piled brush seemed to be at an angle, a little different from the rest, as if it were collapsing into a hollow space beneath the plaza. I stepped closer. It looked very much like the other stones: a square of uncarved limestone unusual only for its reluctance to lie flat. But I have learned to follow my instincts in these matters.

The thirsty trees that set down roots in the sparse soil of the Yucatán are lean and wiry, accustomed to hardship and drought. Even after they have been felled and left to die, the trees fight back, reaching out with thorns and broken branches for the soft flesh of anyone who raises a machete against them. When I tried to pull a branch from the tilted stone so that I could take a better look, the tree clung willfully to the rest of the heap; when I yanked harder, it twisted in my hand and gave way so suddenly that I lost my balance. As I fell back, another branch raked the tender skin on my inner wrist with half-inch thorns, leaving bloody claw marks.

The monte fights back. My efforts had moved the branch slightly and the stone still looked promising. I wrapped my kerchief around my wrist to stanch the blood and decided to wait until the work crew could move the brush. I turned toward camp.

An old woman who did not belong to my time stood in the shade of the tree. The air around me was hot and still. A bird in the jungle called out on a rising note, as if asking a piercing question.

The woman's dark hair was coiled in braids on her head; strips of bright blue cloth decorated with small white sea-shells were woven into the braids. Around her neck was a string of jade beads—each one polished and round, as if worn smooth by the sea. White discs carved of oyster shell dangled from her ears. Her robe, a deeper shade of blue than the cloth in her hair, hung down to the leather sandals on her feet. From her belt of woven leather strips hung a conch shell trumpet and a pouch encrusted with snail shells.

She was not an attractive woman. Her forehead slanted back at an unnatural angle, pressed flat by a cradle board in her infancy. Dark blue spots tattooed on one cheek formed a spiral pattern, marking her as a Mayan noblewoman. Her teeth were tumbled like the stone blocks in an old wall. The front teeth were inset with jade beads, another mark of nobility.

She squinted at me as if the sun were too bright. "The shadow again," she said softly in Maya. She watched me for a moment. "Speak to me, Ix Zacbeliz."

"You see me?" I asked her in Maya. "What do you see?"

She smiled, showing her inlaid teeth. "I see a shadow who talks. It has been long since I have spoken with anyone, even a shadow. I did not know how lonely I would be when I sent the people away.''

''What do you mean?''

''You will learn. We will be friends and I will teach you secrets.'' Her hands were clasped before her and I noticed that her arms, from the inner elbow to the wrist, were bandaged with strips of white cloth.

The sun was hot on my shoulders and back. My heart seemed to be beating too quickly.

''You and I have much in common. You are searching for secrets. I looked for secrets once.'' She spoke quietly, as if talking to herself. ''But in the end, the h'menob of the new religion said I was mad. Wisdom is often mistaken for madness. Is that not true?''

I did not speak.

''Lift this stone and you will find secrets,'' she said. ''I hid them there myself, after I sent the people away. You can find them. It is time for them to come to light. The cycle is turning.''

''How did you send the people away?'' I asked.

The plaza shimmered in the sunlight and I stood alone. Zuhuy-kak had gone. The bird in the monte called again, asking a question that no living person could answer. I headed for camp, glancing over my shoulder only once.

Notes for City of Stones
by Elizabeth Butler

A thousand years ago, centuries before the Spanish conquistadors came, the Maya abandoned their ceremonial centers. After about A.D. 900, they built no more temples, carved no more stelae, the stone monuments etched with glyphs commemorating important events. They fled from the ceremonial centers into the jungle.

Why? No one knows, but everyone is willing to speculate. Every archaeologist has a theory. Some talk of famine caused by overpopulation and years of intensive agriculture. Some claim there was a catastrophe: an earthquake, a drought, or a plague. Some blame the invasion of the Toltecs, a militaristic group from the Valley of Mexico, and still others suggest that the peasant class rebelled, rising up to overthrow the elite class.

I enjoy pointing out the holes in all the theories. I admit—freely and honestly—that I have no idea why the Maya left their cities and scattered far and wide in the monte. My favorite theory is one that a withered Mayan holy man who lived near Chichén Itzá told me over a bottle of aguardiente. "The gods said that the people must leave," he told me. "And so the people left."

Sometimes, I dream of an abandoned city. I dream that each day the sun shines on the walls, fading the bright paints that color the stucco, cracking the plaster that covers the stone. When the evening wind blows, it tatters the cloth that once closed the rooms off from the outside world, carrying leaves and dust in through the open doorways. When the rains come, they flow down the stone steps, knocking loose fragments of stucco, watering the small plants that have taken hold in the cracks. Deer graze on the new grass that sprouts in the courtyard. Mice feast on maize, forgotten in underground chambers, spilled by peasants in the haste of their departure. The mice, rodents of short memories, do not fear the return of the inhabitants. In a temple room, a jaguar makes her home, bearing kittens beneath a statue of the Chaac amid a clutter of windblown leaves.

Sometimes, I dream of quakes—the earth trembling as if it shivered in the cold. The wood beams that support the roofs crack and the thick walls shift so that one stone no longer rests on the other just so. The walls tumble down.

In my dreams, the sun, the face of Ah Kinchil, the supreme god, shines on the temples of the Maya. Small trees reach up to the sun from the cracks between the stones. The rain falls and runs in a helter-skelter course amid blocks that twist this way and that. Birds sing in the trees, and owls hunt here by night, feeding on the arrogant mice that have come to regard this place as home.

Sometimes, very rarely, I dream of a thin man in the white pants of the Yucatecan peasant or a woman in a clean white *huipil*, the embroidered dress of the peasant woman. The man or woman comes quietly to the ruins, cautious lest the gods of the ancestors fail to approve of the visit. The people who return are more fearful than the mice: the people remember the past and know its power. Candlelight chases back the shadows for a time. The visitor burns incense, mutters propitiations and prayers, sacrifices a turkey and leaves it for the gods, then slips away into the night. The jaguar and her kittens eat the turkey, and the shadows return to the ruins.

The city I dream is not always the same. Sometimes it is Uxmal, and I watch swallows build nests in the elaborately carved facades. Sometimes it is Tulúm, and I listen to waves crash below the House of the Cenote and hear the humming of bees as they build a nest in the guard tower on the northern corner of the city wall. Sometimes it is Cobá, and I watch the trees take root amid the stones of the ball court, shoving carved blocks aside. Spanish moss sways on the branches, and *pajaritos*, laughing birds, fly in the branches. The city that I dream changes, but the slow decay is always there. The shadows linger.

I do not know why the Maya left. I only know that the shadows stayed behind.

Chapter Two: Diane Butler

I pressed my forehead to the window of the jetliner and watched the plane's shadow ripple over the brown land below. The plane jerked a little, bucking like a car on a rough road. We were flying through turbulence, and I felt sick to my stomach. My hands were shaking.

Still, I felt no worse than I had for the past two weeks. Not much better, but no worse. At least I was moving. I turned away from the window and rubbed my eyes. They felt gritty and sore from crying and lack of sleep. When was the last time I had slept? Three days ago, maybe. Something like that. I had tried to sleep but when I went to bed I lay awake, my eyes open and staring at nothing. I rubbed my eyes again and covered them with my hands for a moment, shutting out the light. Maybe I could get some sleep now. Maybe.

"Excuse me," said a man's voice. "Are you all right?" Someone touched my arm and I jumped, moving my arm away.

I had not really looked at the man when he had taken the seat beside me. He was Mexican, a few years younger than I was—maybe in his mid-twenties. Dark hair, high cheekbones.

"Fine," I said. My voice was hoarse and I cleared my throat. "Just tired." I tried to smile to reassure him, but my face was stiff and uncooperative.

"I thought you were sick." He was watching me with concern.

31

I knew I looked pale. I felt pale. I felt half dead. "Fine," I said. I could think of nothing more to say. My father is dead, I could say. I just broke off a bad love affair and quit my job as a graphic artist. I could tell him that. I'm on my way to meet a mother I have not seen in fifteen years. And I think I might be going crazy. Then I would burst out crying and hide my face in the shoulder of his sport coat and leave a big damp spot. He looked very earnest and very sympathetic. "I'm fine," I said and turned back to the window.

"Are you going to be spending much time in Mérida?" he asked. "If you are, I can suggest some good restaurants."

I smiled politely, a plastic smile, a Barbie doll smile, a curve of the lips with no intent behind it. "Thanks, but I'll be on an archaeological dig outside Mérida. I don't plan to spend much time in the city."

"You must be going to Dzibilchaltún," he said and smiled when I nodded.

"How did you know?"

He shrugged. "Mérida is not so big. That's the only archaeological dig nearby. I have heard about Dr. Elizabeth Butler, the woman leading the excavation."

"What have you heard?"

"She writes books."

I smiled despite myself. "That, I know." I had read all my mother's books, buying the hardcover editions as soon as they came out.

"How long will you be there?"

"Hard to say."

I leaned back and closed my eyes against further questions. For once, the world inside my head was dark and quiet. The plane was taking me south and there was nothing I could do to speed it up or slow it down. No action was required of me now. I could not stop even if I had wanted to.

My memories of the past two weeks were hazy, but some moments stood out clearly. I remember the night before my father's funeral. I could not sleep, and at some point, around about midnight I think, I got the bottle of Scotch from my father's liquor cabinet, and I started drinking. The liquor did not stop the noise in my head, but the buzz of the alcohol helped drown out the nagging voices that told me about how badly I was behaving, about how ashamed my father would be to see me. I turned on the television and idly flipped from station to station, never lingering beyond the first commercial, until only one station remained on the air, playing old movies until dawn.

I sat in my father's easy chair and watched a pretty blond actress argue with a craggy-faced man. I knew, without seeing the rest of the movie, that the argument would come to nothing. Sooner or later, the craggy-faced man would sweep the blonde into his arms and she would allow herself to be swept, forgetting all past disagreements. I knew that by the end of the movie they would kiss and make up. They always kissed and made up in old movies.

My mother and father had fought, but somehow they never got around to kissing and making up. When they fought, they never shouted—but even when my mother kept her voice down, her words had a bright sharp intensity, like the touch of alcohol on an open cut. And my father was stubborn too—he would not give an inch. I remember the time that he told me that my mother was crazy. There was a hard edge of reproach in his tone, as if somehow her insanity had been her own fault.

A commercial came on, and I downed the rest of my Scotch. I left the television talking to itself and wandered out onto the balcony. My father's house was perched on the edge of a hill, and the balcony offered a panoramic view of Los Angeles, a carpet of twinkling lights, freeway interchanges glittering like distant mandalas, neons flashing, streetlights, houselights, headlights. I stood at the railing, looking down at the city and thinking about my mother. In a moment of sudden dizziness, I closed my eyes.

I opened them to darkness and silence. No lights, except for the pale crescent moon that hung low over the dark valley. No freeways, no houses, no neon. The cool breeze that fanned my face carried the scent of distant campfire smoke. I could hear an owl hooting in the distance and the rapid beating of my own heart.

I clutched the railing with both hands, fighting a wave of vertigo. Panic came over me: I feared I would tumble over the railing and fall into the black void beyond the balcony, plummeting forever in endless darkness. I closed my eyes against the vision and when I opened them I saw the lights of Los Angeles, distant and cold, but infinitely reassuring.

I quit drinking. I did not sleep, but I quit drinking. And in the small hours before dawn, I decided to find my mother. The need to find her seemed linked to my drunken vision of falling and to the restlessness that had plagued me even before my father's death.

I shifted uneasily in my seat, listening to the reassuring hum of the jet's engines. I tried to imagine my mother's face, building it out of the darkness. A thin face, dominated by restless blue eyes. Short and unruly hair, brown with streaks of gray, the color of an English sheepdog. A slight woman whose clothes were too large for her, whose hands were always moving, whose eyes were bright and curious. The picture of my mother that formed in my mind was static, frozen, but I remembered my mother as being constantly in motion: walking, cleaning, cooking.

When I was a child, I had daydreamed about my mother constantly. I dreamed that she would come home. How and why she came changed with each dream. She drove up in a jeep to take me away to an archaeological dig. She roared up on a motorcycle and took me to live with her in Berkeley. She rode into town on a black horse and we galloped away into the sunset. Details changed: she wore khaki, jeans, Mexican costume, ordinary dress. But always the dreams were bright and clear, and always the ending was happy. Fifteen years ago I stopped dreaming.

It was Christmastime. The air had been scented with burning pine; the wine had sparkled in my mother's glass. I was fifteen years old, and I sat on the carpet by the fireplace. Robert, my father, sat in an easy chair beside me.

My mother sat alone on the love seat, an ugly antique with

carved wooden arms and upholstery of heavy tapestry cloth. She had flung her left arm carelessly across the back of the love seat and the sleeve of her shirt, a baggy shirt that was a little too large for her, had fallen back to show the white scars that marked her wrist. Her skin was tanned around the scars.

Robert and my mother were talking politely. "Are you staying in town?" Robert asked.

"At the Biltmore," she said. "I'll be heading back to Berkeley tomorrow. I've been in Guatemala for two months now, and I have much too much to do."

At the time, I wondered what my mother could possibly have to do. She seemed out of place in my father's house, but I could not imagine where she would be in place. She seemed a little nervous, glanced at the clock on the mantel often.

"Where were you in Guatemala?" I asked.

"Near Lake Izabal," my mother said. "Excavating a small site. A trading center. We found some pottery from Teotihuacán, up by Mexico City, some from farther north." She shrugged. "We'll be arguing for months about how to interpret our findings." She grinned at me—a brilliant, open smile very unlike the polite smile with which she had greeted Robert. "After all, archaeologists need to do something in the winter."

"Would you like some more wine?" Robert asked, cutting off my next question. He moved quickly to refill her glass.

He changed the subject then, talking about the house, his business, my schoolwork. When my mother finished the glass of wine, we exchanged presents. Her package for me was wrapped in brown paper, and she apologized for the wrappings. "The Guatemalan market offers a limited choice in wrapping paper," she said in a dry tone that seemed to imply that I had been to Guatemala and knew the market quite well.

I unwrapped a shirt made of a heavy cloth woven of burgundy and black thread. On the pockets and back, a stylized bird surrounded by an intricate border was woven into the cloth. "You can watch the women weaving these

shirts in the market,'' my mother said. ''That's a quetzal bird,
the symbol of Guatemala. It's called a quetzal shirt.''

I pulled the shirt on over my T-shirt. It was loose on my
shoulders, but I pulled it tight around me. ''It's great,'' I
said. ''Just great.''

''It's a little large,'' Robert said from his seat by the fire.

''I'll grow into it,'' I said, without looking at him. ''I'm
sure I will.''

There was more polite conversation—I couldn't remember
it all. I remember Robert congratulating her for her second
book—just out and getting good reviews. My father said
good-bye at the door. I walked my mother to the car. It had
rained that day and the streets were still wet. A car passed,
its tires hissing on the pavement. The Christmas lights that
my father had strung along the front porch blinked on and
off: red and blue and green and gold.

I stood beside my mother's car. When she opened the front
door, the interior light came on and I caught a glimpse of the
clutter on the backseat: two more packages wrapped in brown
paper and tied with ribbon, a dirty canvas duffel bag adorned
with baggage tags, a straw hat with a snakeskin band that
held three brilliant blue feathers. My mother sat in the front
seat and closed the door.

''Where are you going to spend Christmas?'' I asked her.

''I'll spend Christmas day with friends,'' she said. ''I'll
be driving back to Berkeley the day after.'' I heard the click
of metal on metal as she slipped the key into the ignition.

''Can I come?'' I asked quickly. ''I won't be any trouble.
I thought maybe . . .'' I stopped, caught in a tangle of
words.

The colored lights flashed on her face: red, blue, green,
gold, red, blue. I have a clear memory of her face, frozen
like a snapshot. The air around us seemed cold.

''Come with me? But your father . . .'' She stopped.
''You'll be spending Christmas with your father.''

''I want to go with you,'' I said quietly. ''I need to.''

I watched her face in the changing light. She was no
longer frozen: her eyes narrowed and her mouth turned down,

weary, unhappy, maybe frightened. Her hand clenched the steering wheel and the lights flashed red, blue, green. "I'll be leaving soon," she said. "Another dig. I can't . . ."

The dream had gone wrong. I stepped back from the car. "Never mind," I said. "Forget it. Just forget it."

"Here," she said. She reached in the backseat and pulled a blue feather from the band in the straw hat. "This is a quetzal feather. They bring good luck."

I stood in the driveway, holding the blue feather as she backed the car away from the house. The colored lights reflected from the wet pavement, and her tires hissed as she drove away. I threw the feather down on the pavement. When I looked for it in the morning, the wind had blown it away.

I woke to the scratchy sound of a stewardess's voice over the loudspeakers. "Please fasten your seat belts and return your seats to their upright position. We are now landing at the Mérida airport. We hope you have a pleasant stay in Mérida, and thank you for flying Mexicana." The voice repeated the message in rapid Spanish. I understood a few phrases in the flow of words, vocabulary from the high school Spanish I had taken long ago.

The man in the seat beside me smiled at me and said, "Feeling better?"

I nodded, smiled the mechanical smile, and turned to the window to avoid conversation. Through the window, I looked out on a dusty-green carpet pockmarked with cigarette burns, streaks and patches of gray-white. As the plane came in for a landing at Mérida, the carpet became trees and scrubby bushes; the pockmarks, small fields and roads. I could see thin lines of black slicing through the carpet: roads heading for the Gulf of Mexico or the Caribbean coast. Then the plane was down and I could see only the runway and the terminal.

I felt disoriented and peculiar. The world outside the plane window looked flat and unreal, like the image on a TV screen. The sun was too bright; I squinted, but it still hurt my eyes. The plane pulled into the shade of the terminal and the

other people on board were stretching and talking and pushing into the aisles, eager to get somewhere. The man who
had been sitting beside me was standing already. He glanced
at me. "Can I help you with anything?"

"No," I said. "No, thank you." I did not want help. I
wanted to be left alone. When he did not move away, I began
rummaging beneath the seat for my purse. By the time I
found it, he had given up and was heading away down the
aisle. While the other passengers filed out, I took a small
mirror from my cosmetics case and looked at myself. I was
pale. When I lifted my sunglasses, I could see the dark circles
below my eyes. I sat for a while, letting the rest of the
passengers crowd toward the doors. I followed the last one
out.

As I stepped out onto the boarding stairs at Mérida, I
realized that no one was going to stop me. I had flown away
from home, from my job, from my former lover. No one had
stopped me. I hesitated, squinting into the bright sun. The
boarding ramp seemed very high; the terminal, far away.
Remembering my vision of falling, I clung to the handrail,
unable to take the first step down the stairs.

"Is there a problem, señorita?" asked the steward standing
beside me.

"No," I said quickly. "No problem." The metal stairs
made tinny noises beneath my feet. I could feel the heat rising
from the asphalt as I walked to the terminal.

I stepped into the shade of the terminal, my head up, my
smile in place. I waited for my suitcase to roll by on the belt,
letting the crowd surge around me. I tried to catch familiar
words in the babble of Spanish, but had no success. I grabbed
my suitcase when it rolled past and stepped outside the terminal.

"Taxi?" asked an old man standing beside a dirty dark
blue Chevrolet. I nodded and told him in my best high school
Spanish that I wanted to go to the ruins, but he refused to
understand. "*Sí*," he said. "To Mérida." He wore a straw
hat pushed back on his head, and when he smiled he showed
broken teeth stained with nicotine. "Downtown," he said.

"No," I said. "To Dzibilchaltún." I stumbled over the name and the cabby frowned.

The young man from the plane appeared beside me and put a hand very lightly on my shoulder. "You want to go to Dzibilchaltún?" he asked, then spoke to the cabby in rapid Spanish. The two of them argued for a moment, then the man from the plane said to me, "He'll take you there for seven hundred pesos. OK? And if you are in town, you must promise to look me up. My name is Marcos Ortega. You can usually find me in Parque Hidalgo. Look for a hammock vendor named Emilio. He's my friend. He'll know if I'm around." His hand was still on my shoulder. "Promise?"

I nodded and gave him a smile that was almost real. As I drove off in the cab, I looked back to see him standing at the curb, staring after me with a curious expression.

The streets of the city of Mérida are narrow and winding, little better than alleys. The houses and shops crowd tightly together, forming an unbroken wall of peeling facades painted in colors that might have been brilliant once: turquoise, orange, yellow, red. The sun fades the paints to muted shades, gentle pastels.

I saw the city in glimpses from the backseat of the cab: a row of shopfronts, each painted a different shade of blue, all peeling. A dim interior seen through an open doorway and a hammock swaying within. A group of men lounging on a street corner, smoking. A small park with a statue in the center. A fat woman leading a small boy down the narrow sidewalk. A row of stone buildings with carved stone facades bordering on the edge of a park. Trees crowned with red-orange blossoms. My cab narrowly missed a motorbike carrying a man, a woman, a baby, and a little girl, then swerved around a buggy drawn by a weary-looking horse. Finally, we headed out of town along a wider road.

The highway ran straight through a landscape of yellowing trees and scrub, broken now and then by a cluster of small huts. We passed a crew of men who were repairing the road; the cabby tooted his horn and passed them without slowing.

I thought about telling the driver that I had changed my mind: he should turn around and go back to Mérida. But I could not explain that in Spanish and he was already turning off the highway onto a side road. My hands were in fists and I forced them to relax. I tried to take deep breaths, tried to calm down.

I had screwed up royally this time, and I knew it. I was arriving with no warning in a place where I was not wanted. I had been stupid to think that I could do this. I felt sick.

On one side of the road, spiky plants grew in unbroken rows. On the other side, the trees and scrub towered over the cab. The cabby did not slow for potholes; the cab jolted and bumped over rocks and raised a cloud of dust. We passed a cluster of battered stucco houses. The driver slowed to let chickens scatter before us, then drove through an archway and down a dirt road to a cluster of palm-thatched huts that looked even more dilapidated than the stucco houses.

The dust settled slowly. The place seemed deserted. Washing—three T-shirts and a pair of jeans—hung on a line by one hut. The tarp that shaded a group of folding tables flapped lazily in a light breeze.

The cabdriver opened the door and said something in Spanish. I hesitated, then climbed out to stand beside the cab. "Where are the ruins?" I asked. "*Las ruinas?*" He frowned and waved a hand at the huts.

I saw a white-haired man duck through the curtained doorway of one of the huts, squint at the cab, and start walking toward us. The sun burned on my face. I tried to smile at the white-haired old man, but I was glad my sunglasses hid my eyes. "You may want the cab to wait," the man said. He stood, his hands in his pockets, in the scant shade of a tree. "Not much to see here and it's a long walk back to the bus stop on the highway."

"Isn't there an excavation here?" My voice was just a little unsteady.

The old man did not take his hands from his pockets. "That's true," he said. "But there's still not much to see."

"I'm looking for Elizabeth Butler," I said. "I'm her daughter, Diane Butler. Is she here?"

He took one hand from his pocket to push his straw hat farther back on his head. His eyes were blue and curious. "I see," he said. "Well." A pause. "Then perhaps you'd better let the taxi go." Another pause. "Liz didn't tell me that you were coming."

"She didn't know."

"Ah." He nodded.

"Is she here?"

"She's swimming. I'll send someone down to get her." He turned and looked toward the huts. A man was strolling across the plaza toward us. "Hey, John," the old man called. "Could you go get Liz? She has a visitor."

Behind me, the cabby was pulling my suitcase from the trunk. He set it in the dust beside me and said something in Spanish. I fumbled for money, grateful to be able to look away from the old man's eyes for a moment. The cab wheeled around in another cloud of dust and left me there.

The man took my arm in one hand and my suitcase in the other. "You must be hot and thirsty. I'll fix you a drink while we wait for your mother."

"I guess she'll be surprised to see me," I said. I tried to ignore the tears that had started to spill over. I wasn't even sure why I had started crying.

He wrapped a warm, dusty arm around my shoulders. "Take it easy now. It'll be okay."

I could not stop. The tears seemed to come of their own volition, through no fault of mine, and his voice seemed very far away. The bandanna he gave me smelled of dust.

"I'll make you something to drink and you can tell me about all this." He turned me around gently and started me walking.

"Sorry . . ." The word caught in my throat and I couldn't say more.

"Nothing to be sorry about," he said, and he kept his arm around my shoulders. He led me across a central plaza and into one of the huts. The curtain that blocked the doorway fell closed behind us.

His hut was a single whitewashed room, furnished with two lawn chairs, a cooler, a footlocker, a small folding table that served as a desk, and a hammock that was looped over the hut's center beam and pushed to one side of the room. Half the hut was filled with cardboard boxes, picks, jacks, and shovels.

He made me sit in one of the lawn chairs, rummaged in a footlocker for plastic cups, and then in the cooler for a bottle of gin. "I'm Anthony Baker," he told me. "Call me Tony. If you're Liz's daughter, you'll drink gin and tonic."

I nodded and tried to smile. I was having no more success now than I had had outside. The smile kept twisting on my face and turning into something else.

Tony poured two drinks and fished in the bottom of the cooler for ice cubes. I studied his face when he handed me a glass. He looked like someone's favorite uncle. He sat in the other lawn chair and rested his drink on one knee, his hand on the other.

"Do you get many unexpected visitors?" I asked.

"Not many."

I took a sip. The drink was strong and tasted faintly of melted ice and plastic. "Sorry to take up your time," I said.

"No problem. I've got plenty of time," he said. "That's one thing archaeologists come to understand. We've got time. The ruins have been here for thousands of years; they'll wait a little longer." He studied my face over the rim of his glass. "Being in the Yucatán for a while will change your view of time. The people who live here think like archaeologists. Two thousand years ago, their great-great-grandfathers burned over a plot of land in the monte and planted corn with a digging stick. This spring, Salvador will burn over a plot of land in the monte and plant corn with a digging stick. People who work on such a grand time scale don't worry so much about how long it takes to have a drink with the daughter of an old friend." He shrugged. "You stay here a while, and you learn that attitude. You learn to take your time."

I looked down at my drink, turning the plastic glass in my hands. "I had to talk to my mother," I said. "I know I should have written or called or something, but . . ." I shrugged. "It's pretty weird just showing up here with no warning."

"Some people say it's strange for a grown man to spend his summers digging in the dirt. Personally, I try to avoid making value judgments."

"I should have written first," I said.

"I don't see that it's a real problem," he said. "We can always string another hammock. You can learn to sleep in a hammock, can't you?"

I nodded.

He took the empty glass from my hand and poured me another drink without asking if I wanted one. I was taking my first sip when I heard footsteps outside the hut, a knock on the wooden doorjamb. "Hey, Tony," a woman's voice said. "What's this about a visitor?"

The blaze of light when the curtain was lifted aside blinded me for a moment. I blinked, staring toward the figure in the doorway.

My mother's hair had more white in it than I remembered. Her hair was damp, the tendrils curling on her neck as they dried. She carried a towel slung over her shoulder.

She was frowning. I tried to smile, but once again, I had lost the knack. "Hello," I said. "Surprise." I stood up, feeling awkward. I did not know what to do with my hands. She looked worried, I thought, in that first moment. Startled and worried, not angry.

"Diane?" she said. "Are you all right? What the hell are you doing here?"

Tony was making himself busy, pouring another drink.

"My father's dead," I said. "He died two weeks ago." I did not cry and my voice was steady. I waited for a reaction, but my mother's expression did not change. She sat down on the edge of the footlocker.

"I see," she said.

"He died of a heart attack." I was talking too fast, but I

could not seem to stop. "I wanted to talk to you. Dad never wanted me to talk to you. I thought I could come and stay here for a while."

"Here?" She still looked worried, a little puzzled. "For a while," she said. "I suppose you could."

"She could take the place of that student of mine who cancelled," Tony said, handing her a gin and tonic. "Don't you think? We'll teach you to sort potsherds," he said to me.

I was watching my mother. She nodded cautiously and accepted the drink that Tony had mixed. Did she look relieved? Annoyed? Concerned? I could not read her face.

"Do you want to do that, Diane?"

"I'd like to try it," I said. "I promise I won't be in the way. I'll be no trouble at all. Really."

Tony sat in the lawn chair and my mother sat on the footlocker and they talked about which hut I would stay in, which work crew I would be assigned to, and other inconsequentials. I held my glass and watched my mother's face and hands as she talked. For the moment, I relaxed.

Before dinner, my mother took me on a tour of the central part of the ruins. She walked at a brisk pace, talking about people who had been dead for over a thousand years. She seemed quite fond of these dead people. As she walked, she looked at the rocks around us, at the trees, at the ground beneath our feet. She did not look at my face—she did not seem to be avoiding my eyes; she just found the rocks and trees and barren ground more interesting than me. Her straw hat shaded her face. She wore khaki pants and a baggy long-sleeved shirt.

We walked past a low wall and a crumbling fragment of an archway. "The old church," my mother said. "The Spanish built it with Indian labor and the Mayan temple stones."

She spoke in fragments: short bursts of information, a verbal shorthand that eliminated the little words that slow a sentence down. Her way of speaking seemed to match her general attitude; she seemed to be overflowing with the willingness to act, to start new projects, to finish up old ones, to clear jungles and build pyramids. She was a head shorter than me, but I had to work to match her pace.

"Just found an interesting possibility over there," she said, gesturing vaguely. "Underground chamber, I think. We'll start working on that Monday."

The sun reflected off the rocks and I was grateful for my sunglasses. The sky was an uninterrupted blue; no clouds, no hope of shade. Even the jungle did not look cool: the trees looked thirsty and worn. The path was flanked by mounds of rubble from which trees sprouted.

"You'll need a hat," my mother said, glancing at me. "Keep the sun off, or you'll end up with a stroke. You can pick one up in the market."

I nodded quickly, aware that this was the first time she had acknowledged that I would be staying for a time. At the hut, Tony had made suggestions as to where I would stay, what I could do. My mother had simply agreed.

"I didn't know that it would be this hot," I said.

"Sometimes it's not," she said. "Sometimes it's hotter." She flashed me a quick smile, so quick that when it was gone I could scarcely believe I had seen it at all. "When the rains come, it gets stickier, but stays just as hot." She lifted off her hat and ran a hand back through her hair without hesitating or breaking stride.

I had seen pictures of the ruins at Chichén Itzá, Copán, and Palenque: great crumbling heaps of blocky stones, nearly hidden beneath tropical bromeliads and drooping vines; massive pyramids and sculpted facades; tremendous stone heads that glowered from the lush vegetation. I had expected gloom and mystery, the promise of secrets. Here, the sun was too bright for secrets. I could see no pyramids.

At the end of the path we followed, a small building constructed of sand-colored stone stood atop a low platform. The building was a box with a flat roof. On top of the box was another smaller box. On top of that, a third box. Like a stack of three building blocks: big, medium, and small. Except for the roof, the building looked like a child's drawing of a house: a neat flat wall with a dark rectangle for the door, two square windows.

". . . Temple of the Seven Dolls," my mother was saying. "Only building that's been reconstructed. We're working on some of the outlying temples over that way." Another vague wave of her hand toward the setting sun.

I followed her up the steps of the Temple of the Seven Dolls. Two pigeons flew away as we approached the top. "You'll see some bees," my mother said. "They have a hive in one of the beams."

We reached the top. My mother sat down on the top step on one side of the open door where the building shaded her from the sun. "Take a rest," she suggested. I hesitated for a moment, wondering if this were some kind of test. Maybe I should want to explore the building before I rested. Maybe I should ask questions, not just sit.

I sat on the other side of the doorway and looked out in the direction of camp.

My mother lifted a pack of cigarettes from her pocket, tapped one out, and offered me the pack. I shook my head and she set it on the steps beside her.

"Bad habit, I know," she said, lighting the cigarette and leaning back against the side of the door. "Tony's been trying to get me to quit for the last five years." She shrugged. "At my age, it doesn't seem worth it."

Chapter Three: Elizabeth

ON the steps of the Temple of the Seven Dolls, an elderly diviner was casting the *mixes*, the sacred red beans that told the future. His customer was a merchant, a sharp-faced man whose arms and face were tattooed with patterns of swirling lines. A woven bag filled with cacao beans lay on the steps beside him. The old diviner pointed at the red beans that lay on the cloth before him and spoke softly. I could not make out the words.

I took a long drag on my cigarette and wondered what I could say to this young woman who had dropped into my life so unexpectedly. What did she want of me?

She sat with her back to the open doorway; her knees were bent and her arms were wrapped around them. She was prettier than any child of mine had a right to be: her red hair, fair skin, and slim build marked her as Robert's daughter. She wore jeans and an open-necked white shirt. Her eyes were hidden by dark glasses and her hair was tied back in a single braid. "Is it what you expected?" I asked her, waving the cigarette at the camp, the jungle, the overgrown mounds, the diviner and his customer.

"I didn't really know what to expect," she said cautiously.

Robert's daughter: he had probably trained her to be careful, to admit to little. That had been his style: he was careful; he always had to be the one in the know. He had kept himself in check, always carefully controlled.

"Do you want to tell me about how Robert died?" I asked. I tried to speak gently, but the words sounded harsh. I am not good at these things; I deal with dead people better than I do with live ones.

Diane was looking out toward the camp, her chin up, her jaw set. "He died of a heart attack . . . his third one. He was playing tennis at the club."

It seemed an appropriate way for Robert to die. I hadn't seen him for at least five years, but I could imagine him at fifty: out on the court in his tennis whites, smiling his pleasant professional smile, his hair touched with gray at the temples, but nowhere else. I wondered who he had been playing: a colleague from the hospital, a pretty young woman. It didn't matter. I could not manage much sorrow over his death. During divorce proceedings, Robert and I had come to treat each other with a hard-edged polished courtesy. Over the past twenty-five years, that glossy politeness had marked all our infrequent contacts, until at last it seemed like the natural relationship between us. He was a stranger, a vague acquaintance I had once known better. I did not hate him, did not even dislike him particularly, though I did find him dull and opinionated. I could remember the distant times when arguments with him had made me furious, but the fire had burned to ashes and the ashes had blown away on the evening wind. I was indifferent toward him.

"The funeral was two weeks ago," she said. "Aunt Alicia set it up. I guess she didn't let you know."

I remembered Alicia, Robert's older sister, a widow with a smooth, uncrackable personality. I tapped the ash off the end of my cigarette and nodded. "Alicia and I were never exactly friends."

"I know it must be really strange, my turning up out of the blue like this. It's just that Dad never wanted me to talk to you. He never wanted me to know anything about you." She spoke quickly, as if she had to say this quickly or not at all. Her voice had an edge of urgency. "I've read all your books." When she said the last few words, her voice softened and took on a pleading note. She wanted my approval; she wanted me to like her.

I could not look at her. If Diane were crying, I did not want to know. Not now. The jungle was a restful stretch of dirty green. On the steps, the merchant leaned toward the diviner, questioning him closely on a particular point. "So what do you think you'll find here?" I asked her. "What are you looking for?"

"I don't know." Her voice was hesitant. "I guess I just want to dig up the past and figure out what's under all the rubble. That's all."

The diviner waved his hand to the east, the direction governed by Ah Puch, the god of death. Beneath the tattoos, the merchant's face looked mournful.

"You may just find broken pots," I said to Diane. "Nothing interesting at all."

"I'll take my chances on that."

I glanced at her, but I could not read her expression. Her sunglasses hid her eyes. Her back was straight; her arms were still wrapped around her knees, her right hand gripping her left wrist, perhaps just a little too tightly. But she spoke calmly enough. "Right now, all I know is what I remember, and that's just bits and pieces."

The sun was low, and the Temple of the Seven Dolls cast a shadow that stretched away from the camp. The lines of tumbled stones that marked the position of ancient walls stood out in sharp relief. I felt comfortable in the ruins, in the company of dead people and broken buildings. The light of the setting sun shone on my face, warm and soothing. I belonged here among the fallen temples and long-abandoned homes. I watched the merchant pay the diviner in cacao beans, hoist his bag to his back, and trudge down the steps. The diviner faded as the merchant strode into the distance.

I heard the rustle of Diane's clothing when she moved, and I glanced at her again. She was gazing into the distance, looking away from me. I did not know what to say to her. "What do you remember?" I asked at last.

A pause. I took a drag on my cigarette, waiting.

"I remember waiting and waiting after nursery school. Everyone left and the teacher was all ready to go home, but I was still waiting." Her voice was rough, as if she were holding back old tears. Her expression did not change; she did not move. "You were supposed to pick me up. The teacher went and called you, but you weren't home. She called Dad and he came to get me, but he was really mad. We went home and you weren't there. He asked me where you were, but I didn't know." She stopped for a moment, and when she began again, her voice was smooth, her feelings were back under control. "You were gone for a long time. Maybe a month. Then you came back."

"I ran away to New Mexico and enrolled in college," I said. "Supported myself by typing, just as I had supported Robert through medical school by typing. Robert hired a private detective to track me down. When the detective found me, Robert convinced me to come back." I stubbed my cigarette against the step, tapped another out of the pack, and lit it. "What else do you remember?"

"You brought me a Navaho blanket when you came back from New Mexico. You were home for a while—I remember that. I had to be really quiet; Dad told me to be really quiet. Then you left again." Her voice trailed off, but she did not sound like she had finished.

"What else?"

She hesitated. "One night, when I was in bed, I heard you and Dad talking in the kitchen. It was hot and I couldn't sleep. You kept talking louder and louder. I got out of bed and I went down the hall, but I didn't want to go in the kitchen. I stayed just outside the door, where I could see you and Dad. You were holding a breadboard, an old breadboard with a handle on it, and your hand was wrapped around the handle. I couldn't hear what Dad was saying, but all of a sudden you started saying, 'I can't stand it. I can't stand it.' And you started slamming the breadboard against the counter, harder and harder and harder. And you were yelling, 'I can't stand it.' The breadboard broke on the counter and I ran back to bed, I put a pillow over my head and I stayed there, even when I heard shouting. But in the morning, you were gone, and Aunt Alicia was there, and Dad was really upset."

In the long pause, I could hear the pigeons on the roof of the temple.

"You didn't come home for a long time, and then you came home and you left again. Dad said you had gone away because you were crazy. That's all he would say about it. Later on, he told me about the divorce and all that, but that was later."

I remembered the feel of the board in my hand, the thump each time it struck the counter. "Robert was saying, 'You're crazy,' " I told Diane. "That's what you couldn't hear. Other than that, you've got it right." I tapped the ash from my cigarette. "While you were hiding in bed, I locked myself in the bathroom and slashed my wrists. Robert broke down the door, bandaged me, and took me to a private hospital. I was there for two days before I woke up enough to realize that I couldn't go home. Robert had committed me for my own protection."

I remembered being wrapped in cold sheets by white-coated interns. Was that the first night I was there? Hard to say. My memories of the year in the sanatorium were confused. I remembered howling at the ceiling of a cold room, hating Robert and wanting revenge. But I did not know whether that was the first night or many nights later. I suppose it didn't matter. The nights on the ward blurred together; it was a controlled environment, changing only as people came and went.

The spirits I saw there were mad: a pale fat woman with dark smudges for eyes, like chunks of coal in the face of a snowman; a frail old woman who spoke an unknown language, her voice high and small as the chirping of sparrows on the eve of a winter storm; a gaunt woman, thin and dried as a prophet just back from a desert vigil, whose palms and bare feet were marked with bleeding wounds that never seemed to heal.

"I was put in a ward for the seriously disturbed," I told Diane. "I got along all right there. I made friends with a woman who claimed to be Jesus Christ. A powerful old woman with a face like a hatchet.''

I took a drag on my cigarette and exhaled, watching the smoke drift away. Strange memories: I had spent many of my nights screaming at the ceiling that Robert was trying to kill me, that the doctors were trying to kill me. I had been there for a month before I decided to get out. I considered escape, but the bars at the window were quite strong and the interns were muscular. So I decided to behave, to stop screaming all night, to do as I was told, to end my discussions of theology with Mrs. Jesus Christ. I decided to feign sanity, to stop watching the spirits and calling to the moon through the barred windows.

"I was on the ward for three months before I could convince them to move me to a better ward, one for less violent patients. It took me a year to convince them I was cured." I remembered the effort of feigning their kind of sanity. Smiling. Refraining from screaming obscenities even when obscenities were called for. "Robert came to visit me in the hospital. Every other week. Without fail. I was polite to him. I couldn't get out without his help." My voice was very dry, very matter-of-fact. "I wanted to be free of him. I wanted a divorce." I noticed that my hand was shaking as I lifted the cigarette to my mouth; my other hand was clenched in a fist. I forced it to relax. "Finally, he said we could divorce, but only if I would grant him custody of you. I had to agree that I would never try to see you without his permission. I wouldn't try to be your mother. I think that he was seeing someone else at the time and he wanted me out of the way. I had to be free of him, so I promised." I hated the apologetic tone that crept into my voice. I shrugged lightly. "He kept his part of it. He let me out."

"You came back for Christmas sometimes," Diane said.

"I came when Robert wanted me to. On his terms. At one point, I think he was lonely and wanted me back. When I told him that I wasn't interested, he cut off my visiting privileges." I shrugged and smiled a small tight smile. "He wasn't cruel about it. He sent me pictures of you."

"What did you do?" Her voice was controlled and even. Her face was pinched, but she was not crying.

"I went back to New Mexico. For a while, I worked as a typist, then I enrolled in the state university in archaeology. I managed to land a paid position as cook at a field camp that first summer and I was on my way."

"You hated Dad for saying you were crazy," Diane said.

"I hated Robert for a number of things back then," I said. I crushed the half-burned cigarette against the stone. "Locking me up was just one offense among many." I reached for my cigarettes and tapped another from the pack. "So," I said dryly, "you've found what you came to find. You know why I left. What now?"

I looked at Diane. Her arms were clutching her knees and she was rocking back and forth just a little. I regretted my words, I regretted my tone. "Come on," I said softly. "It's all ancient history." I reached out and touched her shoulder, feeling awkward and foolish. She did not react. I wanted her to give me a sign that things were all right between us, but she kept her hands locked around her knees and she did not look at me. "Don't cry over what's long past."

"Can I stay for a while?" she asked.

I shrugged. "I don't know what's here for you."

"Neither do I."

I realized I was still holding the unlit cigarette, and I slipped it into my shirt pocket. "Fine. Stay if you like."

In the distance, I heard the sound of the truck horn. "That's the dinner bell," I said. "Let's go back."

We followed the same path the merchant had taken down the steps and into the light of the setting sun.

Chapter Four: Diane

DINNER was served at a folding table set up in the open area in the center of the cluster of huts. The chairs were metal folding chairs. They looked as if they had traveled too far in the back of a pickup truck, sat in the sun and the rain too long, and generally lived a life unsuited to metal folding chairs. Once these chairs had been painted a uniform gray; now they were marked with rust and dents.

Tony introduced me to the other people at the dinner table. These people, like the chairs in which they lounged, had been exposed to the weather too long. Dirt, broken fingernails, sunburned and peeling faces, chapped lips, and under all that, a lean look, a kind of toughness. The men bore the stubbly beginnings of beards.

Carlos, a tanned Mexican in his late twenties, showed too many teeth when he smiled; he had the look of a friendly barracuda. He wore a tank top and shorts that showed off a deep tan.

John, a Canadian with broad shoulders and what looked to be a habitual slouch, mumbled ''Pleased to meet you'' and barely smiled at all. He wore a baseball cap pushed back on his head, a kerchief tied around his neck, a long-sleeved shirt, and long pants. He seemed to be fighting a losing battle with the sun. His nose was peeling.

Maggie, a blonde with a corn-fed American face, gave me a broad and meaningless smile. She reminded me of all the girls on the cheerleading squad in my high school. Robin, the woman beside Maggie, had hair a shade darker, a smile a shade less bright. Robin seemed born to be a sidekick.

Barbara was the only one to reach out and shake my hand. She was tanned and slender. Her dark hair was cropped boyishly short, and her face was dwarfed by her sunglasses, two great circles of dark glass framed with metal.

"Welcome to camp," Carlos said. He showed me his teeth again. Definitely a predator. "How long are you staying?"

"For a while," I said awkwardly. Hard to admit that I had no idea. A moment of silence as they waited for me to speak cheerful explanations of who I was and why I was there. "I'm on vacation and I wanted to see what a dig was like." My voice was a little hoarse.

"Great place to vacation if you like dirt and bugs," Carlos said. "Have you toured the site?"

"Some of it." I looked to my mother for assistance.

"Have you been down to the cenote?" he asked.

"That's the well. A natural pool formed by a break in the limestone," my mother said. "You haven't seen it yet."

"We use it as a swimming hole," Carlos said cheerfully. "I was just telling Robin about the bones that the Tulane group found at the bottom. Nubile young maidens, cast to their deaths to placate the Chaacob."

"Just what I like to talk about over dinner," Maggie said. "Human sacrifice."

"There was actually more of that sort of thing over at Chichén Itzá than there was here," commented John. He glanced at me. "Have you been to Chichén Itzá? The water level in the cenote there is about eighty feet down. Most of the folks they tossed in died when they hit the water."

A Mexican woman brought out the food—stewed chicken, tortillas, beans—and the conversation went on while everyone ate.

"I'd really rather not talk about this over dinner," Maggie said.

"Oh, come on," Carlos was saying. "Everyone likes to

talk about human sacrifice. It's a great topic. All the tourist
brochures talk about the young virgins who died so horribly."

"I hadn't realized that anyone had determined the victims
were nubile young virgins," Barbara said dryly. "I always
thought it was difficult to tell how virginal a person was from
an old thighbone."

"Now, Barbara," Tony said expansively. "You know we
always assume that they were nubile young virgins until someone proves otherwise. It makes much better news copy. Who
cares if they flung old men and women to the fishes?"

"The old women probably cared," Barbara observed. "I
won't speak for the old men."

"Personally, I'd sooner be flung to the fishes than have
my heart torn out with an obsidian blade," Carlos was
saying. "If I had my choice, I—"

"Can we talk about something else?" Robin asked. Her
request was ignored.

"So," Tony said. "Why would you toss someone in a
sacred well?"

"I wouldn't," Robin said. "I don't see why anyone would."

I noticed that my mother had stopped in the act of slicing
off a bite of chicken. She leaned forward. "Tell me, Robin,
do you believe in ghosts?"

Robin shook her head.

"Then why does it bother you that people have died in the
cenote?" Robin looked very uncomfortable. My mother watched
her, waiting patiently for an answer.

"It just makes me uncomfortable."

"You're uncomfortable because you believe in the power
of the dead," my mother said calmly. "If you didn't, the
bones wouldn't bother you. The Maya who lived here also
believed in the power of the dead. They tried to use that
power to make rain, to placate the gods, to change evil prophe-
cies to good. They felt that those people who had passed near
death were changed—they knew more than ordinary people."

I watched my mother's face as she talked of death. Her
voice was low and earnest, the confident tone of a person who
knows her subject. One of her hands rubbed at a bandage on

her wrist. I wondered what it would feel like to slash the thin skin of my wrists and watch the blood flow. How would it change me?

"Have you read the *Books of Chilam Balam*?" my mother was asking Robin. When Robin shook her head, my mother continued, "When you do, you'll find a fairly extensive description of the sacrifices at Chichén Itzá. Each year, a few chosen people were thrown into the cenote. As John said, most of them died when they hit the water. But some survived. The survivors were hauled out of the well and treated as messengers who had returned from the world of the gods, bringing the prophecy of the coming year. Those who had come near death and survived had a new strength that set them apart from ordinary people." My mother regarded Robin steadily across the table. "You should make an effort to learn about the people you are digging up."

"I have a good translation of that account," Tony said quickly. "You are welcome to borrow it."

Robin nodded.

"Don't mind all this talk of death and dying," Tony said to me. "We're a little preoccupied with death around here. The dead teach us things."

"Speaking of dead people," Barbara said to my mother, "Tony says you may have found a burial site this morning."

"Looks likely," my mother said. "Won't know what we've got for sure until we get the brush cleared away. With any luck, we'll find a burial or two. We could use a few good burials." She used a piece of tortilla to mop her plate. "So far, our success has been severely limited."

"It's only the third week," Tony said. "You're too impatient."

My mother shrugged. "True enough."

Twilight faded to darkness. Tony lit two Coleman lanterns, which cast bright white light, made sharp-edged double shadows on the tables, and attracted moths and flying insects. Carlos, Maggie, John, and Robin moved to another table to play cards. I declined Carlos's invitation to join them. Carlos brought a cassette player from his hut and put on a tape of top ten pop music. I stayed at the dinner table with my mother, Barbara, Liz, and Tony. Tony poured us each a gin and tonic.

"So what will you be doing on Monday?" Barbara asked me softly. With the coming of sunset, she had taken off her sunglasses. Her dark brown eyes were surrounded with circles of pale skin where the sunglasses had blocked the sunlight. Without the glasses, she seemed younger, more vulnerable. "Has Tony assigned you a job?"

I shook my head.

"Want to come on survey with me? We tramp through the monte and look for mounds. Fight with the bugs and try to avoid heatstroke. Lots of fun."

"The monte?"

"Second-growth rain forest," Barbara said. "All this." She waved her hand at the scrub beyond the huts. "The Maya divided the world into the col—the cultivated fields—and the monte—the wild lands. In a week on survey, you'll learn more about the monte than you ever wanted to know. I'll teach you how to read a compass and follow a transect."

"Sure. That sounds all right to me."

"Great." She looked at Tony. "What do you think? She's on survey, all right?"

Tony grinned at me over his drink. "She didn't tell you that you'll have to get up at six A.M."

"That's okay."

Tony lifted his glass as if making a toast. "Barbara wins again. You're on survey."

At the other table, Carlos turned up the volume on the cassette player, and a Mexican version of a Beatles tune filled the plaza. Maggie made an inaudible comment, and Carlos reached over to touch her hand. My mother was drinking a gin and tonic and staring off into the darkness beyond the lantern light.

"You're in the same hut I'm in," Barbara was saying to me. "Want help setting up your hammock?"

"Sure."

We said good-night to my mother and Tony, and headed toward the hut.

"I get tired of watching the courtship rituals," Barbara said as we left the plaza.

The sound of Carlos's cassette player was fading in the distance. Barbara snapped on her flashlight and shone it on the path before us. "The first summer, it was an interesting sociological phenomenon. But you watch it four years running, and it gets tedious. The players change, but the moves never do. I steer clear of it."

"You've come here for the past four years?" I asked.

"Not this site. Last year I was at a site up by Mexico City; year before, I was at an Anasazi site in Arizona. Every site is a little different, but some things don't change. You always feel filthy; there's always a graduate student like Carlos who wants to play late-night games, and there's always someone like Maggie who's willing to play. I got a chance to watch Carlos in action last year. He's smooth, but callous as hell. When he makes a play for you, watch out."

I glanced at her face, but could not read her expression in the dim light. "Who says he will?"

"You've got to be kidding. You're pretty and you're the new kid in town. It isn't a question of whether he will; it's only a question of when."

She stopped by a large black rubber barrel equipped with a faucet attachment. On top of the barrel was a battered metal dishpan. A grimy bar of soap sat in a makeshift soap dish: an old temple stone with an oval indentation. Barbara set her flashlight beside the soap. "Welcome to the washroom," she said. "All the comforts of home. The outhouse is at the end of that path. It's the best outhouse in this part of the country, though that doesn't say a hell of a lot." She rinsed the dishpan, then filled it with water and washed her face. "You can hang your towel in the tree right here," she said, tugging her towel from a branch. "Like I said, all the comforts of home. The showers are down that path, past the outhouse and upwind of it. They remove very little of the dirt, but they do rearrange it a bit. You're better off taking a swim in the cenote instead of a shower except when you want to wash your hair.''

I ran water in the basin and splashed it on my face. The water was lukewarm and even after rinsing I could feel soap on my skin. I guessed that Barbara was right; I never would feel clean. My eyes still felt hot and dry from crying.

In the hut, Barbara lit a tall white candle in a clear glass chimney. The flame cast a pool of yellow light on the footlocker where she set it; shadows wavered in the corners of the hut.

By the candlelight, I found the shelf where Tony had set my bag earlier. I dug through the bag for the oversized T-shirt I had brought to sleep in. Barbara undressed and, casually naked, rubbed herself with insect repellent. She offered me the repellent, advised me to use it, then instructed me on the best method for sleeping in a hammock.

''There's a knack to it,'' she said, laying one hand on her hammock. She took a sheet from the shelf and tossed it to me, took another for herself. She wrapped the sheet loosely around her, held one side of the hammock away from her, spreading the webbing of cotton strings, then sat back in it, lying diagonally. She arranged the sheet around her, tucked one arm under her head, and smiled at me. ''See. Comfortable as your own bed.'' She was rocking slightly. ''Could you hand me my cigarettes?''

I took the cigarettes from the footlocker, used the candle to light one, and handed it to her. She puffed and silently watched me attempt to duplicate her maneuver. My own rocking motion was somewhat more frantic and the edges of the hammock tried to close over me.

''Lie crosswise,'' Barbara suggested.

I managed to squirm around until the length of my body kept the webbing spread. I tucked the sheet around me.

''Comfortable?'' she asked.

''As long as I don't move.''

''Want a cigarette?''

''No thanks.'' I felt more comfortable than I had felt for

many months. I had seen my mother and survived the meeting. "Hey, who's going to blow out the candle?"

"I can get it from here," she said. She leaned over and blew the candle out.

I propped up my head on my arm and my hammock rocked furiously. "Seems like a tough place to make love," I said, thinking of Carlos and Maggie.

"It can be done," Barbara said. "Trust me."

"You sound like an expert." I could see only the glowing tip of her cigarette, rocking slowly in the darkness. For a moment, she was silent, and I thought perhaps I had said too much.

"Stick around here, and you can find out firsthand," she said slowly. "I'm sure Carlos would be delighted to help you learn."

"That's all right. I think I'll pass." I watched her cigarette glow brighter as she took a puff.

"You married?" she asked.

"No. I'm just out of a bad breakup." I tried to sound casual. "That's one reason I'm down here. He was the art director at the advertising agency where I worked." I could visualize his face clearly: dark hair with a touch of gray, blue eyes.

"He was married?"

"Sure enough." I managed to keep my voice light. I was glad the hut was dark.

"Aren't they always," Barbara said. Her voice had softened. "I had an affair with a professor of mine. He was married and had two kids. He finally said it was over, cut me off, wouldn't have anything to do with me. When I was sure it was all over, I changed schools. I couldn't stand seeing him, up there in front of his classes, so very sure of himself."

"I quit and left town." It felt good to tell someone about it. Especially someone who did not know Brian, did not judge me to be a fool.

"I know how it goes," Barbara said. "Well, if you're looking for a place to escape and forget, this is a good one. They'll never find you here."

"Thanks for helping me with everything," I said awkwardly.

"No problem," she said. "Any time you need to talk, let me know."

I watched her silhouette lean over and stub the cigarette out in the dirt on the hut floor. I heard the sheet rustle as she turned over. "Better get to sleep now," she advised.

"Good-night," I said.

" 'Night."

I lay awake for a long time, listening to unfamiliar sounds: footsteps, insects, rustling leaves, the loud ticking of a clock inside the hut. It seemed strange to be able to lie still, not to worry about what would happen when I reached my destination. It seemed that I had spent the last few weeks in constant motion. Pacing up and down the long corridor of the hospital, waiting for the doctor's verdict. Staring out the window of the limousine as my father's funeral procession moved slowly to the cemetery. Wandering in my father's house, confined by four white walls, aimless, unable to settle. Moving slowly, but always moving. Thinking about my mother, remembering my mother. She was shorter than I remembered. Her hair had more gray than I remembered.

The hammock rocked beneath me and I felt like I was still moving, traveling toward an unknown destination. I was just drifting off to sleep when Robin stumbled in and fumbled about in the dark. Finally, she was quiet. I slept.

Notes for City of Stones
by Elizabeth Butler

Robin, one of my students, is a reasonably intelligent, well-educated, young woman. Yet she claims that she sees no reason for human sacrifice. Her attitude, when she speaks of the ancient Maya and their sacrifices to the gods, implies that we are civilized now, we have left that nonsense far behind.

Robin forgets, I think, that her own religion involved human sacrifice. She is a practicing Christian. She partakes of Holy Communion, the body and blood of Jesus Christ, the human son of God who died and rose from the dead to bring back the word of his Father. She believes in the Resurrection, but only as something that happened long ago in a distant land, far removed from her day-to-day life. She believes in God, the Father Almighty. On the other hand, if her next-door neighbor were to claim that God had spoken to him in a vision, she would think him eccentric and possibly dangerous. Her God is a distant patriarch who demands that she attend church and follow a set of ten rules, but he does not deign to pass along new rules through common people. She is accustomed to a God who keeps his distance.

The gods of the ancient Maya are closer and more demanding. At the turning of the katun, the time comes for fasting and drinking balche, for cleansing the sacred books, for dancing on stilts and burning incense. At that time, the people gather at the Sacred Well at Chichén Itzá, a city fifty miles from Dzibilchaltún. The well is a place of power, home of many gods. At the turning of the katun, priests fling jade ornaments, gold bells, copper rings, painted bowls, and incense into the Sacred Well.

With these gifts, they send messengers to the gods. If the messengers do not wish to visit the gods, they are sent— hurled over the edge by muscular priests who only wish to do them honor. The messengers fall, bright feathers fluttering in the sunlight, their voices smothered by the shouting of the crowd, the processional music, the chanting of the priests. Far below, they float, specks of silent color on the jade-green water.

At noon, when the disc of the sun fills the well with light, only one messenger floats on the water. The others are gone, taken down by the Chaacob to the submarine rooms beneath the water's smooth surface. The priests draw out this survivor, who has returned to tell the message of the gods, bringing the prophecy for the coming year.

It is not a simple thing, this human sacrifice, any more than the crucifixion of Jesus Christ was a simple execution. The messengers who do not return are among the gods; the one who does return is the oracle, the interpreter for the gods.

The archaeologist Edward Thompson dredged human bones from the Sacred Well at Chichén Itzá. The bones that Thompson found belonged to messengers who failed in their duty.

Chapter Five: Elizabeth

I tapped a cigarette out of the pack and watched the bright point of Barbara's flashlight move across the plaza to the women's hut. Barbara and Diane were shadows in the distance.

This daughter of mine was as cool as if she were encased in glass, shielded from the world by an invisible protective barrier. She was not unfriendly: during dinner she had smiled and joked with the others. But she seemed cautious, wary, and even when she removed her sunglasses, I could not begin to guess what she was thinking. I lit my cigarette, cupping my hand to protect the flame from the evening breeze, then shook the burning match to blow it out. Tony sat beside me, nursing a drink. I think it was his fourth.

In the corner of the plaza, not far from the table where the students played their interminable game of cards, a loincloth-clad Toltec priest was scraping remnants of flesh from the hide of a newly killed jaguar. A smoking torch cast red light on his bare back and shoulders; at his side, incense burned in a pottery vessel shaped like a jaguar. As he worked, he chanted incessantly, and his voice competed with the rock-and-roll tapes playing on Carlos's cassette player.

"Your daughter is a very nice young woman," Tony said. "I think she'll fit right in."

I said nothing. The priest chanted and the rock-and-roll band sang about love.

"Did you have a nice chat when you took her around the site?"

"Curious, aren't you?"

"Yes." He leaned back in his chair. The hand holding his glass of gin was propped up on one knee; the empty hand on the other. He was waiting. A moth was battering its head against the glass chimney of the lantern. I dimmed the light and moved it to the other end of the table, but the insect circled, found the lamp again, and continued its efforts to die.

"I don't understand what she wants from me," I said finally.

"Didn't you ask her that?" Tony said.

"I did. She said she wanted to dig up the past and see what was under the rubble."

He nodded.

For a moment we listened to the slap of the cards, the low murmur of the students' conversation, and the soft whir of the cassette player rewinding. The priest had stopped his wailing and I could hear the scrape of the obsidian knife against the hide. I realized that I was holding the burning cigarette, but not smoking. I took a long drag and exhaled slowly.

"I don't understand what she's doing here," I said abruptly. "It's all past history. I left her. Why should she look to me for comfort now?"

"Is she looking to you for comfort?"

"She's looking for her mother. I'm nobody's mother."

"Then she'll figure that out," he said. "And then she'll go. Is that what you want?"

I shrugged, unable to say what I wanted. "That would be fine," I said. "Just fine."

"All right," Tony said. "Maybe that will happen."

We sat quietly for a while. The priest resumed his chanting, but the card game seemed to be winding down. Carlos had his arm around Maggie's shoulders and the two of them were laughing a great deal. "She seems to have hit it off with Barbara," I said.

"True. And having another person on survey isn't a bad idea."

"I suppose." I frowned out at the darkness. "I wonder why she's so wary. I suppose that's Robert's doing."

"Give the woman a chance, Liz," he said. "Just give her a chance."

"She seems bright enough," I said grudgingly.

"That's something."

"All right," I said. "It was brave of her to come down here by herself. Is that what you're waiting for?"

He shrugged. "I'm not waiting for anything. I was just thinking that arriving unannounced seemed like the sort of thing that you would have done in her position."

"I suppose you're right," I admitted reluctantly.

"I think I am."

Carlos reached over to the tape player and the music clicked off. Carlos and Maggie headed off, arm in arm, on the path to the cenote, talking in loud whispers. John and Robin headed toward their huts. Tony poured himself one more drink. "You ever going to sleep?" he asked.

"Later," I said. "I'm not tired yet."

"It'll be all right," he said.

I shrugged and watched him walk away. I sat alone at the table.

In the dim lantern light, I could see only the outlines of the huts. The trilling of the insects in the monte seemed to match some internal rhythm, and I knew with a certainty born of experience that if I went to my hut now, I would not sleep. I would watch the shadows on the ceiling swaying as my hammock swayed, and wait until the morning came. I had learned, at times like this, to wait it out. Alcohol would put me out for a time, but when I drank myself to sleep I woke at five in the morning, feeling stony-eyed and wide awake. Sleeping pills would put me out—the university physician had prescribed some for my bouts with insomnia—but I did not like to resort to drugs. A pill would shut the lights out, as surely as a pillow forced down over my face, and there would be nothing I could do to chase the darkness away.

The darkness seemed to be pressing closer. The heat was oppressive. Diane's appearance made the past come back too vividly.

I had walked for miles in the two weeks before I ran away to New Mexico for the first time. Up and down the narrow streets, past fenced yards filled with weeds, past barking dogs and old men on porches and screaming children who always seemed to be running or fighting. Each morning, as soon as Robert drove away to the hospital, I would leave our small apartment. I always wore an oversized sun hat and a loose tent dress. On the days that Diane did not go to nursery school, she walked with me, her short legs working hard to keep up with my steady pace. When she started to whimper and complain, I would carry her for a few blocks. Then I would put her down and she would walk again.

I did not follow any particular route; I had no destination. I just walked—wandering randomly through the rundown section of Los Angeles where we rented our home. I had to walk: when I stayed in the apartment, I had trouble breathing. The walls were too close. I could not stay still.

My marriage to Robert had become intolerable, a cage I had entered willingly, but could not escape. Robert and I met in a chemistry class during my junior year of college. I had been working my way through school—relying on a small scholarship from my hometown Rotary Club and on the cash I could earn by typing papers for professors and more prosperous students. It was a hard life, but no worse than life in my parents' house had been.

I was an only child. My father was a dour straight-backed man who earned his living as a plumber and believed in a dour straight-backed Christian God. He did not believe that women needed a college education. He disapproved of my passion for collecting Indian arrowheads, stone tools, and fragments of pots. My mother, like the female birds of many species, had developed a drab protective coloration that let her blend into the background, invisible as long as she remained silent. She counseled me to adopt the same strategy, to be quiet and meek, but I could never manage it. I always felt like a fledgling cuckoo bird, hatched from an egg laid in an alien nest, a chick too big, too loud, too rambunctious for its adopted parents. When I graduated from high school, my father suggested that I take a job clerking at the local drugstore. I packed my bags and left.

At college, people left me alone. I could read what I pleased, do as I pleased. I led an isolated life, having little in common with the women in my boardinghouse. I was uninterested in mixers, boyfriends, and football games, and far too interested in science classes and books.

Robert was a scholarship student, an earnest young man who was careful in his studies. We started by arguing over an experiment in chemistry class and ended up going to a dance together. We got along. He thought I was clever; he laughed at my jokes. I think, looking back on it, that I never realized I was lonely until, with Robert, I was no longer alone. We went to dances, to movies when we could scrape the money together; we shared ice cream sundaes in the campus coffee shop. And I felt, for the first time, as if I belonged somewhere: I belonged with Robert. I changed for him—softening my manner, becoming less argumentative, paying more attention to how I looked, to the clothes I wore.

One night, after a bottle of wine in the backseat of a borrowed Chevrolet, I lost my virginity. A few weeks later, my period failed to arrive on schedule. We married, the only solution that seemed reasonable at the time, and I dropped out of college, still typing papers to earn a living but also carrying the tremendous weight of a growing child within me. After Diane's birth, during Robert's years of medical school, I typed while caring for the baby, doing laundry, and cooking cauldrons of soup and pasta—soup because it was cheap and pasta because it was filling.

I came to remember with nostalgia the long nights alone in my small boardinghouse room, reading until dawn, then rising to go to classes. In college, my time was limited, but it was my own. As a mother, I had no time. I managed to read sometimes, but only after Diane was asleep. I attended one archaeology lecture at the local college, but Diane grew restless and disrupted the lecture by crying or asking me loud unintelligible questions. The professor asked me not to bring thè child again, but we could not afford a babysitter.

I grew restless and my dreams became vivid: I wandered through exotic jungles filled with bright flowers, strange people, decaying ruins. I was impatient, angry with myself and the world around me.

Robert and I argued endlessly—about Diane, about money and the lack of it, about my housekeeping and the lack of it. I remember one evening at home quite vividly. Diane was asleep and I was darning Robert's socks and trying to watch a television documentary about the Indians of the Brazilian rain forest. Robert was home and awake, a rare combination. He was pacing, filled with nervous energy. At a party given by one of Robert's colleagues, an arrogant man had been talking about the limitations of what he called the "primitive" mind. He seemed to regard all nonwhite races as primitive. I argued with him for a while, and ended up calling him a stupid bigoted fool. Word of this had finally filtered back to Robert.

"Couldn't you have used a little tact?" he asked.

"You want me to kowtow to that idiot?"

"I want you to use a little sense. That idiot is head of surgery and he has a lot of pull at the hospital," Robert said. "You should know better. You used to know better."

I watched an Indian slash a rubber tree with a machete and catch the flowing sap in a bucket.

"What's wrong with you these days?" he asked. "Why are you always so touchy?"

I looked up from the television. "I don't want to be here," I said sadly.

Robert stopped pacing, suddenly sympathetic. "Neither do I." He sat beside me on the couch, put a comforting arm around my shoulders. "Things will get better," he said. "We won't always live here. When I have a good position, we can move to a better neighborhood."

I thought about a better neighborhood and imagined endless vistas of suburban lawns, white picket fences, laughing children. "No," I said.

He squeezed my shoulders gently. "We're almost there. Just one more year of residency. . . ."

One more year would bring me one more year closer to a suburban home that I did not want. "No," I said again. "I want to go to the jungle."

"What?"

I gestured at the television screen, where Indian women squatted by an open fire. "That's my idea of a better neighborhood," I said.

He laughed. "Right," he said. My father had laughed when I told him that I was going to college.

"I don't belong here. I don't know where I belong, but it isn't here."

He shook his head, still smiling. Unbelieving and amused by the whole idea. "For a smart woman, you can be really silly. What the hell would you do there? Besides, one week of the bugs and dirt and you'd be home."

I watched him coolly, suddenly wondering if he had ever listened when I talked of anthropology and archaeology. I could see him clearly, but he seemed very distant, as if a wall of glass had been lowered between us at the moment that he laughed. Diane called to me from her room—she needed a drink of water. Without a word, I left to go to her.

Robert never really understood the nature of my discontent, not even after I ran away from home, not even after I slashed my wrists. He kept waiting for me to turn back into the woman he married, never realizing that she was a sham; she never existed.

And so I strode through the neighborhood, trying to burn off the energy that kept me awake at night, energy that made it impossible to rest at all. It was on those walks that I first started seeing the shadows of the past. A group of Indian men setting forth on a hunt. Four women carrying woven baskets filled with unidentifiable roots. I remember seeing a Spanish friar, mounted on a tired burro, crossing my path on his way to somewhere important. A troop of mounted soldiers raised dust as they trotted down the paved street, disappearing when they continued straight through a building that blocked their way.

I clearly remembered the day that I did not go walking. Diane was five and sick with the flu. I stayed home to nurse her, pacing within the apartment. It was August and the temperature was holding steady at over 100 degrees, a heat wave that the TV weatherman kept promising would end. After hours of fussing and complaining, Diane was asleep. Robert was working a late shift at the hospital. I sat at the kitchen table on a wooden chair that wobbled. It was hot, too hot, and I had been drinking beer all afternoon with a neighbor, a slatternly woman who had nothing good to say about anyone. I had been drinking with her only because I could not stand being alone. I was twenty-six years old, and it seemed wrong to sit alone drinking beer after beer. But at six, when the neighbor left, I kept drinking cold beer and staring at the walls.

In that old apartment, the water heater grumbled, the refrigerator hummed, the floor creaked for no discernible reason. When I listened closely to the refrigerator, I could hear voices, like distant cocktail-party conversation.

After the neighbor left, I became aware that I was not alone. Very slowly, I became conscious of the woman who sat across the table in the seat that the neighbor had vacated. She was watching me. The light in the kitchen was dim—I had not turned on the overhead lamp and the orange light of the setting sun was filtered through smears of dirt on the kitchen window. The woman's face was in the shadows; I could not make it out.

I returned her stare for a moment, wondering vaguely how she had come to be there. "Want a beer?" I asked her.

She shook her head.

"So what do you think I should do? Run away? Or stay here and take care of the child?"

I had told the neighbor woman that I was thinking about leaving Robert. She had laughed at me and said that after a few months out on my own I would come running home.

The woman whose face I could not see did not laugh.

"Run away." Did she speak or was it the rumble of the water heater? The shadows had never spoken to me before.

There was a coldness in my stomach. I felt ill from the beer, dizzy with the heat. "I can't leave the child."

I strained to see the woman's face, but she was hidden in the shadows. "Why are you hiding?" I asked her. "Talk to me. What can I do?"

"Run away." There again, I heard the whisper.

"I can't leave. There must be something else I can do. There must be."

She looked down at her hands and lifted them above the edge of the table to show me what she held. Across her open palms, laid like an offering on an altar, was a knife, a sharp blade chipped from obsidian and glinting in the dim light.

Somewhere in the distance, far away, I heard a child cry out, and I started. I recognized Diane's voice. She was awake after a long nap and calling for me. I looked toward the shadows and the woman was gone.

I sat alone in the plaza and a large moth—maybe the brother of the moth that had tried so hard to reach the light and die—flew out of the darkness, hurled itself at the dim flame of the Coleman lantern, bounced off the glass, and returned to the night. I stood up, unwilling to sit still any longer. I did not want to remember. I walked out toward the Temple of the Seven Dolls, looking for Zuhuy-kak.

The monte was never silent. As I walked, the brush rustled around me with the soft careful movements of small animals. Insects sang and I could sometimes hear the chittering of bats overhead. Harmless sounds—I was accustomed to the monte at night. I passed Salvador's hut and followed the trail that wound through the ancient ruins.

I heard a rustling sound, like skirts against the grass, and looked behind me. Just the wind.

A pompous young doctor at the nuthouse had explained to me that I was having difficulty distinguishing my fantasies from reality. "You just object because I won't recognize your reality," I said to him. "I have no problems recognizing my own reality."

The doctor was a little older than I was at the time, maybe twenty-nine or thirty years old. He was crew-cut, clean-shaven, well-scrubbed, and his office smelled of shaving soap. "I don't see the difference. There's only one reality."

"That's your opinion." My wrists were still wrapped with white surgical gauze from wrist to elbow. The gashes had almost healed, but my arms were still stiff and sore. I crossed my arms across my chest defiantly. "I don't like your reality. I don't like my husband's reality either, but he won't let me change it."

The young doctor frowned. "You must cooperate, Betty," he said, looking genuinely concerned. "I want to help."

"My name is Elizabeth."

"Your husband calls you Betty."

"My husband is a fool. He doesn't know my name. My husband wants to kill me."

The young doctor protested that my husband cared very much for me, my husband wanted to protect me. The young doctor did not understand that there are shades of reality. Metaphor is reality once removed. I said that Robert wanted to kill me. Really, he wanted me to be quiet and compliant, as good as dead. He was not evil, but he did not understand what I needed to live. He wanted me to be dead to the world. When I saw the walls of the ward closing in, that was a kind of truth too. The world I lived in was small and getting smaller.

The young doctor believed in only one reality, the one in which young doctors are in charge and patients are very grateful. He would never admit to a reality in which spirits of the past prowl the streets of Los Angeles. That would not fit; that would not do. The doctor was a young fool then; probably an old fool now.

By the Spanish church I smoked a cigarette and listened for the sound of footsteps on the path. Nothing. I was alone. I fingered the bandage that covered the claw marks where the tree branch had raked my skin. My wrist ached, and the feeling brought back memories. My daughter slept nearby and that brought back memories too.

Sometimes, memories of my attempt at suicide return to me, unbidden and unwelcome. The scent of the aftershave that Robert favored, the wet warmth of steam rising from a newly drawn bath, the touch of cold glass to the skin of my inner wrist—these things recall the time that I locked the flimsy door to the bathroom, turned on the hot water so that it thundered into the tub. The rumble of the water covered the crash of breaking glass when I shattered a drinking tumbler in the sink. I did not like the thought of slicing my skin with a razor blade, cold metal against my skin. I held a long thin shard of sharp-edged glass in my hand and smiled; this was better, more appropriate.

It hurt, I remember that, but mixed with the pain was a sense of anticipation. I stood on the edge of something enormous, like the feeling just before orgasm when the body burns with a new intensity and every nerve is alive, so alive that each movement carries with it joy and pain. There are sensations so great that the body cannot contain them. We label these feelings pain for lack of a better word. I felt more than pain as I drew the glass edge along my wrist, more than the cold edge of the glass and the thin line of pain and the warm flow of blood down my arm. I could see the blood pump in time with the beating of my heart and I let it flow into the tub, where it mingled with the rushing water.

I was nearly unconscious when Robert broke the lock on the flimsy door and found me sprawled over the tub, my arms hooked over the porcelain lip, my wrists submerged in the hot water that overflowed the tub, pouring onto the floor, onto my naked body. I would have fought him, but my energy was gone. I had passed beyond fighting into a large empty place that roared with the sound of the sea. I was ready to go on, but Robert pulled me back.

Sometimes, I remember. I try not to.

Chapter Six: Diane

JUST after my father died, during the two weeks when I could not sleep and could not eat, my friend Marcia suggested I visit a psychologist. I went to see Marcia's counselor, a square-shouldered woman with soft gray eyes that looked out of place in a face composed of angles and harsh planes. On the wood-paneled walls of her office hung watercolors in black frames—an odd combination of softness and severity. She sat in a rocking chair. I sat in an easy chair that was too soft.

She asked me to talk about myself. I considered, for a moment, telling her about the night before my father's funeral. The memory had haunted me. For three nights running, I had dreamed of the great dark valley spreading beneath my father's balcony. I remembered the dreams only vaguely, waking each time to a feeling of panic and a memory of falling. While awake, I avoided the balcony, especially at night.

I spent my days sorting through my father's things—deciding what clothes would be donated to charity, what papers might be of interest to my father's colleagues at the hospital. Aunt Alicia kept asking me when I had to be back at work. I had not told her that I had quit work and given up my apartment. By night, I drank, watched television, and tried to sleep. But whenever I managed to doze off, I woke from strange dreams, restless and unhappy.

I told the counselor that my father was dead, that I could not eat and I had trouble sleeping, that I was very nervous and upset. She asked me about my father and my relationship with him, and I told her that my father and I had had a good relationship, a very good relationship.

She asked about my mother and I told her that my mother did not enter into this at all. I told her that I had not seen my mother in fifteen years.

"How do you feel when you think about your mother?" she asked. Her voice matched her eyes—pale gray and gentle.

I shrugged. "I don't know. Sad, I guess. Sad that she left."

She waited, studying me. "What are your hands doing?"

My hands were clenched in fists. I did not speak.

"Can you give your hands a voice and let them tell me how they feel?"

I shook my head quickly and forced my hands to relax. "Holding on," I said in a thick voice that did not sound like my own. "I guess they were holding on. I didn't want her to go."

The gray eyes studied me dispassionately and I thought that she did not believe me.

On my first morning in camp I woke to the sound of a blaring car horn. The clock on the footlocker said it was 8:00. Already the air was hot. Barbara's and Robin's hammocks were empty. Maggie was still asleep, curled up with the sheet pulled over her head. I felt more relaxed than I had in months, and I resolved, lying in my hammock, to adopt Tony's easygoing attitude and take things as they came.

I slipped out of my hammock and dressed quickly. Barbara was at the water barrel, washing her face. I wished her a good morning and hung my towel in the tree.

"I wish you wouldn't be so cheerful before I have my coffee," she grumbled, but she waited for me to wash up. On the way to the plaza, we passed the kitchen, a small hut constructed of slats. Through the open door, I could see a thin woman in a white dress tending a small fire and cooking tortillas on a flat black pan.

"That's Maria," Barbara said. "She's married to Salvador, the foreman." A small girl with large dark eyes stood by Maria and watched me solemnly. In one hand, she held a tortilla. When I smiled at her, she hid behind her mother. Maria looked over her shoulder to see what the child was watching.

I smiled but Maria did not smile back. She studied me seriously, suspiciously I thought. After a moment, she turned back to the fire and the tortillas. The little girl smiled at me, then hid her face behind her mother's skirt.

Tony and my mother were already at the table. Breakfast was *huevos rancheros* with tortillas, strong coffee, and fresh orange juice. My mother looked tired, but seemed filled with nervous energy. She greeted me and waved me to a chair, then went on making out a shopping list. "Yes, yes, pineapples, I'll get fresh fruit. What else? I know I've forgotten something important."

My mother finished checking over her list, then glanced at me. "I'll be going to the market in the afternoon," she said. "If you'd like to come along, we can get you a hat."

"Sure," I said. "I'd like that."

Tony's eyes were red-rimmed. His voice, when he spoke, was hoarse, rough as wool cloth against the skin. "I'll be going for a swim right after breakfast," Tony said softly. "Do you and Barbara want to join me? You have time."

Barbara and I agreed.

The other students were just wandering down to breakfast when Tony, Barbara, and I finished our coffee. Barbara and I returned to our hut to change into swimsuits, then followed Tony down the path.

At the crest of a small rise, I stopped to look around. In the distance, the Temple of the Seven Dolls stood above the barren ground. "According to the guidebook I read, this is one of the largest sites in the Yucatán," I said. I looked at the jungle that surrounded us and shook my head. "Am I missing something? Where are all the buildings?"

Tony stamped his foot lightly on the ground. "Underneath you," he said. "All around you." He waved a hand in the direction of the temple. "You have to learn how to look. Don't the mounds look a little more regular than hills should look? And you see how they're arranged so that they make a nice path from here to there." He drew a line in the air with his hand. "And look at the rocks that are scattered around. They aren't your average rocks."

"I suppose so," I said doubtfully.

"We're standing right on top of an old temple," he said.

"How do you know it's a temple?"

Barbara broke in. "Everything's a temple until someone proves otherwise," she said in a mildly derisive tone. "We could even give it a name: Temple of the Sun, say. Or Temple of the Jaguar—that sounds good. The names are arbitrary anyway."

"Careful," Tony said, smiling faintly. "You're giving away professional secrets."

"She'll keep it in the family," Barbara said. "She's trustworthy."

She started down the trail and we followed. I studied the rocks around us as we walked. Occasionally, I saw one that bore the remnants of carving, but most just looked like rocks.

The cenote was a pool of clear blue water, set in the limestone rock. Right beside the path, the rock sloped gently down to the water. On the far side, the rocks rose out of the water in a sheer face that leveled off several feet above the water's surface. I could not see the bottom of the pool. Water lilies floated at the far end.

We left our towels in the sun on the sloping rock. Barbara and I climbed in slowly. The water was cold, a shock after the heat of the morning. I swam a dozen laps, down to the water lilies at the far end and back. I could see tiny fish, each no longer than my finger, hovering just under the water lilies. When I swam toward them, they scattered, heading down into the darkness.

Tony sat on the sloping rocks, basking in the sun like an ancient reptile trying to absorb the warmth. He had leaned back on his hands and tilted his face to the sun. Now that he had taken off his shirt, I could see how thin he was. His skin, tanned to the color of old leather, seemed to fit him badly, like a shirt handed down from a larger man.

I climbed out on the rocks beside him. Barbara was still in the water, floating contentedly on her back. I spread my towel beside his and he acknowledged my presence with a nod.

"How deep is this pool?" I asked him.

He shrugged without opening his eyes. "Deeper than you think. According to the team from Tulane University, it goes straight down to a hundred and fifty feet. Keeps going at an angle from there. They did quite a bit of underwater work."

"Will you be diving this summer?" I asked.

Tony shook his head. "No budget for it. The university doesn't think this is a glamorous enough site for the big money."

I could understand that attitude. So far, I had seen nothing that looked particularly impressive.

"It's an important site," Tony was saying. "The oldest continuously occupied ceremonial center. But to convince the university to let us come back next year, we need to find something spectacular."

"Like what?"

"Jade masks, gold, pottery painted with pictures of important rituals. Or maybe a set of murals like the ones at Bonampak in Chiapas." He lay back, setting himself down gently as if his bones might shatter. "Something flashy—a tomb filled with treasure would be ideal. Something that can double as a tourist attraction."

"You think the chances are good?" I asked.

His eyes were still closed against the sun. He shrugged without opening them. "Hard to say. We're gambling. We always have to gamble. Liz likes gambling, I think. But then, she's never lost big. She has luck. The academics don't like her. But she has luck."

"I hope I won't be in the way here," I said. My voice sounded thin and weak. "I don't want to get in her way."

He opened his eyes halfway and squinted at me. "What do

you expect to find here?'' he asked. His voice was a low rumble, like the thunder of ocean waves on a warm beach or like rain on a tin roof on a winter morning. "Some come looking for secret knowledge; some, for adventure. What do you want here?''

I shrugged. "I don't really know.''

"You'll find something, that's certain. But it's never what you expect.''

"What do you want here?'' I asked him, closing my eyes against the sun.

"Warmth and peace,'' he said. "I used to want more, but the years have changed that.''

"What should I do?'' I asked lazily, my eyes still closed. "Expect nothing and see what comes?''

He was silent for a moment. "That might work.'' He hesitated. "Your mother doesn't know what to do with you—I can tell you that. That's why she's a little stiff. She doesn't know what role to play.''

I opened my eyes and wrapped my arms around my knees. The sun had dried my skin and the rock was warm beneath me. "Neither do I,'' I said.

"You've been doing okay,'' he said. "Just keep on the way you're going.''

I did not look at him. I watched Barbara dive beneath the water and pop up like a cork.

"I think that having you here will be good for Liz,'' he said. "I think she needs people more than she is willing to admit.'' I heard him shift position, but I still did not look at him. "Someone once told me that archaeologists are anthropologists who don't like live people. They dig up dead ones because dead ones can't talk back. That's not quite true. But I think live people are too fast for most archaeologists. We're a slow-moving lot. We look at a change in pottery technology that took a hundred years and say that that's pretty quick. We're used to taking our time. You'll have to give Liz some time to get used to the idea that she has a daughter.''

"All right,'' I said slowly. "I will.'' I lay back on my towel and let the sun warm me.

After a time, Barbara left the water and lay down beside us. Tony left after about fifteen minutes of sunbathing, saying he had some reading to do back at the camp. Barbara propped her head up to watch him go. He waved from the crest of the hill, then vanished from our sight.

"Ten to one he'll be on his third gin and tonic by the time we get back," Barbara said in a matter-of-fact tone.

I looked at her sharply.

"Don't get me wrong," she said. "I like Tony. Everyone likes Tony. And we all see that he drinks too much." She rolled over and lay on her back, her head pillowed on one arm. Her dark hair was slicked back and still glistening with water from the cenote. "It hasn't interfered with his work so far. He's still a brilliant teacher, from what I've heard. It's just in the field that he lets himself go."

I remembered what he had said about warmth and peace. Barbara glanced up at my face and shrugged. "Sorry. I suppose I shouldn't have mentioned it. After a while, there's not much to do in camp except gossip about the other people. Dead people, fascinating though they may be, are not nearly as interesting as the live ones." She turned her head and opened one eye to squint at me. "Don't you agree?"

"I suppose you're right."

"Of course," she said. "Now—what do you suppose Carlos and Maggie and Robin are saying about us?"

"What makes you think they are talking about us?"

"I thought we just went through that. They're talking about us because live people are more interesting than dead ones. You don't think that archaeologists talk about archaeology all the time, do you? No, they talk about other archaeologists. So what do you think they're saying about us?"

"Ten to one, Maggie thinks that I'm stuck up," I said, adopting her tone. "Probably thinks you are too."

"No bet there," Barbara said. "And Robin will go along with that, because Robin goes along with anything Maggie says. She has the mark of the eternal sidekick. What about Carlos?"

"If Carlos has any brains, he'll stay out of it."

"Ah, your first error of judgment. Carlos has no brains. I'd bet that he will try to defend us—at least he'll defend you. Carlos and I aren't the best of friends."

"So I'd noticed," I said dryly.

Barbara shook her head. "I can hear those wheels turning," she said. "And you can just stop. No, I never slept with Carlos. But I watched him sleep with four different women last summer—courting each one with equal energy and passion—and dropping each one just the same." She shrugged. "The first of the women was a very good friend of mine. She had to hang around the rest of the summer and watch Carlos make his moves on numbers two, three, and four. All of them were very nice women. All of them were burned." She shrugged again. "I don't know why he does it, but I think he likes trouble. Be careful."

"Thanks for the warning. I'd figured that out already."

"John, on the other hand, is a workaholic. I doubt if he even realizes women exist." She closed her eyes against the bright sun overhead. "So, do you want to place a bet on whether Maggie and Robin will wear mascara on survey tomorrow?"

We lay in the sun and chatted. Barbara had a sharp eye and a sharper tongue and she was quite amusing at the expense of the others.

After an hour or so, we heard shouting and laughter on the trail. A group of Mexican boys, ranging in age from five to fifteen, came scrambling down to the cenote. Barbara and I watched them swim for a time, but packed up to leave when the older boys started a contest to see who could make the biggest splash by leaping into the water from the sheer rock face. The rock where we were lying was right on the edge of the splash zone and retreat seemed the wisest course.

"It belongs to them the rest of the year," Barbara said as we headed back. "We only borrow it."

"Do they live near here?"

"Up at the hacienda, I think. You know, the ranch out by the highway. In the middle of the henequen fields."

"Long walk down here," I said.

She shrugged. "When there's only one place to swim, I suppose it doesn't matter much how long the walk is."

The camp was quiet. Tony sat in the shade by his hut, a drink balanced carefully on the arm of his lawn chair. My mother was apparently working on her book—I could hear the tapping of her typewriter. Barbara declared that the only thing worth doing was taking a nap. I borrowed a book from her, took a seat in the shade at one of the tables, and settled down to read.

Chickens scratched in the dirt around me, clucking bemusedly to themselves. A small black pig lay by the wall near the kitchen, taking a prolonged siesta. I could hear the cook's daughter singing to herself. She was just on the other side of the wall, scratching in the dirt with a stick. I could not understand the words of the song. They could have been nonsense or they could have been Maya. When she peeked over the edge of the wall, I smiled and said, "*Buenos días.*" She ducked back behind the wall and was silent for a few minutes. Then I heard the scratching of her stick in the dirt and she returned to her song.

The first chapter of Barbara's book gave a general history of the Mayan empire, profusely illustrated with photos of Chichén Itzá and Uxmal. Dzibilchaltún was mentioned as the oldest continuously occupied site, but the text included no photos. I understood why.

The Maya had occupied the Yucatán peninsula since 3000 B.C. They absorbed several invasions from Mexico. From the book, I got the impression that the Maya's strength was not in their military prowess, but in their ability to absorb invaders, adopt some of the new customs, retain some of their own. For the most part, they held their own until the Spanish came along. The Spanish conquistadors overcame the Mayan armies; the Catholic Church subdued the survivors. The friars seemed, from the book's account, to be concerned with saving the heathens' souls even if that meant ending their lives.

I took a break and drank a glass of water from the barrel in the shade. I considered going back to the cenote for another swim, but the prospect of the long, hot walk discouraged me. The plaza was hot, even in the shade. Tony had gone into his hut for a nap or another drink, I supposed.

The second chapter described the Mayan view of time, saying that the philosophy of time was an essential part of their way of thinking. The book failed to make it seem at all essential. I had read the first paragraph over three times and was considering a stroll through the ruins, when the jeep drove up in a cloud of dust. Carlos and Robin were sitting in the front seat; Maggie was alone in the back. "Hey, Robin," I heard Maggie say, "let's take this stuff to the hut and go for a swim."

The two women headed off together with their laundry bags, never looking back at Carlos. I suppressed a grin and looked back down at my book, considering the comments that Barbara might have on this particular sequence in the courtship rites.

I tried to concentrate on the book, but the description of the Mayan calendar was as dry as my throat. I had moved on to the second paragraph, but it was little better than the first. Cycles of twenty days made a month; eighteen months made a year. Each day had a name and the Maya believed that each day was the responsibility of the god of that name. There seemed to be an inordinate number of names and gods and cycles.

"Would you like a beer?" I looked up. Carlos was holding out an open bottle. The brown glass was beaded with condensation and a wisp of cold vapor curled from the open neck. Carlos set it on the table in front of me without waiting for my answer. He sat in the chair across from me and took a long drink from his own bottle.

I put the book down and took a long drink. The bottle was cold in my hand and the beer was cold running down my throat. "Thanks," I said. "That was a quick trip to town."

He nodded and grinned. He was tanned and handsome, and he knew it. He wore white shorts and an air of confidence. He pushed his chair back away from the table and propped his feet up on another chair. "Just long enough to do laundry and have an argument."

"An argument? What about?"

He seemed at ease, sleek and content as a well-fed cat. "I got myself in trouble with Maggie by commenting on how pretty you are."

"Barbara mentioned that you liked trouble," I said.

He glanced at me, then threw back his head and laughed. "I suppose I do," he said. "I seem to find it often enough."

"Are you sure you don't go looking for it?" I asked.

He shrugged, still grinning. "Could be. You are pretty, though. You're from Los Angeles, aren't you?"

"That's right."

"I spent about five years in Los Angeles. I'm from Mexico originally, Mexico City. L.A.'s a nice town. Why the hell did you decide to spend your vacation in this godforsaken spot?"

I did not look at his face; I considered the condensation on the beer bottle. One drop traced a path through the other drops and reached the table. I shrugged. "I really just wanted to spend time with my mother."

"I see." He turned the book, which I had set down on the table, and read the title. "I would have thought you knew all this already. Being Liz's daughter."

"I don't know much at all," I said. "This is my first dig." On the wall by the kitchen, a small blue lizard marked with yellow stripes was sunning itself. The black pig shifted its position, sighed, and continued its nap. I could still hear the little girl singing softly. The chickens were scratching in the dirt. I watched the chickens and regretted having accepted the beer. I did not want to talk about my reasons for coming here.

"Why don't you tell me something interesting about the ancient Maya?" I asked.

I could see him weighing possible comments. "Your eyes are the most beautiful shade of green I've ever seen," he said at last.

I raised my eyebrows. "That has nothing to do with the ancient Maya."

"That's true." He paused, and when he spoke again, he spoke slowly, as if choosing each word with care. "The ancient Maya carved elaborate ornaments of jade using nothing but stone tools. The jade that they carved was just the color of your eyes."

I couldn't help smiling a little. "A little better. Try one more time, and leave my eyes out of it."

He tapped a cigarette from his pack and lit it, studying my face as he did so. Then he said, "The people who have put their minds to translating the Mayan hieroglyphics have come to the conclusion that many of the symbols are puns and puzzles. '*Xoc*,' for example, means 'to count.' It is also the name of a mythical fish that lives in the heavens. So the Maya used the head of the fish to represent counting. But since the fish was difficult to carve, they substituted the symbol for water, since that's where fish live. The symbol for water is a jade bead, since both are green and precious. So jade means water means fish means to count." Carlos paused, took a drag on his cigarette, and blew out a cloud of smoke. "And as confusing as all that sounds, it is simplicity itself compared to the mind of a woman." He tapped the ash from his cigarette and looked at my face. "Is that better?"

"I don't think so," I said, but I couldn't help smiling. He worked so hard at being charming. "Somehow, I think that I'll learn more about the Maya by reading a book."

"Could be. But I'm much more amusing than a book. You did smile there for a minute."

"You got me there." I studied his smiling face. Clever and dishonest and charming. "How many times have you used that line before?"

He shrugged. "I never use the same line twice."

"Was all that about the hieroglyphics true?"

"It may not be true, but I didn't make it up. I leave that to the professors. When I get to those exalted ranks, I'll make up my own outlandish theories." He leaned back in his chair, his arms locked behind his head, his legs outstretched.

I believed him when he said he never used the same line twice. He was a fisherman, choosing his bait carefully with a certain fish in mind.

A moment of silence. The lizard suddenly lifted its head and ran away across the wall. The little girl's singing had stopped. As I watched, she peeked over the wall at us.

"What's the little girl's name?" I asked Carlos. "She won't talk to me."

"That's Teresa. *Qué tal, Teresa?*"

She smiled at him and muttered something in Spanish. He said something else to her, but the only words I caught were *"la señorita."* Teresa shook her head and said something quickly that I could not begin to understand. She turned and ran away to the kitchen hut.

Carlos looked at me. "I asked her why she wouldn't talk to you. She said that her mother told her not to."

"I wonder why."

Carlos shrugged. "Maybe she's worried that getting to know loose American women will corrupt her little girl."

"What makes her think we're loose?" I said.

He raised his eyebrows and grinned. "All American women are loose," he said. "Ask any Mexican man."

"Somehow, I wouldn't trust you as an expert on American women." I leaned back in my chair and noticed my mother watching us from the door of her hut. I waved to her and she strolled out into the plaza.

"I'll be leaving for town in fifteen minutes or so," she said.

I finished my beer and stood up. "I'll be ready."

She glanced at Carlos, and turned away without saying anything. "You know," he said when she was out of earshot, "I don't think your mother likes me."

The ride to town was hot. The truck hit the potholes in the road hard and the seats were poorly padded. The roar of the engine made polite conversation impossible. Now and then, my mother would shout over the engine to point out a landmark—the road to a small village, the henequen-processing plant, a local high school.

The market in Mérida was housed in a corrugated-steel building: a place of noise, low ceilings, strong smells, and confusion. A beggar woman wrapped in a fringed shawl huddled beside the doorway. My mother dropped a coin in her hand and started into the crowd. I followed a few steps behind.

A woman in a white dress, embroidered with flowers at the neck and hem, carried a plastic basin filled with strange yellow fruits. She balanced it on her head, steadying it with one hand and making her way purposefully through the crowd.

A man shouted behind me and I stepped aside. He carried three crates in a stack on his back, secured with a rope wrapped around his forehead. I let him pass, then hurried after my mother.

An old peasant woman held out a plastic bowl filled with peppers, calling out the price. A younger woman, her daughter I think, squatted beside her, carefully arranging glossy peppers in a neat pile on a square of white cloth.

My mother stopped by a stall in which a wizened old man stood, surrounded by burlap sacks filled with beans. Each sack was open to display its contents—red beans, black beans, rice, dried corn. My mother fingered the black beans and exchanged a few words with the man. He shoveled several scoops of black beans into the metal dish of a scale and poured them into a smaller sack.

My mother glanced to make sure I was with her, beckoned me to follow, and continued through the crowd. "Maria does most of the shopping," she commented. "She's better at bargaining. I'm just picking up a few things."

Another stop—this one for chickens. My mother bargained and the chickens watched her nervously from between the wooden slats of their crates. Chicks peeped from the back of the stall, and three large turkeys, exhausted in the heat, lay in the dust of the aisle. The three black hens that my mother bought pecked at the hands of the boy who carried them, still crated, to the truck.

My mother made her way through the crowd with confidence, not stopping to glance at the butcher's stall, where vacant eyes stared from the face of a butchered pig. She seemed undisturbed by the warm sweet scent of overripe fruit and the underlying aroma of decay. She stepped around the squatting women who haggled over the price of tomatoes. She sidestepped to avoid the small dog licking at a crushed mango on the pavement. Now and then, she nodded to a shopkeeper, stopped to buy something—a plastic bag packed with ground pepper the color of blood, a bunch of bananas, a bag of small yellow squash.

I followed her, carrying her packages, stopping when she stopped. I was out of place here—I did not understand a word of the rapid transactions that were taking place all around me. But as long as I followed my mother, I felt protected. She obviously belonged here. I stayed close to her.

"Are you doing all right?" she asked just as we were about to plunge down another aisle of stalls, through the dim light and tropical heat. Without waiting for a reply, she said, "We'll stop for a drink soon." She bought two pineapples, a bunch of radishes, and two heads of wilted lettuce.

We left the food in the truck with the squawking chickens and she bought me a Coke—too sweet but at least it was wet. We sat at a counter and the crowd surged past us.

"It's confusing," I said.

She shook her head, smiling. "At first, I suppose. You get used to it."

"I'd like to." And that was good. Maybe I would have the chance to get used to it.

When we finished our drinks, my mother led me to another area of the market: a line of stalls filled with dresses, hammocks, shawls, sandals, blankets, tourist trinkets. She stopped at a hat-seller's stall and chatted with the man behind the counter. Something in her manner had changed. She had slowed down, relaxed a little. She lit a cigarette and laughed at something the man said. I stood to one side, fingering the brim of a hat, grateful for the breeze that blew in from the street, fanning away the heavy scent of decay.

The man held out a broad-brimmed hat with a high crown. "Try it on," my mother said. The man nodded and smiled and said something in rapid Spanish that made my mother

laugh again. When she replied, he shrugged and spread his
hands in a gesture of denial.

"He says that you look very pretty," my mother told me.
"And he says that you look like me." She smiled and leaned
against the counter. "I told him that he was just trying to
make a sale." She looked younger when she laughed, her
blue eyes caught in a net of wrinkles, her face shaded beneath the broad brim of a straw hat similar to the one I wore.
"What do you think?"

I glanced in the mirror that the man held out. "Great."

Bargaining for the hat took longer than bargaining for
food, proceeding at a more leisurely pace, with more smiles
and laughter. Final sale and my mother dropped the stub of
her cigarette, ground it into the asphalt at her feet, and used
both hands to adjust the hat on my head. She eyed it critically
and nodded. "Looks good. Wear it on survey."

That was it. We drove back with our produce, and the
chickens squawked each time we hit a bump.

Notes for City of Stones
by Elizabeth Butler

Why do we come here to dig in the dirt, living in huts and going without showers, battling insects and trudging through the afternoon heat? Some people think that archaeologists look for treasure—jade masks, delicate shell jewelry, beaten-gold ornaments. In truth, we search the gray stone past for something much more elusive.

We are looking for patterns. We search for pieces of the past and try to reassemble them. Who lived here? How did they live? Who ruled them and how was that determined? Who were their gods and how did they worship them? Did the people of this place trade salt and carved shell from the gulf for pots from Tikal, obsidian tools from Colha, molded figurines from Isla de Jaina? What news traveled with the merchants who journeyed along the *sacbeob*, the limestone roads that connected the cities? Did merchants talk of the rise of new rulers, the festivals held to honor gods, the failure of the cacao-bean crop, the overabundance of quetzal feathers this year, the new fashions in Uxmal, the rumors of war in the north?

Each of us looks for patterns in his own way. Anthony Baker, my co-director, is a good man with a trowel and a brush, possessed of awesome patience and the dexterous hands of a grease monkey. In his youth, Tony dismantled and reassembled clocks, electric motors, gas-powered engines, mechanical toys, and, on one hot summer day, the fiendishly intricate planetary-gear-shifting mechanism hidden in the hub of a three-speed bicycle, a device constructed of gears within gears and wheels within wheels.

These days, Tony deals with intricate constructions of a different kind. Tony studies pots. Or, to be more accurate, he studies pieces of pots—potsherds, broken fragments of bowls and pitchers and vases and incense burners and little pipes and ceremonial vessels. Long ago, the vessels broke and the shattered pieces were tossed in the trash heap, thrown into the fill for a new building, kicked aside, cast off, ignored. Tony gathers these fragments and considers them with affection.

When Tony finds a potsherd, chances are he'll pop it in his mouth to clean it with spit. Archaeologists get used to the taste of dirt and Tony claims he learns about a sherd by its taste and its texture. Each sherd carries its history with it. What kind of clay did the potter use? What was added to the clay to temper it? How was the pot shaped, decorated, burnished, fired? Tony concerns himself with these things, and sometimes I think that he would be quite at home chatting with the artisans of A.D. 800 about the merits of organic paint over mineral paints, sand-tempered clay over untempered clay. Behind his home in Albuquerque he has a studio where he turns and fires pots.

Fashions in pottery changed steadily over the years, and potsherds are durable records of changing times. The presence of certain types marks the passage of certain eras. Finding a broken bowl in the fill of a palace lets us date the structure.

John, one of Tony's most trusted graduate students, has a different preoccupation. Though I have never asked, I believe that his father was a bricklayer or a carpenter, a builder of some sort. John admires a well-built wall. He will talk for hours about arches—noting the difference in construction methods used in A.D. 400 and 800. I think he would be happiest if he were funded to rebuild a temple or two, mortaring temple stones in their rightful places. He draws elegant reconstruction sketches, extrapolating from the tumbled stones of the structure back to the plans from which it could have been built. In his sketches, he realigns the walls, returns the roof combs to their lofty position, carefully sets each stone of the arches back in its place, canting them inward to make a smooth line. His drawings are black and white—fine ink lines on smooth white paper. John knows that the Maya painted their stucco and stone—traces of red and black paint still cling to sheltered stones. But his imagination stops short of color. He likes the stones—solid, massive, and gray—and does not embellish upon them.

And what do I like? I like asking impossible questions about remnants less tangible, but no less durable, than pots and walls. Ancient gods, myths, legends, modes of worship, belief systems—these are my concern. What motivated the potter to shape an incense burner, a mason to build a wall? When a small child woke crying in the dead of the night, what frightened him and to whom did he pray for comfort? When a woman was dying in childbirth, what god did the h'men call on for power?

The questions are impossible; the answers, elusive. I have fewer clues than Tony or John: ancient texts in unreadable glyphs, unreliable records kept by Franciscan friars on the pagan religion they sought to destroy, ceremonial objects cast in cenotes and sealed in tombs, fragments of knowledge retained by the current h'menob. And the embellishments of my own imagination. In my dreams of the ancient past, the buildings are always painted in vivid colors. I people them with ghosts.

Tony makes pots; John builds walls; and I construct castles in the air.

Chapter Seven: Elizabeth

"**W**HO are your gods?" The old woman smelled sour. Her costume was constructed like a Mayan temple: layers rested on layers upon layers. An orange turtleneck showed through the ragged holes in a thick brown fisherman-knit cardigan. The hem of a wine-colored skirt dangled beneath her green dress. She was dressed for a colder climate than Berkeley in the spring, bundled to withstand arctic winds. She had singled me out of the crowd of browsers in the used bookstore, recognizing me as a fellow outcast.

"Who are your gods?" Her voice was cracked, a parody of a confidential whisper. She stepped closer and the smell of unwashed clothes enveloped me.

I had been a lecturer on the Berkeley campus for one year and I had gained a reputation for being hard-nosed, unyielding, uncompromising. But when I looked into the bag lady's eyes—innocent blue eyes with the color and luminance of cracked antique glass—I backed away. "I don't know," I muttered before fleeing down another aisle of books.

She pursued me, waving her finger with greater energy. They know me, these strange ones with crystalline eyes that see what others do not.

"Sorry," mumbled the clerk who had followed us both. He was talking to us and to himself. He was sorry that he was the one who had to throw the woman out. "Sorry, but you are disturbing the other customers." He was looking at the bag lady, but somehow I felt that he included me as a troublemaker. "I'll have to ask you to leave."

"She's not hurting anyone," I said in a feeble voice that no student of mine would have recognized.

Too late. The old woman was shuffling toward the street, mumbling and clutching her sweaters about her. The clerk cast me a doubtful look, and I knew that I was tagged as a strange one, a woman who talked to the human flotsam that drifted down Telegraph Avenue. I left the store soon after.

John, Tony's favorite student at the dig, always looked at me with an air of faint doubt that reminded me of the bookstore clerk. I did not trust John and he did not trust me.

After breakfast, Tony and I lingered over our coffee. Diane had left with the survey crew, wearing her new broad-brimmed hat and a liberal coating of Barbara's sunscreen. Barbara seemed to be taking care of my daughter, making sure she was properly dressed, instructing her in the use of a compass. Diane was smiling when she left. In the light of day, memories of my personal past were less urgent than they had seemed at night. My daughter seemed happy enough; we would talk to each other and the uneasiness between us would dissolve. My immediate concern was a past of considerably greater antiquity.

Tony had assigned John to supervise the workmen who were moving the brush heap away from the broken stone that might hide an underground chamber. I had wanted to supervise the work myself, but Tony had insisted that we let a student oversee the operation. "You have to let them have some fun," he had said.

John was fired with a fierce dedication that was uncomplicated by imagination or eagerness to speculate. He was meticulous, given to caution and obsessed by details. His field reports were noteworthy for the amount of information he packed into a page of small careful printing.

Tony poured me a second cup of coffee. He would not let me leave for the site right after breakfast. "You'll just pace around, getting in the way and doing your best to get heatstroke."

The morning was really too warm for hot coffee, but I ignored the heat and drank the coffee, sweetening it with unrefined sugar that was the color and consistency of California beach sand. The condensed milk that substituted for cream added a slight tang of metal.

"When have I ever been in the way?" I asked.

He grinned and leaned back in his chair. "Save your energy," he advised. Even as a young man, Tony had been slow-moving. Not lazy—he would work hard if the situation called for that. But he was always careful to ascertain exactly what work was needed and what work could be avoided. He considered each problem carefully before he acted, never wasting a movement. My own inclination was to attack a problem at once, trying various approaches in succession until one seemed most productive. "You chase problems like a city dog chases rabbits," Tony had observed once. Tony waited until the rabbits came to him.

We gave John an hour's head start. Maybe a little more—Tony insisted on strolling to the southeast site at an irritatingly leisurely pace. We arrived just as the workmen were hauling away the last branch. John was directing the work, his baseball cap pushed back on his head and a bandanna tied around his neck. His face was red with exertion and yesterday's sunburn. Beneath his arms, his T-shirt was already dark with sweat. His arms were laced with red scratches from the thorns.

I squatted beside the tilted stone. It measured about three feet by three feet; one edge was about three inches out of flush with the plaza, cracking the plaster that covered it. Dirt had filled the depression where the stone tilted down.

"Maybe a chultun," Tony said and grinned. The underground storage chambers called chultuns often contain unbroken pots, a rarity at this site.

"Maybe a burial," I said. "A high-ranking individual, perhaps, buried just outside a major temple." The tools and artifacts found in tombs are a rich source of information on the Mayan view of the afterlife.

John deals in the actuality, not in speculation. "I don't

understand how you happened to notice it,'' he said. "Can't
say I would have given it a second glance.''

I shrugged. "Go for a walk at dawn sometime,'' I suggested. "The shadows are better then.'' But even as I made
the suggestion, I doubted that John would profit by it. Even
at dawn, his imagination was limited. I doubted that he
would notice a Mayan woman who stood in the shadows. I
glanced at the spot where Zuhuy-kak had stood, but there
was no sign of her. In the jungle, a bird called on a rising
note of interrogation, but I had no answers.

"It's cemented in place pretty well,'' John said. "It'll take
all day to work it loose, I'd guess. And I'll need to take two
workers from the crew on the house mounds to do it.''

Tony frowned. The house mounds were his favorite site;
he was hoping to find vast quantities of sherds and he be-
grudged any attempts on my part to shift workers away from
that project. "Think it's worth it?'' he asked.

"It's only a day, Tony.''

He shook his head, but did not argue further.

We checked in on the investigation of house mounds near
the plaza, an operation that was also under John's supervision.
Four men were digging a test trench across one mound. The
de facto leader of the crew, an older man who went by the
nickname of Pich, grinned at me and climbed from the trench
when I greeted him in Maya. He pushed his straw hat back
on his head, wiped his hands on his white pants, already
marked with smears of powdery soil, shook my hand, and
bemoaned their lack of luck so far. Removing wheelbarrow
after wheelbarrow filled with dirt had revealed only fragments of plainware—potsherds with no markings—and as-
sorted tools for grinding corn. I patted Pich on the shoulder,
suggested that the crew take a short break to smoke, handed
around cigarettes, and offered a few words of encouragement.

On the far side of the clearing, the shadow of a woman
who had died long ago was grinding maize, rubbing the
kernels between two stones and leaning into each stroke. Nearby,
a naked little boy played with a small dog. I suspected that

no matter how much dirt we moved in this area, we would find only broken plainware and grinding tools. At this spot, I had seen only the shadows of peasants going about their daily chores. But I could not tell that to Tony.

We left John, Pich, and the crew and followed the winding path around the mound to the far side, where Salvador was supervising a group of men. The sun was high. The shadows were sharp-edged patches on the barren earth. We climbed the mound in the afternoon heat, following the path worn by the workmen. For the past two weeks, the men had been stripping away the dirt that covered the top of the mound. It still didn't look like much: a heap of rubble with a recently flattened top; a jumble of flat-sided boulders. The work had exposed one wall of the temple on the crest, and we were using that as a guide to establish the orientation of the building.

Mayan buildings were constructed using tremendous quantities of stone and limestone cement. They used corbeled arches, building up a curved opening by placing each block farther in than the block on which it rested. Sometimes, they used beams of sapodilla, a local hardwood, as supports. When the beams collapsed and the roofs caved in, the rooms filled with stone rubble and the building became a mound.

"Good thing I trust your judgment, Liz," Tony said from behind me. He had stopped in the trail, resting in the scant shade of a tree. He had been trailing a few steps behind me as we walked up the mound. "If anyone else had insisted on excavating that area at the expense of the house mounds, I might have argued."

"Good thing," I said. I waited for him to move from the shade.

"Come now, Liz," he said, pushing back the straw hat he wore to keep the sun out of his eyes. "Tell me why you think we should take two men from the house mounds to loosen that block."

"Looks promising."

"A better reason."

"A hunch," I said. "I just don't think we'll find much more than we already have at the house mounds."

"Son of a bitch," he said. "I wish your hunches weren't right so often. All right. I give up."

I smelled Salvador's cigarette before I saw him waiting for us at the top of the path. "How goes it?" I called to him in Spanish.

He squatted to crush his cigarette against the ground and dropped the stub in the pocket of his loose-fitting white pants. "We have found something," he said in Spanish and gestured for us to follow him around the crest of the mound.

The test pit was a two-meter square, sunk in the rubble on the far side of the mound. Since the last time I visited this site, the crew had taken the pit down to a depth of more than a meter. Tony crouched on the edge of the pit and began fanning himself with his broad-brimmed hat.

I stood over him and peered into the pit. The men grinned up at me. The floor of the unit was a jumble of large stones that could well have been part of a roof. On one, I could see the traces of worn decoration. Others had obviously been shaped.

"Over there," Salvador said, pointing to the far corner of the pit, which was slightly higher than the others. The workman—I recognized him as Salvador's nephew—stood aside to give me a clear view. Between two stone slabs, a great stone head lay wedged in the floor of the pit.

I told the men to take a break and climbed down into the pit carefully. It was pleasantly cool after the sunshine of the mound. I used a stiff brush to clear the loose dirt away from the face. The head was about three times life size. It was not actually stone; it had been sculpted in the durable stucco that the Maya had manufactured using local limestone. I recognized the spiraling tattoos that decorated one cheek. Zuhuy-kak, the ghost who haunted me, had been a woman of power in her time. Carved shells decorated her carved braids. Below the headdress, the forehead was flattened. Long ago, the tip of the nose had been chipped. A crack ran through the forehead, through the left eye and the left cheek.

I ran one finger along the crack, but could not tell if it was only on the surface or if it went all the way through. Offhand, I would have guessed that it had been at least a thousand years since those staring eyes had last seen the sky.

"Looks like it could have been part of the roof comb or a decorative facade," I said to Tony, trying to suppress my excitement. "If that's so, there should be others. Would you say ninth century or eighth?"

He shrugged and grinned at me and I found myself grinning back. "Doesn't much matter, does it?" he said.

"It's too late to do much now. Looks like it will take a few days to get it free. Tomorrow, let's start by getting this out of the way," I said, tapping on the smaller of the two slabs beside the head. "And maybe we can get her out intact."

I reached up for Tony's hand, and he helped me climb back into the sun. Salvador was standing by. "Good find," I said. Salvador shrugged and smiled. "We'll work on it tomorrow." We left the head where it lay, staring up at the sky from the rubble of an ancient roof.

Chapter Eight: Diane

"A ruin is never going to speak, except if
one's mind gives it magnetic power, gives
it force. For this reason, we should not
confuse ourselves that the spirit, that the
evil shadows, frighten us, kill us. One
frightens oneself; it is not the shadow that
frightens us."
>   —Eduardo el Curandero,
>   the Words of a Peruvian Healer

EVEN at six in the morning the air was warm. Lizards basked
on the rocks, running a few feet as we approached, then
stopping to watch us.

Barbara led the way and I walked beside her, wearing the
hat my mother had given me. Carlos, Maggie, and Robin
trailed behind.

"We're walking on history," Barbara told me, stamping
one boot on the ground beneath our feet. "This is a limestone
causeway, built by the Maya. They built miles of them all
over the place. God knows why. Trade, religious ceremonies
. . ." She shrugged. Her mannerisms and speech reminded
me of someone, but for a moment I could not place them.
Then I remembered walking with my mother to the Temple

of the Seven Dolls. Barbara had adopted the same staccato style: abbreviated and to the point. "They called the roads *sacbeob*. The singular form of the word is *sacbe*. Plural is *sacbeob*. We're using this one as a reference line for the survey."

Trees crowded close on either side. Grasses and scrub had grown underfoot, but the way was clear compared to the monte around us.

Like my mother, Barbara did not wait for questions. She assumed that I was interested. "Aerial surveys are just about useless here," she said. "They give you a great view of trees, but that's it. The only way to map a site is to walk it and get personally acquainted with every tree, rock, stinging bug, and thorn. This causeway runs east. We'll be mapping the quadrant between here and a line due south. That means we've got to walk over every square foot and note every ruin, mound, and monument. Maybe we sample some of the ones that look promising."

"Then what?"

"Then I figure out a theory based on what we find, get my Ph.D., and you call me Dr. Barbara." She stopped beside a tree marked with a blaze and waited for the others to catch up. When they did, she turned into the monte, following what looked like a deer trail to another blazed tree.

The concept of the survey, as Barbara described it, was simple enough. The survey team spread out, leaving about twenty paces between people. Carlos was on one end of the line and Barbara was on the other. Carlos made a blaze on trees as he passed them; Barbara followed the line of blazes from the previous day. We were to follow a compass course due east. Barbara instructed me on the use of the compass and put me in the middle of the line.

It was hot work, sticky work, boring work—trudging through the monte, ducking branches, climbing over rocks, shouting out when I stumbled over something of interest, and then waiting while Barbara carefully noted its location on her map. The first three mounds we found had already been noted by the Tulane University crew several years before, but Barbara methodically checked location and noted minor corrections.

Flies hovered just in front of my eyes, dancing and buzzing, a constant irritation. I trudged through the heat, listening to the shrill cries of insects, the rustling of small animals and birds, the sound of footsteps, the occasional crash when someone blundered into a low-slung branch and the curses that followed. At regular intervals, the sounds of the monte were punctuated by the solid impact of Carlos's machete against the innocent trees. I stabbed myself several times before I learned to watch for thorns. It took a great deal of effort to keep looking for the lines of rocks that Barbara said marked where walls had once been, the overgrown low mounds that had once been huts or temples.

Conversations grew shorter as the day grew hotter. Even when we were waiting for Barbara to complete corrections on her map, we maintained our positions in line, unwilling to move together just to move apart again. Early morning was hot; midmorning was hotter. At about eleven, beside the largest mound we had yet encountered, Barbara called a lunch break.

We sat in the thin shade of a ceiba tree, saying little, drinking water, and eating the tortillas and cheese that Maria had packed. Maggie was still pissed off at Carlos, I think. She and Robin sat a little way apart from us, sharing food and laughing at private jokes. Carlos tried to start up a conversation with me and Barbara, but Barbara ignored him and I was too tired to be drawn into talk.

I leaned back against the solid trunk of a tree and, drowsy from the heat, let my eyes droop closed. Such a peaceful place, I thought. I was still tired from my sleepless nights in Los Angeles, and I was at peace for the first time in weeks. I relaxed.

The bark of the tree at my back had a strong sweet aroma, like the smoke of incense carried on the breeze. In the distance, a bird called with a long low breathy note, like the sound of a child blowing across the top of a bottle. The call ended, then came again, a hollow tone that rose in pitch. The buzz of the insects seemed to grow louder and harsher, as if in response to the bird's call. A warm breeze fanned my face, and the sweet smell was stronger.

I dreamed that I heard voices, unfamiliar voices. In the private darkness behind my closed eyes, I listened, but I could not understand the language that the voices spoke.

I opened my eyes, but I was still dreaming. Across from me, a temple built of carved limestone blocks glistened in the afternoon sun. I squinted against the reflected light.

The voices continued, muttering softly in a foreign tongue. I could see two men, standing in the bright sunlight and looking down at a carved slab of stone. They were dressed in white loincloths and their bare chests were decorated with intricate tattoos in great swirling patterns, like the waves of a turbulent sea. At their feet was an incense burner in the shape of a crouching cat. Smoke escaped from the cat's mouth, white tendrils curling past sharp teeth and dissipating in the breeze.

I knew somehow, with the certainty of a dreamer, that the men were a threat to me. I did not like them. There was something cruel about their faces. They did not smile and their voices were harsh, hard-edged.

I sat very still, not even moving to wipe away the sweat from my forehead. If I did not move, perhaps they would not notice me, perhaps I could get away. I felt the same panic that had touched me on my father's balcony.

A drop of sweat trickled down my forehead and dripped into my eyes. I blinked and the men were gone. The voices were gone. The temple was gone. I sat alone beneath a tree, staring out at the sunlight that filtered through the thin leaves. A twisted tree grew where the men had been standing. At its base was a fallen log, overgrown by creeping vines and thornbushes.

Disoriented, I stood and went to where the men had been standing. The air was as warm and stuffy as the air in an attic. The flies droned, flickering like spots before my eyes. Sweat trickled down my back, making my shirt cling to my skin. A vagrant branch, lined with thorns and eager to make mischief, grabbed at my shirt as I squatted beside the fallen shape beneath the tree.

It was not a fallen log. Thorny creepers had overrun a large block of limestone, covering the surface completely. I gingerly pulled one aside and caught a glimpse of the carved surface underneath. I looked around and saw Barbara, poking in the bushes on one side of the mound. "I've found something here," I called to her.

She picked her way slowly through the brush to reach my side. She knelt beside the limestone block and used the trowel that she carried at her belt to scrape away more vines. She cut away the branch of one bush with the edge of her trowel and held back another, careless of the thorns and of the black bugs that ran away from the sudden light. I could see the weathered surface of a carved slab of stone, half buried in dirt and debris.

"It's a stela," she said. I must have looked at her blankly. "A monument," she said. "They put them up to commemorate certain dates: religious festivals, historic events, astronomical happenings. Usually, they're carved with glyphs. Some sites—like Chichén Itzá or Copán—had dozens of them. They've only found a few around here."

The stone was worn by centuries of rain. I could make out the profile of a face, outlined by dark fragments of decayed leaves. Here and there, I could see the remnants of other carvings.

"We'll get a crew to raise it," Barbara said. "Maybe the other side is better preserved." She was grinning. "Good work. I was hoping to find something that can help date the outlying sites so I'd know whether they were inhabited at the same time as the main area. That'd help us get an idea of the population that this center supported." She stood up and looked around as if she expected to find more. "You're as lucky as Liz at this game."

We searched the rest of the area and found no more monuments. Maggie discovered a tree filled with stinging ants. I found a tree loaded with thorns and managed to forget about the two men in the dream. Nothing else of note. On our way back, we laid a transect line adjacent to the line we had laid going in.

Chapter Nine: Elizabeth

AT dinner that night, Maggie sat beside John and kept up an animated conversation over the chicken and stewed tomatoes. I assumed that she had quarreled with Carlos and wondered how long it would take for them to make up. Diane and Barbara were talking quietly about the book that Diane was reading.

"I read about the Mayan calendar today," Diane said to me. "It seems confusing: twenty days to a month, eighteen months to a year, twenty years to a . . . ." She stopped. "I've forgotten."

"A katun," I said. "It gets worse. From the sound of it, you were reading about the Long Count. There's also the haab, a cycle of three hundred and sixty-five days divided into eighteen months, with five days at the end for bad luck. There's the tzolkin, a cycle of two hundred and sixty days divided into thirteen months. And then there's the cycle of the katuns, which repeats every two hundred and fifty-six years. But you don't have to worry about the names and numbers. You just need to understand the intent. The calendar let the Maya follow the cycles of time and predict the future by knowing the past. Whatever happens at a particular time will recur when that time returns. If the last Katun 8 was a katun of upheaval and discord, this one will be too. A *h'men*, a Mayan priest, can determine which gods influence a certain day—and because he knows the gods, he can predict what will happen at that time. He can advise you on whether you should expect a particular day to be lucky or unlucky, good for planting corn or for hunting or for burning incense. The Maya looked for patterns.''

Diane nodded and smiled in a strange sort of way. We were in a little island of quiet: Tony was talking with Robin; Carlos was watching Maggie flirt, his face expressionless; Barbara was listening without comment. ''It makes a sort of sense,'' Diane said. ''They believed you must know and understand your past to understand your future.''

''Yes,'' I said slowly. ''I suppose so.''

She nodded again and said no more about it.

I stayed in the plaza to drink coffee after dinner. Barbara was discussing her survey plans with Tony. Tony nodded sagely and smoked his pipe. Diane had moved to the edge of the plaza. She sat in a folding chair in the fading light of the setting sun. She was reading a hardcover book—one of Barbara's texts on the Maya.

I found myself watching my daughter. She had been swimming in the cenote before dinner and she had combed her hair out to dry. It flowed down around her shoulders. Her hands, holding the book open before her, were soft and slender, each nail perfectly shaped. She was leaning forward, and the collar of her loose shirt had fallen open to show the strong muscles of her neck. She lifted one hand to her head to push back the tide of hair, and I watched the muscles of her arm flex and shift.

She glanced in my direction and caught me watching her. Her eyes widened and a look of doubt crossed her face, but she smiled. I believe that she smiled in self-defense, using the open vulnerability of her smile as a shield, the way a puppy bares its neck to a stronger dog. The smile was a peace offering, made before the conflict began.

The inevitable card game had begun at the other table. Maggie, Robin, and John were playing. Carlos had not joined them. He was still at the dinner table, smoking a cigarette and looking pensive. A calculated pose, I was sure. He held the cigarette loosely in one hand and leaned back in his chair, his white shirt open at the collar and his head back to look at the sky.

I listened to the slap of the cards on the table, the soft mutter of conversation, and I watched as Carlos strolled across the plaza to where Diane was sitting. He stopped beside her and laid a hand on her shoulder. I could not hear what he said. Diane tilted her head a little to one side and leaned back in her chair. I did not like the way Carlos smiled at my daughter. I had never liked Carlos much.

"Tony," I said quietly across the table. He had been listening to Barbara, but now he looked to me. "What would you think of shifting a few assignments? John could use Carlos's help on the southeast site for a few days. The house mounds are a bit far from the other excavation. And I'd imagine that with Diane on survey, Barbara has enough help."

Barbara gave me a considering look, then nodded. "I wouldn't miss him."

Tony followed my gaze to Diane and Carlos. "You want to keep Diane on survey?"

I nodded.

He rattled the ice in his glass and nodded. "I'm surprised I didn't notice the need myself."

Carlos laughed and touched Diane's shoulder again. Tony stood, taking his drink with him. "I'll mention it to Carlos," he said, and headed toward the couple. I watched him join them, pulling up a chair and settling down as if he planned to stay a while. Tony would handle it well. He was very good with people. I watched for a moment as Tony spoke to Carlos. Carlos frowned, but nodded. I could not see Diane's face.

That evening, I worked on notes for my next book. My hut was oppressively hot even though I had opened the door wide to let the evening breeze blow through. I worked by the light of a small candle lantern that was too dim to draw many moths. As I typed on my travel typewriter, a compact Olivetti that had served me well for the past five years, the wooden table wobbled and the candle wavered. I had completed a description of Zuhuy-kak when I noticed the figure that stood in the shadows just beyond the lantern light. I turned in my chair to face her. In the darkness, I could see the white shells on her belt and in her hair. I lit a cigarette from the stub of the one I had just finished and greeted her softly in Maya. She did not speak. She remained in the shadows. I could smell incense, a warm resinous smell like burning pitch.

"I dreamed of you," I said. "I dreamed of the day that they threw you into the cenote at Chichén Itzá."

"I did not know that shadows dreamed," she said. She took a step toward me and stopped at the edge of the lantern light. Though she stared in my direction, I do not think she saw me clearly. She lifted one hand, as if to shade her eyes.

"I dream," I said.

She shook her head, as if to clear it. "I had enemies," she said in a soft voice, like a woman who is muttering to herself. "After the ah-nunob came, I had many enemies. I knew too much, you understand. I was too strong. The h'menob of the new religion did not approve of a woman who knew too much." Her hands fingered the conch shell at her belt, as if for comfort.

That dated her: I recognized the word "ah-nunob" from the *Books of Chilam Balam*. It meant "those who speak our language brokenly" and referred to the Toltecs from northern Mexico, who had invaded the Yucatán in about A.D. 900. As near as we could tell from the archaeological record, the invaders had displaced the Mayan nobility and modified the religion by adding Kukulcán, the feathered serpent, and other gods to the Mayan pantheon. The invaders had taken Chichén Itzá as their stronghold.

"I served Ix Chebel Yax, goddess of the moon and the sea, the protector of women in labor and madmen, she who weaves the rainbow and brings the floods." One of Zuhuy-kak's hands stroked the smooth inner surface of the conch shell. "When the ah-nunob came, they took my temple. They tore down the facades that honored the goddess and replaced them with serpents that twisted and curled around the arches." One hand gripped the conch shell as if to use it as a club. She remained silent for so long that I thought she might be fading into darkness again.

"How did you come to be given to the gods?" I asked, trying to catch her attention, to keep her talking.

She held her head proudly and straightened her shoulders like an aged general reminded of past battles. "The h'menob could not kill me. They feared bad luck. But they said I was one of the chosen messengers to the gods. Twelve were chosen by the gods to visit the well; one would survive. One would return with the prophecy for the coming katun, Katun 10."

She was gazing into the distance as if unaware of my presence. "It was a long journey, seven days on foot to Chichén Itzá. On the day named Cimi, the women prepared me: anointing my skin with blue paint, dressing me in a feather robe, lacing quetzal feathers in my hair.

"I walked from the women's quarters to the mouth of the well. Priests of the ah-nunob walked on either side of me, their hands hot on my arms. The crowd parted before us; smoke from the incense burners followed. The sound of the tunkul led us on.

"Some of the chosen ones were weeping. A slave from Palenque cried with a constant wearying whimper. The daughter of a nobleman who had fallen from power wept with short gasping sobs that rose and fell, almost stopped, then started again. There was a beautiful young boy, I remember, also a slave. He had drunk the balche that the h'menob offered us. He leaned on the priest beside him as he walked and sang a childish song that kept time with the tortoise shell rattles. I walked just behind him, listening to his song, saying nothing. The h'menob led us to the edge of the well and threw us in."

She stopped speaking, as if she were remembering the howling of the crowd. Outside, I could hear the soft voice of the palm leaves, rubbing one against the other.

"I fell for a long time." She was cradling the conch shell in both hands and running her finger along the smooth lip of the shell, stroking the polished edge. The shell's interior was

as smooth and pink as the skin of a baby. "The murmur of
the crowd became the rush of the wind past me, dragging on
my robes, tugging the quetzal feathers free of my hair and
scattering them in the sky. Then the cold water slapped me. I
remember rising to the surface like a bubble. And I remember that one leg ached with a fierce pain." She shifted her
position, as if the remembered pain affected her now. Her
voice had taken on a singsong rhythm. "For a time, I floated
on the surface among the reflections of the clouds. For a
time, I heard someone crying—one of the slaves, I think—
but the whimpering grew weaker and weaker, then stopped at
last. My leg was numbed by the cold water, and I floated in
the sky among the clouds, considering the prophecy for the
coming year. I could hear the tunkul and the rattles and the
shouting of the crowd, coming to me from the earth far
below.

"The h'menob did not expect me to survive. They would
have been glad to pull out one of the others—the slave, the
noblewoman, the beautiful boy. But the others had not enjoyed floating in the sky. They were done with their crying
and only I remained. At noon, when the sun rose over the lip
of the well, I lifted my hands and welcomed it. The h'menob
pulled me from the water, reluctantly, I thought, and roughly,
considering how holy I had become.

"I knew the prophecy for the coming year. I smiled when
I told them. 'Give yourselves up, my younger brothers, my
older brothers. Submit to the unhappy destiny of the katun
that is to come. You must leave the cities and scatter in the
forests. You must cast down the monuments and raise no
more. That is the word of the katun that is to come.' " Her
voice had grown louder and more powerful, like a strong
wind driving the rain before it. "I said to them, 'Submit to
the unhappy destiny. If you do not submit, you shall be
moved from where your feet are rooted. If you do not
submit, you shall gnaw the trunks of trees and the leaves of
herbs. There shall come such a pestilence that the vultures
will enter the houses. There shall be an earthquake over the
land. There will be thunder from a dry sky. Dust will possess

the earth, a blight will be on the face of the land, the tender leaf will be destroyed, and the people will scatter afar in the forest.' ''

She smiled when she turned to look at me. ''I spoke loudly so that the crowd could hear. And the h'menob wrapped me in soft cloths and rushed me away to the palace where the holy women lived. I think I fainted from the pain in my leg, and I don't remember the journey to the women's quarters. I woke on a soft pallet, tended by a frightened young woman who was sweet and attentive but told me nothing. The h'menob came and spoke to me, and I told them the prophecy again.''

She straightened her shoulders, still smiling. ''It took some time for my words to be heard by all. The h'menob softened the prophecy, but they could not deny it or destroy me, for either of those would have meant bad luck. So the people began leaving the city, slipping away into the forest. Stoneworkers toppled the monuments that they had carved, workmen threw down their tools and left temples half finished. After the farmers left, the fields were poorly tended and there was famine. There was pestilence. It takes time for a city to crumble. But it happened, here and in the other cities. My enemies were destroyed because they had tried to destroy me. That was the order of the katun. That was what Ix Chebel Yax said would be.''

She laughed and the sound was like branches rattling against one another in a high wind. ''The h'menob said I was mad. I was mad because I said words they did not wish to hear, because they could not control me, they could not drag me along like a tethered dog. And so they said I was mad.''

The Mayan empire was overthrown and the cities abandoned because of an angry prophecy from a vengeful goddess.

''You know that I am not mad,'' she said. ''You and I understand each other. We have much in common.''

Someone knocked on the lintel of the door to my hut.

''I had enemies,'' Zuhuy-kak said softly.

''Liz?'' I recognized the questioning tone as my daughter's.

''Yes.'' Zuhuy-kak was gone, vanished back into the shadows. ''Come in.''

Diane stopped just inside the door, as if unsure of her welcome. Her hair was still down around her shoulders, and her eyes were large in the candlelight. She had the look of a lost child wandering in the night.

"What's wrong?" I asked her.

"Couldn't sleep," she said. "I saw your light." She shrugged, then sniffed the air. "What's that smell?"

I sniffed, smelling the lingering aroma of incense. "Candle wax," I said. "And a hint of insect repellent." I tapped a cigarette from my pack and lit it.

She kept standing in the doorway, looking uncomfortable.

"Sit down," I said.

She perched awkwardly on the corner of my footlocker. "I'm just feeling restless. It happens sometimes. If I sleep when I'm feeling like this, I have nightmares." She shrugged. "So I stay up. Why are you still up?"

"I was planning to go to bed soon. After this cigarette."

"I didn't mean to interrupt. I mean, if you were working on something . . ." She slurred the words ever so slightly. She had been drinking with Tony—that explained why she was brave enough to come visit me, yet still feeling awkward enough to require an invitation to sit down.

"It's all right. Has Barbara already gone to sleep?"

"A while ago. The whole camp seems to be asleep."

"You never liked being in new places when you were a baby," I said, surprising myself a little by remembering. "You cried whenever we traveled. And when you were little, you had bad dreams."

She would walk at night, a diminutive child dwarfed by her flannel nightgown. I would tuck her back in, rock her to sleep, curl up beside her, and listen to the whisper of her breath coming and going.

Diane shrugged a little, leaning forward. "I still have bad dreams. I always have trouble sleeping in a new bed. When I went to college, I was insomniac for a month. I told Dad about it and he prescribed sleeping pills. I don't use them much."

"Robert always did prefer external remedies," I said dryly.

"He always treated the symptom, not the cause." A pause. I took a puff on my cigarette and watched Diane's face.

"What's the cause?" she asked.

I shrugged. "If I knew that, I'd sleep better myself."

She nodded, staring into the darkness, avoiding my eyes. "Tell me . . ." she began, then stopped and started again. "Tell me what it was like when you started to go crazy."

The hut was very quiet, a crystalline silence that seemed ready to shatter. A pool of darkness had gathered at her feet. "Robert called me crazy," I said softly. "I never agreed."

"You don't think you were?"

"I think that a great many people we call insane are just in the wrong place at the wrong time." I shrugged. "I opposed the societal norms, so I was crazy by Robert's definition. Out here, no one calls me crazy." I studied her in the dim light. Her head was bowed and her hair hid her face. "Why do you ask?" I wanted to go to her, to touch her on the shoulder and stroke her hair, but I could not make myself move.

"I think . . . I thought before I left that I might be going crazy. I thought coming here was crazy." Her voice was low. "After Dad died and I quit my job, I didn't know what to do. I kept walking and walking—pacing from one room of the house to another, moving a knicknack from a shelf to a side table and back. Just walking and walking, with no purpose." One of her hands rubbed the other, scratching a mosquito bite and raising a red welt. "I thought about killing myself, just so I could rest."

I took a long drag on the cigarette. "When Robert had me committed, the doctors at the nuthouse had to tend to my feet. I had infected blisters, all over the bottoms and sides of both feet. The doctors asked me why I hadn't stopped walking when my feet hurt." I shrugged. "I wanted to leave and I couldn't. Walking seemed like a reasonable reaction."

She was looking at me now. "Was coming here a reasonable reaction for me?"

"I suppose it was," I said.

Her smile was tentative. "Last night was the first time I

slept a night through in weeks. I had dreams, but I slept the night through."

I glanced at the clock on the shelf. The luminous dial showed midnight. "I'll walk you to your hut," I said. "Survey comes early tomorrow."

She nodded slowly but did not move. "You and Tony took Carlos off survey."

"Yes," I said. "We thought that Barbara had a large enough crew and John needed a little help."

Her expression did not change. "I wanted to tell you: I've been taking care of myself for a long time now. I'm not stupid."

"I know that. I—"

"It's not that I don't appreciate your concern. But you made me feel like a fool." She was watching my face.

"I didn't intend that."

I could not read the expression in her eyes. "All right."

"I'll walk you to your hut," I said.

"Never mind," she said. "I'll be fine." She ducked through the door and left me alone with the shadows.

Tony and I walked out to the plaza by Structure 701 on Tuesday morning. We walked slowly, and the shadows of Mayan women passed us on the path. They carried gifts to the temple: baskets filled with maize, pots of freshly brewed balche, woven cloth, cured deer skins. Preparations for a festival, no doubt. I tried to eavesdrop on two old women who were chatting about the misbehavior of their neighbors— particularly about the bad housekeeping of one woman. But the women spoke quickly, and Tony kept interrupting with comments about the weather and the dig, and I could not follow their conversation.

The shadows faded before we reached the plaza. The sun was hot. The three workmen who had levered the stone from its place stood in the shade, smoking and sharing water from a gourd, while Tony and I squatted by the upturned slab, brushing away the loose dry dirt that clung to the stone surface. On its underside, the slab was carved with a series of glyphs.

The stones on all four sides of the area that the slab had covered looked like they could have been walls. The center was a tumble of boulders and fill. I sat back on my heels. "A corridor, I'd guess. Intentionally filled." I looked at Tony. "Leading to a burial filled with pottery, jade, and obsidian artifacts."

"I suppose that you want to take some men from the house mounds to continue the excavation," he said.

"I suppose so."

He frowned.

"Jade masks," I said. "Discs of beaten gold. Pottery in a known context."

"An empty chamber and a lot of wasted time," he said gloomily.

I reached in my pocket for my lucky piece. "I'll flip you for it," I said. "Heads, I get two men from the house mounds and two from Salvador's crew. Tails—"

"Forget it," he said, shaking his head. "I always lose when we flip. If I hadn't made that coin myself, I'd swear it was rigged." He shrugged. "Take the men and see what you find."

I grinned at him. "That sounds like a fine idea."

In the afternoon, I hiked out to the fallen stela and made plans to raise it, a project that would require additional equipment and workmen who were currently excavating the house mounds. Tony would complain, but I would convince him.

That evening, I worked with Tony on deciphering the glyphs that I had copied from the face of the stone that had covered what I insisted on calling the tomb. The glyphs gave a date in the Mayan Long Count corresponding to A.D. 948, around the time that the Maya had abandoned the cities. That fit with Zuhuy-kak's story.

The men began the excavation and I sat back and did the thing I found most difficult: waiting to see what we would find.

Notes for City of Stones
by Elizabeth Butler

A society defines what is normal and what is crazy—and then says anyone who challenges the definition is crazy. In our society, for instance, self-destructive acts—self-mutilation or suicide—are considered mad. If you slash your wrists, you are locked up as a crazy person.

In Mayan society, suicide was a perfectly respectable act. The patron goddess of suicide was Ixtab. She is generally pictured as a woman dangling over emptiness, supported only by the noose around her neck. Her eyes are closed, her hands are relaxed, and her expression is calm, as if she were raptly contemplating an inner vision. Ixtab escorts people who die by suicide or sacrifice directly to paradise. Self-mutilation was also an essential part of many rituals: piercing the ear-lobes, lips, and tongue so that they bled profusely was an act of worship.

The gods of the Maya were demanding, much more de-manding than the distant patriarch of a God that most Chris-tians worship. Mayan gods governed each day's activities, and each day a different set had to be praised and propitiated. And a Mayan who ignored the dictates of the gods and decided to behave as he pleased would be as mad, relative to his society, as a resident of Los Angeles who ignored the traffic regulations and decided to drive as he pleased.

You may consider the comparison a frivolous one. Maybe you believe that traffic laws are for your protection and ignoring them would be dangerous. If you asked an ancient Mayan, he would explain that the rules for behavior laid down by the gods are for your protection. Ignoring them would be very dangerous. It would be dangerous, for example, not to offer a share of the honey to Bacab Hobnil, god of the bees; foolish to offend the Yuntzilob by hunting on the wrong day.

We find the Mayan pantheon peculiar. By our standards, suicide and human sacrifice are unacceptable. We tend not to notice the peculiarities of our own culture. We accept the thousands of children who wear braces to correct their teeth, yet we consider the Maya odd for filing teeth to beautify them. Each culture defines its own idiosyncracies and then forgets that it has done so.

Chapter Ten: Diane

"The twilight is the crack between the worlds."
—Carlos Castaneda,
The Teachings of Don Juan

WHEN I went to my hut, I crawled into my hammock, bone-tired after the long day of hiking. I remember scratching a few mosquito bites, thinking about getting up to get a drink of water, then falling into a darkness as quiet and deep as the bottom of the cenote. I woke to the blare of a horn. In the warm bright dawn, I did not remember my dreams.

The second day on survey was much the same as the first. We searched a new transect on the way out to the site where we found the stela. We were hot and sticky, plagued by flies, set upon by stinging ants. Dutifully, we mapped the site where we had found the stela. Using a rope line and small wire flags for markers, we divided the area into squares and Barbara designated certain squares to be searched for potsherds and worked stone: a random surface sample. I had the bad luck to draw a square that was covered with thornbushes that fought me at every turn. By the time I finished the search, my arms were laced with bright scratches.

We were resting in the shade when my mother arrived at

the site, tramping cheerfully through the monte, knocking aside thorny branches with her walking staff, fanning away her escort of flies with the other hand. A workman followed her and they were chatting in Maya about something as they walked. "Hello," she called out.

Barbara opened one eye and peered out from under her hat. "It's too hot to be so cheerful," she said.

"I came out along the sacbe," my mother said. "It's much easier going."

Barbara grunted. "I know. But we have to go back through the monte. So I don't really care."

"I take it you haven't made any wonderful finds today," my mother said.

"We decided to limit ourselves to one wonderful find every other day," Barbara said. "We didn't want to overdo it." Barbara opened the other eye and went to show my mother the stela. Through eyes half-closed against the brightness of the day, I watched them. I could not hear the words of their conversation, only the sound of their voices rising and falling in the distance. My mother used her staff to hold back the branches and stooped beside the fallen monument. I wanted to get up and join them, but I felt as if I would be intruding. Barbara and my mother seemed to get along well. They did not need my help.

I heard them laughing about something, high laughter like exotic birds in the trees, and I closed my eyes against the sun, jealous of Barbara's ease with my mother, jealous of her knowledge of archaeology. She was my mother's daughter, and I was a city dweller who was misplaced here among the flies and the thorns.

A shadow fell over my face and I opened my eyes. My mother stood beside me. "How are you doing?" she asked hesitantly.

I opened my eyes and propped myself up on one elbow. "Fine. Just fine."

"You'll want to put some antiseptic on those scratches when you get back to camp," she suggested.

I glanced down at my lacerated arms. "It's not so bad."

Barbara was still out by the stela, taking several pictures with the camera that my mother had carried with her. Maggie was giving her advice that she did not want. Robin was napping on the other side of the clearing.

"You're doing very well for someone who has never been on a dig before," my mother said quietly. She was not looking at me. She seemed to be watching something on the far side of the clearing, but when I followed her gaze I saw only sunshine and trees. "Don't compare yourself to Barbara. She's been doing this for years."

"I know."

"That's good," she said. "Remember that." She touched my shoulder lightly. "Come to my hut for the first-aid kit when you get back to camp."

Several hot and dusty hours later, with new bug bites and lacerations, I went to my mother's hut. She was alone, sitting at the table that served as her desk, examining a few typewritten pages.

"I came for the first-aid kit," I said. "Sorry to bother you."

"That's all right," she said and pointed to the shelf that held a metal box painted with a bright red cross. "Wash those cuts with peroxide. You've got to take care of yourself out here."

Half of the cool interior was crowded with supplies and equipment: a bundle of burlap sacks bound with twine; a stack of folded cardboard boxes; a box filled with folded paper bags; another box filled with a jumble of paper bags that had been marked with numbers and letters.

I was swabbing my cuts when my mother spoke again. "I wanted to apologize for taking Carlos off survey."

"That's all right."

"I'm not very good at dealing with people."

I looked up at her. Her face was unnaturally still; her hands held a pencil that she rolled between her fingers, a senseless incessant motion.

"It really is all right," I said, with sincerity this time. "It was just a mistake. It's OK."

She nodded, set the pencil down on her desk, and smiled tentatively. "Have you seen the latest find?" She gestured toward the stone head that stared from the shadows at the far end of the hut.

Leaving the first-aid kit open on the shelf, I went to examine the head more closely. It lay on a burlap wrapping and stared up at the ceiling. I did not like the look of the face. It sneered at me, the lips drawn back, the eyes wide open and hostile.

I squatted beside the face and laid my hand on the elaborately carved headdress. It was cool to the touch. With one finger, I traced the crack that ran through the face. For no particular reason, I shivered.

"They brought her down from the site today," my mother said from behind me. "I'm a little surprised she survived the trip with that crack."

"Was it part of a sculpture?"

"More likely part of a building facade. It's made of limestone stucco," my mother said.

I nodded and sat back on my heels. "Who was she?"

My mother shrugged. "Hard to say. There has been evidence, here and there, of a few women rulers. But I think more likely she was a priestess. Out on the Caribbean coast—on Cozumel and Isla Mujeres—there were shrines for a goddess named Ix Chebel Yax, goddess of the moon. I would like to think that the structure we're excavating was a temple for the goddess. If it is, it's the first evidence of such a cult on this coast." She squatted on her heels beside me and ran a finger along the spiral on the cheek. "Ritual tattooing," she said softly. "Very common among priests and nobility." She touched a long barbed needle that was woven with the shells into the woman's hair. "Stingray spine," she said. "Usually used in bloodletting ceremonies. The devout would run spines or needles through their earlobes or tongues and offer the blood to the gods."

"Seems like a cruel way to live. Human sacrifice, offering blood to the gods."

She sat back on her heels. "Ah, now you are starting to sound as provincial as Robin. Don't tell me that you're afraid of the bones in the cenote too?"

I shrugged. "I didn't say that. It just seems like a cruel way to live."

"People always talk about human sacrifice as if it were an unusual and aberrant activity," she said thoughtfully. "Over the centuries, it's really been fairly common in a number of societies. Think about it. There're a number of religions in the United States whose worship centers on a particular human sacrifice." She glanced at me.

"Jesus Christ on the cross," I said slowly.

"Certainly. Thousands of people consume Christ's body and blood each Sunday."

"That's different."

She shrugged. "Not really. Christ died long ago in a faraway place, and that might make it seem different. His worshipers claimed he was God incarnate, but the Aztecs claimed the same for the god-king they sacrificed. It happened only once, and that speaks for moderation on the part of the Christians, but that's not a fundamental difference, just one of degree." She smiled at me, obviously enjoying herself. "Besides, I suspect that people overestimate the number of human sacrifices made by the Maya. One sometimes gets the impression that Mayan priests spent most of their time beating their fellows over the head and tossing them willy-nilly into the nearest well. And that's not so. It was a rare and important occasion. And you must be careful about applying your standards to another culture. They have rules of their own. This woman may have participated in human sacrifices— but by her standards, that was good. The sacrificial victims went to a sort of paradise, and all was well."

She stood up and went to her desk for a cigarette. She tapped it out of the pack and held it without lighting it, still looking at me. "The fundamental bloodiness of the act is the same—whether it's the Roman soldiers hammering the nails into Christ's hands or the h'menob slicing out the heart of a captive soldier. Blood has a power to it, a strength and a magic." She had rolled up the long sleeves of her shirt and I could see the scars on the pale skin of her wrists. She lit the cigarette, inhaled deeply, and blew out a cloud of smoke.

Then she grinned at me. "Sorry. I get carried away sometimes. Occupational hazard of being a professor."

"You sound almost like you prefer the Maya to the
Christians."

She laughed. "Understand them better, anyway." She put
her cigarette in a jar top that served as an ashtray and walked
over to the first-aid kit. "Maybe you should let me bandage
those cuts," she said, and I heard no more about the ancient
Maya that afternoon.

The daily rigors of survey left me tired, but the restlessness
that had kept me pacing to and fro in my father's house had
not deserted me. Here, I had more room to pace. When I
woke in the morning before the blast of the truck horn or
when I was restless after dinner, I went walking—past the
kitchen where the air was always touched with woodsmoke,
past the cenote and out to the tomb site, past the arch of the
Spanish chapel and out to the Temple of the Seven Dolls,
where I could look down on the green-brown trees of the
monte. Often, I met my mother on these walks. I found her
by the Spanish chapel, sitting on a fragment of wall and
staring out toward the Temple of the Seven Dolls. I found
her alone by the cenote, dangling her legs over the water and
watching the birds swoop low over the surface. I met her by
the tomb site, muttering to herself as she inspected the excavation. When we met, she seemed genuinely glad to see me.

The air was cooler at dawn and dusk, and my mother
seemed slower, more contemplative. We walked together
when we met. I told her little about myself—life in Los
Angeles seemed distant and unimportant, a faded snapshot
where the colors were muted and the figures blurred. My
mother's world was painted in vivid colors with crisp lines
and edges. As we walked together, she talked slowly and
carefully, as if she pieced together the ideas as she spoke
them, groping for the next fragment and slipping it in place.
Her sentences had the feel of written text—scripted thoughtfully, but as yet unedited.

She told me about the Maya and their gods. "For each

yield that the Maya took from the monte, a return was due the gods. A turkey, a bowl of balche beer, a *jicara* of atole, a kind of corn gruel sweetened with wild honey. The offering to the gods was given freely in a spirit of goodwill. Wise men did not haggle with the gods. A mean man who gave grudgingly would suffer bad health, his crops would fail. The Maya recognized that what they made, they made with the permission and protection of the gods. It was only temporarily theirs. In the end, it belonged to the gods. Our society tends to regard the monte, the wilderness, as an enemy. Christians battled and subdued the wilderness. The Maya have a much saner way of looking at the world, I think.''

She was a strange woman, my mother. When I was fifteen and she came to visit my father's house at Christmastime, I recognized that she did not belong there. But I did not realize then that she did not really belong anywhere. She walked with me, but she did not belong in the world I knew. She did not look at me as we walked together. She was always staring off into the monte, peering into the mounds as if something fascinating were out there.

We sat by ruins of the Spanish chapel and I asked about her books. ''In the last chapter of your first book, you said, 'There's more to be seen in the world than most will admit.' What did you mean?'' I asked.

She stared into the distance, where the light of the rising sun already shimmered on the sparse grass and barren ground. ''Over there, on the edge of the plaza, a stoneworker once sat and shaped irregular lumps of obsidian into sharp sacrificial blades for priests, into spearheads for hunters. He squatted on the ground, shaded by an awning of bright blue cloth. His skin glistened with sweat as he bent over his work. He was a well-fed man, fattened by the venison and wild turkey with which the hunters paid him, unusually stout for a Mayan.'' My mother leaned forward, as if to get a better view of the stoneworker. ''Do you see him there, sitting in the sun and patiently chipping an edge on an obsidian blade? I see him. He's a very careful workman. You can choose to see him. Or you can choose to see the bare earth." She glanced at my face. "That's what I meant. Do you see him?" Her tone was light and casual.

I felt uncomfortable, staring at the bare place in the earth. I remembered the dream that had led me to discover the stela. But that had been a dream—I was awake now. I shrugged. "I see the sunlight on the rocks, that's all."

She nodded. "Nothing wrong with that. I sometimes think that to see the past clearly you must give up a good deal of the present." She shrugged. "It's a choice I made long ago. A sacrifice of sorts."

"Do you mean you really see him? In the same way that you see me?"

She was silent for so long that I thought she had decided not to answer. When she spoke, she spoke softly. "Sometimes, I think I see the shadows of the past more clearly than I see any living person." She shrugged, as if to rid herself of the thought, then quickly stood to return to camp.

I did not follow all that she said to me. I was reluctant to ask questions, because questions seemed to disturb the spell, to break some unspoken rule. If I asked too many questions, my mother would shrug and fall silent, or suggest immediately that we return to camp. Sometimes, it seemed like our morning walks were waking dreams, unsettling, subtly disturbing. Thoughts and feelings that I could not pinpoint were tapping at the back of my skull. I liked my mother, but I did not understand her. I did not understand her at all.

In the heat of the day, my mother was a different person— brisk, fast-moving, impatient that the excavation went so slowly. She argued with Tony about where the crew should be digging, about the significance of the stone head, about the likelihood that the underground chamber would really turn out to be a tomb.

By the fourth day, I felt at home at the dig. It seemed that I had always washed my face in gritty lukewarm water from a black barrel that smelled faintly of plastic, had always blundered to a pungent outhouse in the darkness each night.

Barbara asked me if I wanted to go to Mérida with her that weekend. She knew a cheap hotel with a pool. We could take hot showers, maybe see a movie and eat popcorn in an air-conditioned theater. I asked my mother if she thought that a trip to Mérida would be worthwhile, and she said I should go.

On Saturday morning, I woke early. Barbara had not set her alarm: we had planned to sleep late and leave camp sometime in the middle of the morning. When I woke, I glanced at Barbara, who was just rolling over to look at the clock.

"What time is it?" I whispered. Maggie and Robin were still asleep.

"Seven-thirty," she whispered back. She leaned back in the hammock, one hand tucked under her head. She was frowning. "I can't even sleep late anymore," she grumbled. "This is ridiculous."

We dressed quietly, packed clean clothes, and slipped out of the hut. We stopped at the water barrel to wash, and the splash of water into the metal basin was loud in the hot morning air. The camp was still asleep; the only sign of life was the small curl of smoke rising from Maria's kitchen.

"Ah," Barbara said. "Perhaps we can convince Maria to spare us a cup of coffee."

I hung back when Barbara went to the door of the kitchen. The look that Maria gave us was far from friendly. Teresa hid behind Maria's skirts. Barbara stepped away from the kitchen, frowning. "I guess we'll get coffee in Mérida. Maria says she hasn't made any this morning."

I followed Barbara to the car. When I glanced back over my shoulder, I caught a glimpse of Teresa, peering out the kitchen door after us. "I don't think Maria likes me much," I said to Barbara.

"Of course not. She doesn't like me either. You and I are young women, but we dress in pants and spend all our time with men." Barbara shook her head. "We don't behave properly. She doesn't approve."

"She talks to Liz."

"She doesn't like Liz either. She doesn't approve of any of us."

I nodded, relieved at Barbara's certainty that I was not alone in Maria's disapproval.

Barbara's battered Volkswagen bug jounced over every bump and rut in the road out of camp, finding every pothole, dropping into it, and emerging triumphant on the other side. Barbara drove with gleeful enthusiasm and unnecessary speed, tromping on the gas whenever the road looked clear for a stretch, only touching the brakes for an instant when the car hit a bump. "What's the hurry?" I shouted over the roar of the engine.

"I'm tired of moving slow, that's all," she shouted back. She swerved to avoid one pothole, struck another one dead-on, gunned the engine, and kept moving. "I'm tired of dirt and flies." She hit another pothole. "I want a hot shower, coffee, breakfast, bright lights, and men who want to talk about something besides potsherds." She looked away from the road to grin at me with bright-eyed malice. "I want to look for trouble." We hit another pothole.

"I know one person in Mérida who might know where to find trouble," I shouted. "Someone I met on the plane."

"Man or woman?"

"Man."

"Of course. Fast worker." I didn't know whether she meant that I was a fast worker or the man was a fast worker. It didn't seem to matter. "Cute?"

I thought for a moment. My memory of Marcos was rather vague, but I thought he had been presentable enough. "Not bad."

"Good. He'll have a friend. They always do."

We reached the main highway, the road that had seemed so narrow on my way to camp. It felt like a freeway now. The car picked up speed, and we rolled down the windows to let the wind blow through. We passed a truck filled with workmen on their way to somewhere, and we waved and honked the horn like high school kids who had escaped the campus for a field trip. We roared by a cluster of huts and waved to a woman who was hanging out the clothes and to a troop of children who were playing by the road.

"We'll have hot showers first, then breakfast," Barbara shouted.

"Great," I said. Everything was great. The wind, the road, the promise of breakfast.

The hotel was an old establishment, a few blocks from Mérida's main square and right beside Parque Hidalgo, the park that Marcos had mentioned. A little shabby. The desk clerk spoke bad English. A thin black cat seemed to live in the lobby. The banister on the curving stairs leading down to the lobby was ornately carved, but in need of polish. The blue and gold tiles of the lobby floor needed sweeping; dust hid behind the potted palms. But the sun streamed in through the open arch that led to Parque Hidalgo and there were fresh flowers on the check-in counter.

We registered and took hot showers before breakfast. I sat on one of the two twin beds while Barbara showered, rubbing lotion on my legs, working around the mosquito bites and scratches. For the first time in a week, I was wearing a skirt and sandals rather than jeans and sneakers, and my hair felt clean. Overhead, the ceiling fan turned with a steady rattle. Barbara was singing in the shower.

Parque Hidalgo was a small brick-paved plaza. Tall broad-leaved trees shaded the plaza and dropped small yellow blossoms on the men who spent the day idling on the park benches. In the center of the square a tall bronze man stood on a white stone pillar atop a stone platform. I never did learn his name.

We ate breakfast at a sidewalk café beside the hotel and on one side of the park. Ornate metal tables, fringed umbrellas, red-and-white tablecloths, and a matronly waitress who seemed harried.

"*Hamacas?*" asked a stout man in a yellow baseball cap. On one shoulder he carried a bundle of plastic-wrapped hammocks. Over the other shoulder, he had slung a loose hammock, which he held out for our inspection.

"Is your name Emilio?" I asked. "I'm looking for a

hammock vendor named Emilio.'' He shook his head heavily and went to the next table, where there were tourists with simpler needs.

Barbara flipped through the pages of a tourist guide to Mérida, which she had picked up from the hotel lobby. It told the way to the zoo, to the market, to the ruins at Chichén Itzá, to the best places for lunch and for dancing. She read aloud bits of information that she found interesting.

"The main square is called the *zocalo*,'' she told me.

I nodded, watching the people strolling by on the street. The coffee was good and I was content. I had not realized that I was nervous about being at the dig until now, when I had relaxed.

"You interested in a tour of Chichén Itzá?'' she asked me. "It's only about an hour's drive from here.''

"Maybe tomorrow,'' I said.

"We could tour Casa Montejo, the mansion built by the Spanish back in 1549,'' she said. "Or we could visit the cathedral. Or we could go to the market.''

"Whatever you like.''

We decided to go to the market, figuring that we would have time to stop in the cathedral on our way back and still have time for a siesta before dinner.

We were finishing breakfast and drinking coffee when I spotted Marcos at the far end of the café. I nudged Barbara. "He's better-looking than I remembered,'' I said. He was a thin, small-boned young man with dark brown eyes, white teeth, high dark cheekbones. He was grinning as he watched a hammock salesman—I assumed it was Emilio—display a hammock to an American couple: a woman in a sundress and a man in a Hawaiian shirt. Emilio had looped one end of a hammock around the arm of one of the wrought-iron chairs. He hesitated for a moment, holding the hammock in a bundle, then he flipped it open with an elegant flourish—the way a waiter uncorks a bottle of wine. The gesture conveyed the importance of the act and the value of the product. The hammock was a rich shade of purple that caught the sunlight and held it.

Marcos saw us then and joined us at the table. "Hello," he said to me. "How are you?" He pulled out a chair. We watched Emilio close his sale; the American couple walked away with two hammocks, and Emilio stuffed a handful of paper money into his pocket.

He came to the table and dropped his bundle of hammocks by a chair. "It's going to be a good day," he said. "I have luck today." He was a head shorter than I, compact and broad-shouldered. Dark eyes, dark skin, and a smile like an all-American boy except for the gold filling that showed around the edges of one front tooth. "You are Marcos's friends." The easy charm of a born salesman. "You want to buy a hammock? I'll give you a good price."

"We've got hammocks," Barbara said. "In fact, we're sick to death of hammocks."

"How could you be sick of hammocks?" Emilio asked, and Barbara went on at length on how she could be sick of hammocks, so very sick of hammocks.

"Buy one for a present," Emilio suggested and then bought a round of coffee with the same sort of flourish with which he displayed a hammock. We talked about tourists and the weather while the morning wore on. Emilio and Marcos seemed quite at home in the café, familiar with the waitress. A line was forming outside the nearby movie theater. The smell of popcorn hung in the warm air.

After a time, Emilio was trying to talk Barbara into visiting an isolated cave at a place called Homún. An underground river in a limestone cave with stalactites. "Beautiful," he said. "Really beautiful."

Marcos was watching me. "*Qué piensas?*" he asked. "What are you thinking?"

I shrugged. "Not much."

"You looked like you were thinking about something."

I shrugged again. Emilio was using both hands to describe the stalactites in the cave. Barbara looked unconvinced.

"On the plane, you looked sad. What was wrong?" Marcos asked.

I said nothing. Shrugged.

He glanced at Emilio, who was growing more eloquent in his attempts to persuade Barbara that a visit to the lonely cavern at Homún was the perfect thing for any young American's summer vacation. "I am tired of sitting here," Marcos said. "Come on. We'll walk and come back here." We left Barbara and Emilio talking about underground rivers.

They walk, in Mérida. Out in the small parks, where the breezes are a little cooler than the air pushed about by the ubiquitous ceiling fans. We wandered through the main square. "What were you doing in Los Angeles?" I asked Marcos.

"I went to visit my uncle." He shrugged. "But there was no work, so I came home. There is no work here, but I have friends."

He led the way through the square, past small horse-drawn carriages in which tourists rode.

"What made you sad?" Marcos asked. "You can tell me."

I shrugged and told him about coming to the dig to find my mother, about how I had not seen my mother in many years.

He listened and nodded. "So, what do you want from your mother?" he asked.

I shrugged.

"You don't know what you want."

"I guess not."

"Tonight," he said, "I play basketball for the university. You want to come?"

"Basketball? Let me see what Barbara thinks."

He took my hand. "Even if Barbara does not want to come, you come and watch me play, OK?"

"All right."

Back at the café, Emilio was asking Barbara what we were planning to do that day.

"Go to the market," she said. "Wander around Mérida."

"And tomorrow?" he said. "What are you going to do tomorrow?"

"We talked about going to Chichén Itzá," she said. "But it's a long drive."

"I'll help drive," Emilio said. "No problem. I'll bring

hammocks to sell. All right?'' Barbara was laughing, but Emilio did not let up. "I'll tell you what. If you want to go to Chichén Itzá, you meet me here tomorrow in the morning. I'll help drive. It'll be good." He grinned, showing his gold-rimmed tooth.

We finished our coffee, and Emilio and Marcos went to the zocalo to sell hammocks. Barbara and I went to the market, heading away from the zocalo on Calle 60, a narrow street with narrow sidewalks. All the streets were narrow. The houses and shops pressed close to the street and stood shoulder to shoulder, presenting a solid front to the world.

We passed the open door of a room filled with the smell of beer and the sound of men talking. A young man standing in the doorway smiled at us, but we did not smile back. We smiled at children, dogs, and women. The children smiled back; the dogs and women did not.

A middle-aged man was selling coconuts from a pushcart. We watched him skillfully chop the husk from a nut, break the shell away, pierce the round white fruit, and insert a straw. We each bought a coconut and sipped the sweet milk as we walked.

I recognized the market but could not begin to remember the way through the maze of tiny stalls. We peered down long corridors that led into darkness. In the dimness beyond where the sunlight reached, I could see boxes of fruit and vegetables, crates of chickens, hanging meat. Barbara consulted her guidebook and dragged me to the corridor where clothing was sold. It was on the edge of the market and the sun shone in. Every stall was bright with hanging shawls, dresses, shirts, skirts.

"I like that one," I said to Barbara, pointing out a very pretty burgundy-colored shawl with a painted floral border. The woman who sat in the stall called to us, smiling and beckoning. She had gold earrings that matched her gold tooth and she seemed fascinated by my hair and determined to sell me the shawl. I bargained in bad Spanish and, I think, ended up paying too much for the shawl. Barbara bought a white dress that was embroidered with a pattern of dark blue squares. It was just past three when we headed back to the hotel.

"Time for a nap," I said.

"Let's stop at the cathedral," Barbara said. "It's on the way and it'll be cool inside."

I put a coin in the hand of the beggar woman who sat just outside the arched door. She blessed me with the sign of the cross.

The interior was cool and dark. Light filtered down from high octagonal windows. White columns rose to a high vaulted ceiling, crosscrossed with stonework that was lost in the shadows. An emaciated Christ hung wearily on his cross at the far end of the hall. Old women knelt in the front pew. A young boy sat in the back, doing sums in a school notebook.

A few other tourists were wandering around the hall. I hesitated just inside the door. I felt uncomfortable—more than just awkward about entering an unfamiliar church, but somehow reluctant to move closer to the figure of Christ. But Barbara had already started up one of the side aisles, and so I followed her.

Plaques on the white stone walls depicted Christ's suffering and death. I did not linger to look at them. I remembered my mother's contention that Christianity was a religion of human sacrifice and I was inclined to agree. Halfway up the aisle, I paused to look at an elaborately carved statue of the Virgin Mary. Candles burned on a small table before the statue, and the warm air was thick with the scent of incense and burning wax. The candlelight flickered on the Virgin Mary's carved wooden robes.

Mary's hands were spread in acceptance; her mouth was curved in a half smile. But something about her expression seemed wrong to me. The artist who painted her features had tinted her skin several shades darker than the usual anemic white. Her eyes were dark; they caught the shadows. She lacked the delicacy that I had seen in other depictions of the Madonna; her features seemed more Indian than Spanish. She seemed older than the usual pale maiden Mary. Older and wiser. Her smile was knowing.

The candlelight on her cheeks cast spiraling shadows and her forehead seemed strangely flattened. I could smell incense more strongly now, a sharp resinous smell, like burning pine. The same smell had filled my mother's hut. The Madonna was watching me from the shadows. She had gathered the shadows around her, and the burning candles shed just enough light to let me see her clearly. I recognized her then: her face matched that of the stone head in my mother's hut.

I felt dizzy and sick to my stomach. I looked away from her face, stepped back and put one hand on the edge of a pew for support. I closed my eyes and waited for the wave of dizziness to pass.

I opened my eyes when the stone floor felt steady beneath my feet once again. The Madonna was staring over my head, her features set in a benign expression of acceptance. She was not watching me. This corner of the cathedral was as well lit as any other.

I hurried to join Barbara on the far side of the hall. She was strolling toward the door. When we stepped out into the sunshine, I immediately felt better. I put another coin in the beggar woman's hand and received her blessing once again.

"You look pale," Barbara said. "You all right?"

"I felt a little sick in there," I said. "Just for a minute."

"Touch of the touristas?"

"Could be. I feel better now."

"You'll be better after a siesta."

Our hotel room was stuffy, but cooler than the outside. Barbara turned the ceiling fan to a faster speed, stripped to her underwear, and flung herself on one bed. "Siesta," she said, turned her back on me, and fell asleep immediately. I lay awake for a long time, watching the ceiling fan turn, listening to Barbara's steady breathing.

Notes for City of Stones
by Elizabeth Butler

Today is Saturday, March 17, 1984, by our reckoning of time. A simple set of numbers and names, designating the day but granting it no particular power, no special value.

In the Mayan system of dating, this day would be assigned a number and a day name in the tzolkin, or sacred almanac, a different number and a different day name in the haab, or vague year. In the Long Count, the system of dating used on stelae, this date would be written as 12 baktuns, 18 katuns, 10 tuns, 13 uinals, and 15 kins, designating this day as being 1,861,475 days since the starting point from which the Maya count time. By Mayan reckoning, each of these numbers and names has a meaning and an importance.

The tzolkin and the haab are part of a system of interlocking cycles, known to modern Mayanists as the Calendar Round. The haab is a cycle of 365 days: eighteen months of twenty days and one month of five evil days at the end of it all. The tzolkin is a cycle of 260 days: thirteen months of twenty days. The two cycles are interlocked: one can think of them as two great cogs—one with 260 teeth and one with 365. As one wheel turns, so turns the other. Every fifty-two vague years, both cycles begin a new year at the same time.

That's one system for counting the passage of time. The other is the Long Count, a system for counting from an established date long ago. Our notation of the year 1984 indicates the number of years that have passed since the birth of Christ: one period of one thousand years, nine centuries of one hundred years, eight decades of ten years, and four years of 365 days. A Long Count inscription indicates how many days have passed since the beginning of the Mayan time count by noting the passage of baktuns, or periods of 144,000 days; katuns, or periods of 7,200 days; tuns, or years of 360 days; uinals, or periods of 20 days; and kins, or days.

All this is important, but the heart of the matter lies in the power of the days, not the methods used to calculate or record them. Many years ago, I learned of the importance of these numbers and names from a shriveled woman with a clubfoot, who, for reasons I never ascertained, had moved from a mountain village to the city of Mérida.

She was bargaining for herbs in the market when I met her; she glanced at me with bright sharp eyes and commented to the shopkeeper on my poor selection of produce, saying that gringas did not know how to shop. She spoke in Maya and I, hot and tired from a long day of shopping, spoke up in the same tongue, saying that I would gladly take lessons on how to shop if anyone would offer to teach me. She grinned and beckoned to me.

For the next hour I followed her as she trudged from stall to stall. She taught me to shake my finger to indicate disinterest, told me when to push for a better price, when to give a little, when to walk away, when to joke. The shopkeepers stared at us—an American and a Mayan crone—but no one commented. I thanked her at the hour's end and bought her a Coke, which she drank with great enthusiasm.

A week after my tour of the market, I met her again, this time in the zocalo in the early evening. She sat alone on a green bench at the west corner of the square and she hailed me, beckoning. She had been drinking aguardiente—to stop the pain, she said. I do not know what caused her pain; she would not talk about that. She asked me the hour and the day, and when I told her, she gripped my wrist so tightly that her nails cut into my skin. I asked her what was wrong, but her answers made no sense. She wanted to talk about time.

She said that this was the last day of an evil year; she was distraught, but I could not make out the reason for her agitation.

I bought her another bottle of aguardiente—her pain seemed real and that was the only help she would allow me to offer. Over the bottle, she began rambling, reciting something. "Imix, he is the first one: earth monster, dragon head, root of it all. He rules the corn; a very good day for planting. Ik, he is the second, and he brings the wind, a very good day. Akbal is dark, a prowling jaguar who devours the sun. He lives in the west, where he drinks the dark water, and the rain he brings is not good. He kills the corn. Offer him bebida and do not plant this day."

I realized, as she continued, that the names she called, praising this one and warning against that, were the names of the days in the tzolkin. "Ben is lord of the maize, a good day for planting. Offer him atole, made of the best maize. Oc wears the head of a dog; he brings the sad rain that makes the maize rot in the ground and gives the children sickness. Cauac wears the head of a dragon; he brings thunder and violent rain." She shook her head, let her breath out in a great gasp, and gripped my hand more tightly. She was staring at me wildly, but I did not think that she saw me. She recited the almanac of days for an apprentice, a daughter, a son, a person who would learn and benefit from this knowledge. "You know them, do you not?"

"Yes, grandmother," I said to calm her. "I know them."

"There is Lamat, the lord of the great star that rises with the sun. There is Muluc: give him jade and the rain that comes will favor the corn. You must remember these things!"

She gripped my hand with both of hers and breathed warm brandy-scented breath in my face. Around us, the square was quiet. The lovers and loiterers who strolled here favored the far side, closer to the café that sold sweet fruit ices.

"You must know them all: Etz'nab is the lord of the sacrifice; he carries a blade of sharp obsidian. Behead a turkey in his name; feast for him."

The moon had risen. Its pale light filtered through the leaves of the shade trees to dapple the cement paths that crisscrossed the square. Somewhere across the square a guitarist played a ballad, doubtlessly for lovers who would rather have been left in peace. The old woman stared up at the moon as if she had never seen it before.

"And you must know the day named Men, governed by the old woman moon goddess, Ix Chebel Yax. She is a trickster, that one, bringing rainbows and floods, healing and destruction. She gives children stomach pains, helps women in childbirth, teases madmen, brings sleep to the weary, snarls the thread of weaving women. On her day, you can divine the future, but you cannot trust her."

"Rest, grandmother," I said to the woman, laying one hand on hers. "I will remember this. But now you must go home. Let me take you there."

"That does not matter," she said. Her voice was softer now. "Today is the last day of the five unlucky days. Cimi is dark and deadly; he knows Ah Puch. When he flies to you, you never hear him coming; his feathers make no sound. On this day, you must burn the blood of a turkey with incense."

"Yes, grandmother. But now I will take you home."

"I will die this night," she said, standing like an obedient child as I tugged on her arm. "It is the end of the old year: the cycles have returned to the place that they were when I was born. The year is out and Cimi has come for me."

She followed me to the curb and I hailed a taxi. Apparently she had finished the recitation of the days; she was quiet, acquiescent. She told me her address and I told the cabby to take her there, paid him in advance, paid him extra to help her inside. I stood under the full moon, listening to the distant guitar serenade. The hag's fingernails had left marks beside the old scars on my right wrist. I rubbed them idly and watched the taxi drive away.

On the next day, which I called Sunday for lack of a better name, I took a taxi to the address that the old woman had given the cabby, a shabby house in a row of shabby houses. The woman who answered the door frowned when I asked after the old woman and said in Spanish, "She is dead now. What do you want here?"

I backed away, unable to tell her of the strange evening under the moon, unwilling to describe the feelings that had pulled me here. I needed to ask the old woman what day this was and what that day meant, but I said nothing. I caught the same taxi—he had waited for me at the corner—and went home to my hotel.

Today—the day I write this—is Saturday. I do not know its Mayan name and number. I do not know the gods that influence this day. I know very little.

—— Chapter Eleven: Elizabeth ——

> Gods that are dead are simply those that
> no longer speak to the science or the moral
> order of the day . . . every god that is
> dead can be conjured again to life.
> —Joseph Campbell,
> *The Way of the Animal Powers*

ON Saturday morning, before I woke, Diane and Barbara left for Mérida. Having Diane leave was a relief in a way. In the one week that she had been in camp, she had managed to interrupt my moments of solitude more than I could have imagined possible.

Every morning, at dawn and dusk, I wandered the site. I watched a potter—a young woman with glossy black hair that glistened in the morning sun—molding a vessel in the shape of a pot-bellied dog. I stood in the shade and listened to the scraping of an obsidian chisel on cedarwood: a withered old man was carving the statue of a god. I did not see Zuhuy-kak. At the times that I most expected to see the old woman, my daughter would wander by instead.

At dawn, as I sat on a fragment of wall by the Spanish chapel watching a stonecutter, Diane strolled toward me on the path from the cenote. At dusk, as I lingered by Structure 701, watching the shadows gather, I heard the sound of Diane's boots on the path from camp and the shadows fled.

In the early evening, I stood on the edge of the cenote, watching the bats skim low over the water. Diane waved cheerfully as she walked along the path from the camp.

She was willing and eager to walk with me and listen to me talk about the site. I talked a great deal. Sometimes, in the bright light of day, I thought that I talked too much.

During the week, excavation had continued on the house mounds, the Temple of the Moon, and the tomb site. Work went slowly; the dirt had to be cleared away from each boulder before it could be moved, and each bucket of dirt had to be sifted for potsherds and flakes of worked stone. Hot, tedious, and dusty work.

At the tomb site, the workmen had uncovered eight stone steps leading downward to the beginning of an underground passageway. The rubble they removed from the stairway had yielded little of interest: a few plainware potsherds, a few carved stones with glyphs too badly battered to decipher.

Early Saturday morning, I walked alone to the tomb site. As I crossed the open plaza, I saw a flash of blue by the excavation. Zuhuy-kak was standing beside the tarps that covered the open pit. Her eyes followed me as I walked toward her. She stood in the sunlight and cast a shadow of her own. I greeted her in Maya, sat in the shade by the excavation, and lit a cigarette. Zuhuy-kak remained standing, staring out toward the mound.

"You see," she said, pointing to the mound. "You see how the ah-nunob have desecrated the temple. But soon their time will be over. Soon, the cycles will turn."

I followed her gaze but saw only the rubble-strewn mound, the path worn by workmen snaking around it. An iguana stared back at me from its perch on a weathered temple stone.

"What day is it, Ix Zacbeliz?" she asked.

I knew that she wanted to know the day in the Mayan calendar. "I don't know," I said. "We use a different calendar now."

She frowned. "You don't know? Then how do you know what to do each day?" She seemed more confident than she had when she first appeared. She stood straight, with her hand resting lightly on the conch shell at her belt. "Don't you know the cycles of time, Ix Zacbeliz? You know that what has passed will come again, repeating endlessly. You must learn what day this is, so that I can advise you. The time is near for Ix Chebel Yax to return to power."

"I'll try to figure it out."

"You must." She was watching me with a disconcertingly direct gaze.

"Yes, I will," I said, a little sharply. "But right now I am concerned with this excavation. Can you tell me how much further we will have to dig here? And what will we find in the end?"

But she was not there. The wind hissed like snakes in the dry blades at my feet, rattling the tarps and sending dust devils scurrying about the mound.

At dinner that night, I missed having Diane and Barbara there. Only John and Tony had remained in camp; all the others had run away to Mérida, to sleep in clean beds and take hot showers. The three of us sat together in the plaza, drinking coffee and aguardiente while the sun set. John and Tony talked while I stared out into the dusk beyond the plaza. The moon was just above the trees—a thin crescent with the horns pointing aloft. For once the shadows were quiet: the priest had finished scraping the jaguar skin; no wood-carvers worked by moonlight.

"What do you think, Liz?" Tony asked.

"What? I wasn't listening."

"John was talking about problems at your favorite site."

I looked at John, suddenly attentive. He hunched his broad shoulders forward slightly, as if to protect himself against me. "What sort of problems?" I asked.

John wrapped both big hands around his coffee cup. "Work's going slowly. I leave to check on Carlos's crew, and when I come back, the men have always been delayed. The sifter is torn. The head of a pickax has come loose. A man is stung by a scorpion. Someone saw a rattlesnake. Always something."

"You put Pich in charge of that crew, didn't you? He's usually very hard-working."

John shrugged. "Not this time."

"I'll ask Salvador what he thinks," I said to Tony. "Maybe we need to shift the crews around."

"Sounds like it," he said.

After a time, I excused myself and wandered by Salvador's hut. I could see the silhouette of a man standing in the yard, having a smoke. I called to Salvador and he came to the *albarrada*, the wall of limestone fragments that surrounded the *solar*, the yard around the house. Lighting a cigarette, I leaned against the wall beside him.

Here, the air smelled of greenery. Within the *solar*, the growth was lush. Maria kept a careful garden: an avocado tree shaded the doorway to the house; chili plants and herbs grew beside the albarrada. I could smell the sweet oranges that hung from the tree on the far side of the yard.

"How goes it?" I asked.

"Well enough." I watched the red tip of his cigarette glow brightly for a moment, then fade to dull red. I could not see his face.

"It's quiet with the others gone," I said.

"Yes. It is always quiet here."

"John tells me that the work goes slowly at his site," I said. "He says that there always seems to be a problem."

He ground his cigarette out on the limestone wall, and red sparks scattered on the rough stone. "This is not a lucky time of year. And that is not a lucky place," he said. "The work goes slowly because the luck is bad."

I offered him another cigarette and lit it for him. By the brief flame of my lighter, I saw his face: calm, considering, steady. When the cigarette was burning, he spoke again. "When we had cattle here, the animals would always spook near that place. It is unlucky."

"You did not speak of this before."

The cigarette hesitated halfway to his mouth. "You would not have listened before," he said. He was invisible in the darkness, and he knew that.

"We have to dig there," I said. "It's the most promising site we've found." A pause. The tip of his cigarette glowed brightly as he drew in the smoke. "Can we use more men there? Would that help?"

"It is a narrow passage," he said. "Only three can work there at a time: one to move rocks, one to move dirt, one to sift."

"Perhaps a different three workmen," I said. "Men who do not know or care that it is an unlucky place."

"Perhaps." His tone was noncommittal. "I will assign a different three."

That evening I sat in my hut, consulted my reference books, and calculated the date according to the Mayan calendar. It wasn't an easy task. Sylvanus Morley, a noted Mayanist active in the early 1900s, had derived a formula for the conversion of Mayan dates to dates in the modern calendar, but apparently it had not occurred to him that someone might want to convert from the modern calendar to the Mayan.

After much calculation, checking, and rechecking, I decided that today was Oc in the tzolkin or sacred almanac, the fourth day of Cumku, the last month in the haab or vague year. The Mayan year was almost over. The year's end, a period of five days of bad luck, would be upon us in sixteen days. I wondered if the proximity of the year's end was the reason for Salvador's fear of bad luck. We were also, according to the Long Count, about to reach the end of a katun, a time of change.

In any case, the day Oc was not too bad a day. In the glyphs, it is portrayed by the head of the dog that guides the sun in its nighttime journey through the underworld. I suppose, if I were writing a newspaper horoscope based on Mayan days, I could interpret it as something like "A day to receive guidance."

That night I dreamed clearly. I dreamed of Los Angeles, the tacky battered crackerbox of a city that I left so long ago.

The sun was just up and the morning light was pale. The world had no hard edges: a soft blur of gray-green formed the shrubs in a neighbor's yard; a slash of dark brown was a broken fence that marked the property line between two pale brown lawns, splashed with dark green where crabgrass grew. An old Volkswagen bug—dull blue flecked with rust—rested on its wheel rims in a weed-filled drive. The tires were flat; they had been flat for many years. The city was silent. No dogs barked; no birds sang; no cars drove past. The people were gone.

Diane walked beside me, a round-faced five-year-old with solemn green eyes. Her small soft hand was in mine and she trudged beside me without complaint though we had been walking for a long time.

Under our feet, the sidewalk was cracked and buckled. Diane tripped at a place where one cement square was higher than another and I caught her as she fell. When she looked up at me, her eyes were filled with tears.

"What's wrong?" I asked her. "Did you hurt yourself?"

She shook her head, but the tears started to spill over. I was caught by the strange restlessness that forced me to keep walking despite the blisters on my feet. "Come on," I said. "We have to keep going." She did not move, even when I took her hand and tugged on it. "If you won't come," I said, "I'll have to leave you here."

The tears were rolling down her round cheeks and falling to make dark spots on the cement. I swung her into my arms, arching my back to lift her. "Don't cry," I said. In that moment, I heard the coughing roar behind us. I glanced back to see a jaguar slip from behind the Volkswagen and begin to pace us, following without haste, as if confident of his prey.

I started to run, but I ran at dream speed: my feet moved slowly; my steps took me nowhere. Diane had locked her arms around my neck; she was a burden that I could not drop. My foot caught on the edge of a sidewalk stone, and I fell heavily to one knee. Diane lost her grip around my neck and fell away from me.

I heard the coughing roar of the jaguar behind me and

knew that I did not have the time or the strength to save the child.

I woke in my hammock. The thunder sounded again, a rumble like a jaguar's roar, like the hoofbeats of the horses that the Chaacob were reputed to ride. No rain yet, just thunder. Thunder from a rabbit sky, the Maya called it. A bad sign. The Chaacob rode, but they brought no rain. A particularly unlucky sign for us if it presaged the end of the dry season. When the rains began, excavation would have to end.

I stood in the doorway of my hut, looking out across the plaza. Though my watch said quarter past one, a burning lantern still hung from the corrugated tin roof that sheltered a small area just in front of Tony's hut. I pulled on my clothes, knowing it would be hours before I could sleep again, and crossed the plaza.

Tony sat in one of his two lawn chairs. His old plaid robe—the same robe he brought to camp each year—was belted tightly around him. He wore scuffed leather slippers. Above them his legs were painfully thin and marked with the red swellings of mosquito bites. A wooden crate served as a side table, holding Tony's pipe, a box of wooden matches, a glass, a bottle of gin, and a bottle of tonic water. Tony was reading a thick blue book that I recognized as a reference on Mayan pottery types.

He looked up when he heard my footsteps, smiled, and set the book aside. "You're still up," I said. "The thunder woke me. Do you think the rains are starting early?"

"Not a chance," he said. "It's just a summer shower. Come have a drink with me. It'll help you sleep."

When he ducked into his hut to get me a glass, he seemed a little uncertain of his footing, a trifle unsteady. I had never worried about Tony's drinking until his wife, Hilde, died two years ago. Before that, I knew he drank in the field, but assumed that Hilde kept him from drunken excesses at home. Now he lived alone in Las Cruces, and I suspected he drank heavily throughout the year. I had noticed that the circles under his eyes were darker this year than last. He seemed thinner, paler, a bit more battered and scuffed.

The drink that he poured for me was warm and the tonic was flat, but I did not mind. The lawn chair creaked beneath me when I sat down and stretched my legs out in front of me. The air was muggy and still. The thunder rolled across the sky like the stones of falling empires.

My first dig was a Hopi site located in Arizona's Mogollon Mountains. For two months, I lived in the motley village of leaky tents that New Mexico State University called a field camp. On my first night, I woke to the sound of thunder, to the trickling of running water, and to a feeling of dampness. I snapped on my flashlight and the beam glinted on the shifting surface of a minor waterfall that cascaded down the side of the tent—a foul-smelling army surplus model supplied by the university. A puddle had soaked my shoes and was creeping toward the tent flap. Outside, the rain whipped against the side of the tent, shaking the poles. The wet khaki-colored canvas shifted uneasily around me.

I had crawled out of my wet sleeping bag and was pulling on my clothes when I heard the creaking of poles shifting position, the sharp crack of a rope giving way, and the soft sigh of wet canvas released from tension. One side of the tent gave way and the rest followed, soddenly collapsing into itself, relaxing into its natural folded state.

I abandoned my possessions and groped my way to the door, cursing with a passion, swearing exotic oaths I had learned from the madwomen in the nuthouse, kicking at the dripping canvas and beating at it with my fists and flashlight, flinging the tent flap aside and escaping into the downpour. The tent lay like a dying animal, twitching sporadically in the wind.

The rain beat on my head, hammering my hair to my skull, soaking my clothes. I was barefoot in the mud. I heard someone chuckling. He stood in the open doorway of another tent, his hands in the pockets of his flannel robe. He was dry, clean, and amused, and I started over to kill him.

He stopped laughing when he saw me coming. "Stop

grinning or I'll kill you," I said. I had not been out of the nuthouse long, and I managed to remain socially acceptable only through a conscious effort. Without that effort, I slid easily back into a more primitive state.

"Sorry," he said. "Want to come in and dry off?"

I think it was his voice that won me. Even at thirty, Tony had a husky comforting voice with a soft rasping quality, like a fine wool blanket against bare skin or the warm coat of a friendly dog. He offered me a towel, loaned me dry clothes that did not fit, made hot chocolate over a camp stove, and, in the morning, helped me resurrect my fallen tent.

We were never lovers, Tony and I. We were good friends, best friends for a while, but we never slept together. I thought it better that way.

I can remember Tony's wedding more clearly than I can my own. Thinking about my wedding to Robert is like seeing stones at the bottom of a clear running stream. I can see them, but I know that their shapes are distorted by the water's movement, that the colors I see are not their true colors. I know that the stones are not as smooth as they look, but I can't touch them to be sure. The water is too cold and too treacherous; I cannot venture closer to investigate. I must keep my distance. I think, as I recall that time, that I married Robert in an effort to become a person I wasn't. An ordinary normal person.

Thinking of my wedding, I imagine Robert and me, dressed neatly and uncomfortably in our best clothes, standing before a justice of the peace in an office that smelled of dying flowers. I feel cold, thinking of it now. I cannot remember if I felt cold then.

Tony's wedding was in a church filled with flowers and well-wishers. I stood in the back, having declined a place in the bridesmaid lineup. Hilde had asked me, but I would have felt strange and awkward in a lacy gown. I remember watching Tony stride toward the altar, fumble for the ring, lift the white lace veil and kiss the tow-headed bride. I can even remember what I was thinking. I was wondering why I did not hurt. I was considering how curiously empty I felt. I felt like the shell of a half-constructed house or like a broken pot. The hollowness was centered in the pit of my stomach and I wondered if I might be catching the flu.

After the wedding I wished them well and drank champagne. The bubbles rose and burst in the great void inside me, but failed to fill it. I danced badly with men I did not like.

A little after midnight, I returned to my home. Sitting at my desk in the cramped ill-furnished one-bedroom apartment, looking at the flowered wallpaper and the ugly green rug, I worked on my thesis project, reading and taking meticulous notes. At dawn I went to the campus library so that I would be there when it opened, and I passed an Indian hunting party on my way. When Tony returned from his honeymoon, I welcomed him back and we picked up our friendship without a hitch.

Now we had come to this: old friends drinking warm gin and tonic and listening to thunder.

"I like your daughter," Tony said easily. "She's a lot like you were on that first dig."

"Yes? And how was I?"

"Careful," he said. "Very cautious. She's friendly, but she never lets her guard down completely. Something's going on under all that calm, but I don't know what it is."

"Neither do I."

The thunder rumbled and Tony waited for it to pass. The wind was blowing harder and our shadows rocked as the lantern was buffeted by wayward gusts. "I don't think you need to worry about Carlos. Diane's too smart for him."

"You're probably right."

The rain began with large drops. Each one made a wet spot the size of a dime on the hard-packed dirt of the plaza. The wind blew behind us, sweeping the rain over the tin roof and away from us.

"What about you?" he asked. "How are you getting along with your daughter?"

I shrugged, staring out at the rain. The memory of the

dream was still with me. My world was filled with uncertainties that I could not explain. "All right, I suppose."

"I've been wondering—it seems like you've been worried about something. Anything you want to talk about?" He was leaning forward, holding his glass in both hands.

I do not like it when friends lean forward and ask me what is wrong, particularly when they are asking about worries that I have not yet admitted to myself. I had a vague feeling, still less than a hunch, that a balance somewhere was shifting and I was losing control.

"That first summer in Arizona you held everything tight, sealed up, smooth like glass," Tony said. "But I knew there was something explosive inside. If anything nicked the surface, you would blow up. You're like that again."

My arms were folded across my chest. I shook my head. Somewhere in the darkness beyond the swaying circle of lantern light, the shadows were gathering. The world was out of balance.

"What's wrong?"

"I just feel like . . ." I made a quick helpless gesture with my hands. Empty. Open. Vulnerable. "I don't know."

He leaned back in his chair. "I've always wondered which of us has it worse. You keep everyone at a distance, shut them out so they can't hurt you. I drag people in so close that they can't help but hurt me." His voice was slow and steady, only slightly blurred by gin. "Neither of us can find the middle ground." He reached out and took one of my hands in both of his, holding it carefully and gently. I liked the feel of his hands on mine. His voice was warm and comforting. His hands were rough from the acid bath he used to clean lime deposits from potsherds.

I find it difficult to let people help. I always have. Tony knew that. He would not push me. "I'm afraid," I said.

The thunder roared and rain clattered on the tin roof above us. In the flash of lightning that illuminated the plaza I saw a shadow step into the open space, moving with the rain that swept across the hard-packed dirt, yet oblivious to it. In her world, it was not raining.

"Don't be afraid," Tony said.

Another flash and I saw the shadow more clearly: a young woman dressed in blue, her face illuminated by a moon that I could not see. I recognized her by the tattoos on her face: Zuhuy-kak, when she was much younger. I heard the steady beat of a drum, a hollow wooden sound. The woman was dancing, lifting her arms over her head and leaping toward the sky. Another lightning flash: she was whirling and the light glinted on the obsidian blade in her hand. The drumbeats blended with the thunder. Her expression was joyful; her eyes were enormous and filled with power. I felt the moonlight running in my veins, and for an instant, I wanted to join her, to dance with her under the moon.

"Liz?" Tony squeezed my hand to get my attention. "Just remember that you can talk to me."

"I'll remember," I said.

The lightning flashed and the plaza was empty except for the rain. I held Tony's warm calloused hand and tried not to be afraid.

I was tired. The rain let up soon after I left Tony, but I slept sporadically, awakened again and again by ordinary sounds: the rattling of the door in the wind, the croaking of a frog, the thunder. At dawn, I was glad to leave my hammock and walk out to check on the southeast site.

The ground steamed in the early-morning sun. Most of the water had already seeped away into the soil. Birds bathed in the few remaining puddles. One of Maria's pigs was napping in a wet spot beside the albarrada.

At the excavation, all was well. Some water had leaked past the tarp that covered the opening, but only a little. The stones were damp.

I went down the steps. A centipede rippled across the floor to hide in the rubble. When I stood erect in the passageway, my hat just brushed the stone slabs. The passageway was about five and a half feet high, three feet wide. Its construction was nothing remarkable: the walls of the stairway were smooth masonry, square blocks stacked neatly. At the top, protruding stones formed a lip on which the flat slabs that made the roof of the passageway rested. The plaster of the plaza had been laid on top of these slabs. The passageway was interesting only because I expected it to go somewhere interesting. I climbed the stairs and stepped out into the sunshine.

Zuhuy-kak squatted in the shade, as if she were waiting for me. I greeted her and she nodded to me, accepting my presence. I sat on a nearby rock and lit a cigarette. "Yesterday was the day Oc," I told her. "The fourth day of Cumku."

She smiled. "Yes," she said. "The year ends soon. The time is near. Have you seen my enemies, Ix Zacbeliz?"

"Last night, I dreamed of a jaguar who stalked me and my daughter," I said slowly.

"He knows that the time is coming for change," she said. "Cycles are turning." She fingered the conch shell on her belt thoughtfully. "My enemies will try to stop the goddess from returning to power. You must be careful." She turned away from me, her eyes tracing the line of a building that had long since fallen. "It is so quiet here since the people have gone," she muttered. A lizard the length of my forearm watched us from a sunny rock on the mound. The grasses whispered softly. "I did not know it would be so quiet."

She looked sad and weary. I started to reach out to her, wanting to give her comfort. My hand passed through her as if she were smoke and I sat alone beside the tomb, talking to myself in the growing heat of the morning.

Chapter Twelve: Diane

The bush covers almost everything; it is
the background within which lie all other
special features of earth's surface. It is
never reduced permanently to man's use;
the milpas are but temporary claims made
by men upon the good will of the deities
who animate and inhabit the bush. . . .
—Robert Redfield,
Folk Culture of the Yucatan

THAT night, we went to the university basketball game and
watched Marcos's team lose. The game was played in a
central courtyard, surrounded by tall stucco buildings. A few
stars showed in the dark patch of sky above our heads.
Spectators' shouts echoed from the yellow walls, and a small
boy kept the score on a large blackboard. Marcos's team,
long-legged young men dressed in bright green, ran and
shouted and stole the ball from long-legged young men dressed
in blue. High over the courtyard, the stars moved slowly
across the rectangle of the sky.

Barbara and I sat at the top of the concrete bleachers, the
only North Americans in the crowd. Barbara leaned against
the building that served as the back of the bleachers and put
her hands behind her head. Her eyes followed the men as

they ran from one end of the court to the other. "Wrap them up," she said softly. "We'll take them all home."

On the court, Marcos fumbled the ball and lost it to a blue-clad giant. I could recognize Marcos only by the number on his shirt. "Somehow I think Liz would object."

"Yeah, she would. She deals with sex by avoiding it." I glanced at her and she shrugged lightly. "As far as I can tell."

"How long have you known her?" I leaned back too, imitating Barbara's casual pose.

"Seven years," she said. "We've been working together at the university for three years." She lifted her eyes from the court to look at the stars overhead. "She's not an easy person to get to know. She likes to keep people at a distance. I'd been working with her for a year and a half before she ever invited me to her house."

"Where does she live?" The question was out before I stopped to think.

"It's a little apartment in an old building. One-bedroom. Crammed with books and pots and artifacts. Tiny kitchen. I think she eats out mostly." Barbara glanced at me, still casual. "You know, you still haven't told me the story here. You're Liz's daughter, but you don't know her and she doesn't know you. You turn up here unexpectedly and you stay." She shrugged without looking at me. "Tell me if you want to."

"She and my father were divorced when I was five. My father raised me," I said. "I only saw my mother a few times after the divorce. My father didn't want her to have anything to do with me. So I don't know her. I don't know her at all."

"Your father kept her from seeing you? Didn't Liz have anything to say about that?"

I shrugged. "Apparently not."

The courtyard erupted with cheers when Marcos's team grabbed the ball and made a basket—their first in ten minutes. Barbara waited for the echoes to die, her eyes following the running men. "So, do you think you'll sleep with him?"

I shrugged, grateful that she had changed the subject and knowing that she had done so for my benefit.

"Don't expect much if you do," she said. "Mexican men play by a different set of rules."

"That sounds like the voice of experience."

"I've heard tales," she said.

I did not get to hear any of the tales. Emilio hailed us from the bottom of the bleachers and made his way up to where we sat. He sat on the level below us, leaned against Barbara's legs, and grinned up at her, showing his gold-rimmed teeth. "I knew Marcos and I would have luck today," he said.

Sunday morning, Barbara and I woke early to the sound of church bells calling the people to Mass. Marcos and Emilio arrived at the café just as we were finishing breakfast.

Emilio dropped a stack of hammocks beside the table, collapsed into a chair, and waved for the waitress to bring two more coffees. "*Qué hacemos?*" Marcos asked, sitting beside me. "What are we going to do?"

"Want a hammock?" Emilio said to a passing couple, and what we did for a while was watch the intricate quick-step of careful negotiations. The woman said no and the man said yes, then after a while the man said maybe and the woman said maybe. Then finally, after much bargaining, the woman said yes and the man said yes. Emilio returned to the table smiling.

"So what are we going to do?" Barbara asked, but Emilio, distracted from romance by the promise of profit, had spotted two French tourists on the other side of the café and was watching another hammock vendor try to convince them to buy a hammock.

"I will sell them a hammock tomorrow," he said.

"Let's leave these guys here and go somewhere cool," Barbara suggested to me.

Marcos leaned forward and said, "We could go to the park. You haven't seen the park, have you?"

We caught the crosstown bus, a battered vehicle that had come to Mérida to die. Clattering, wheezing, overloaded, and much abused, it had, I would have bet, served many years hard time in the States or in some wealthier province of Mexico before it reached Mérida. The bus took us to the park, which was not cool, but was a little cooler than the café.

We rode the small train that circled the park, squeezed in one corner of a car packed with fat women in peasant dresses and sticky happy children who smelled of cotton candy and hot sauce. We rented a small boat with clumsy wooden paddles and journeyed slowly across a tiny cement pond filled with pale green water no deeper than waist-high. Barbara and Emilio paddled enthusiastically. Halfway across, we collided with a boat piloted by a solidly built Mexican father; his wife and two children watched us with round eyes as we called out apologies in English and Spanish. On the way back, we rammed a boat piloted by two high school boys, who seemed to regard the collision as a challenge of some sort. The taller boy smacked his paddle against the water to send a cascade of green water in our direction, and we hastily retreated toward shore.

We rode in red-and-gold skyway cars, passing over the pond and dropping potato chips on the high school boys and, accidentally, on the father, who still paddled valiantly in a vain and foolish effort to reach the far shore.

We watched high school students on roller skates careen around a small concrete rink. Marcos bought me a balloon from a withered old man. Barbara and Emilio tried to sell a hammock to two young American men.

Two old women in huipiles sat at a small metal table by the refrescos stand, drinking Coca-Cola and eating potato chips. A troop of noisy children ran along the paths; a middle-aged woman carrying an oversized purse trudged after them. Four high school boys strolled along the path with their hands in their pockets and sunglasses shading their eyes. Emilio bought us all melon-flavored *helados*, sweet fruit ices that had cantaloupe seeds mashed in with the fruit juice. Marcos held my warm, fruit-juice sticky hand, and we strolled behind the high school boys, taking the day at its own pace.

The zoo was small and smelled of warm animals, warm hay, warm manure. The owl, a small brown-feathered bird with delicate ear tufts, perched in the far corner of his cage, as far as possible from the path. When Barbara hooted at him softly, mimicking the call we heard in the camp at night, he blinked at us, ruffled his feathers, then closed his eyes again.

The jaguar was pacing in his cage, one foot crossing over the other as he turned, took three steps to the far end of the cage, turned again and took three steps back, weaving an endless pattern. He returned my gaze. Marcos leaned on the railing beside me.

"Are there still jaguars in the monte?" I asked him. "I'd hate to meet one out by the camp at night."

He shook his head. "Not here. Not near Mérida. Not anymore." He put his arm lightly around my waist. "Are you afraid, being alone in the camp at night? I will come back with you and keep you safe at night."

I laughed. "Ah—there may be no jaguar, but there are wolves in Mérida."

He frowned. "I don't understand."

I laughed again. "Nothing. Never mind. It's not important." I spotted Barbara and Emilio over by the camel's enclosure and started to lead him in that direction. He held my hand and pulled me back to him, put his hand lightly on my shoulder, and kissed my lips quickly.

"You should not laugh at me when I don't understand," he said. "I don't laugh when you don't understand."

I think I blushed. "I'm sorry," I said. "I didn't mean. . ." He kissed me again, then led the way to where Emilio and Barbara were feeding the camel popcorn through the bars.

By the time we returned to Parque Hidalgo, the day was fading. The line for the movie theater stretched along one side of the square, and vendors sold balloons to the people leaving the church on the corner. Marcos and I shared a concrete love seat on one side of the park; Emilio and Barbara shared another. The love seats in Mérida's parks are two concrete chairs joined in an S curve—the person in one chair faces the person in the other chair, yet the two are separated by a wide concrete armrest. Intimacy with separation. I still wore my sunglasses and they made the world seem dim and far away.

Marcos was holding my hand in a companionable way and I was watching Emilio and Barbara. Emilio was trying to persuade Barbara to stay one more night and go to bed with him. Barbara was saying that she would see him next weekend. I knew their conversation because the discussion had started on the bus back from the park. Barbara was laughing and shaking her head.

The heat of the day weighed upon me. On the brick plaza, two pigeons were courting. The male was circling the female, cooing and puffing out his neck feathers so that they caught the light. The female was searching for bread crumbs, oblivious to his attention.

Two small children, a boy in a blue shirt and jeans and a little girl in a faded dress, came to us with a bouquet of flowers. Marcos bought me a flower and I tucked it behind my ear. The little girl grinned: her teeth were crooked and her hair needed combing. I patted her on the shoulder—the way you pat a kitten or a puppy—and gave her a coin.

"Will you come here next weekend?" Marcos asked me.

"Sure," I said. "I think so."

He squeezed my hand lightly. "Sometimes," Marcos said, "you look like you are very far away from here. What happens with you then?"

"Just thinking, I guess. I can't explain it."

He studied my face, then shrugged. "Whatever it is, it will be OK. You are in Mérida with us." He squeezed my hand lightly. "It will be good. We will be good friends."

Across the way, Emilio's attempts to persuade Barbara had been interrupted by the flower-bearing children. As I watched, Emilio tried to shoo them away and continue his conversation with Barbara, but the boy just grinned and thrust the flowers out again. Clever urchins, they kept grinning and holding out the flowers and watching Barbara laugh. Finally,

Emilio threw up his hands with impatience, bought a flower from the boy and bribed the little girl with a coin.

"Don't look sad," said Marcos. "You will come back in a week. One week will pass just like that." He waved a hand in the air.

Barbara was walking toward me, twirling a white flower between her finger and thumb. Emilio, defeated but still hopeful, walked at her side. Barbara and I drove away in a car filled with the scent of dying flowers.

—— Chapter Thirteen: Elizabeth ——

DIANE and Barbara returned to camp late on Sunday, roaring in about an hour after sunset. Tony, John, and I were sitting beside Tony's hut when they drove up. Barbara waved to us from the car, immediately brought over a bottle of red wine that she had purchased in Mérida, and insisted that we all share it. She seemed exuberant, happy to have gone to Mérida, happy to be back. Diane was more subdued.

Barbara dragged over a few folding chairs, and we drank wine and listened to Barbara's tales of selling hammocks to tourists. The wine was too sweet. Diane said very little, and I found myself watching the shadows shift and move. The dancing woman did not return. I felt restless and out of place and I excused myself after finishing a single glass of wine. Alone, I walked to the cenote.

I fingered the lucky piece that I carried in my pocket. Tony had given me the coin on the same day he told me that he loved me. I don't remember what I said to him. I have a better memory for what others say than for what I say myself. We were walking home from the movies. Tony had insisted on taking me; he told me I was working too hard, that I needed some time off. When we reached my apartment door, he pulled a dark blue box from his pocket and handed it to me. "I made you a present," he said.

"You realize," he said as I was opening it, "that I care a lot about you." He was shy, a little awkward. I remember hoping, as I opened the box, that a collapsible rubber snake would jump out, or that a joy buzzer would sound, or somehow the whole thing would be a joke. The coin glistened in the light. "I love you, Liz. You know that?" Tony said quietly.

I did know—though I had not admitted it to myself before. I said, I think I said, "I don't want this. I'm sorry." I think I held the coin out to him, hoping that he would take it back and hide it away again.

He took my hand and gently closed it around the coin. He kept his hands on mine for a moment. "Think about it," he said. He turned and walked away, leaving the coin in my hand.

I remember sitting in my apartment. I didn't turn on the lamp; I could see the dim outlines of the furniture by the light of the streetlamp, filtered through the window shade, and I wanted no more light than that. What I had told Tony was true—I could not love him. Somewhere at my center, with the madness I had locked away, I had sealed off the part of me that knew how to love. It was too close to the part of me that knew how to hate, and that was at the center of the madness. I had sealed them all away, leaving a dead place, a place where nothing hurt because there were no nerve endings there. I had severed connections, cauterized the wound. I sat in the dim light in an ugly apartment that needed painting and I probed the dead spot, thinking about Robert, thinking about the pain of madness. Nothing.

I don't think I cried. I don't remember crying. I remember taking a shower and letting the warm water run over my body. I remember thinking, I feel the water, so I must be alive. But the warm water did not reach the part of me that I had sealed away.

Tony and I remained friends—very good friends. I tried to give him the coin back, but he insisted I keep it. We went to lunch together, to dinner now and then. Eventually, he mentioned to me that he was dating Hilde, one of the secretaries who worked in the department.

The cenote was dark and still. I stood on the edge of the

pool and held the coin lightly in my hand. Something was stirring in the back of my mind; something that I did not want to examine too closely. Feelings that I had buried long ago were surfacing in me. I turned the coin over and over in my hand.

I heard the rustle of fabric behind me. Zuhuy-kak stepped to my side, smiling in the moonlight. "Ah, you are here," she said. "That is well: you belong here."

I smiled back. Seeing her helped ease the restlessness. I did belong here; I had always felt that.

"I came to tell you that a day of bad luck is coming," she said. "The day Ix, three days from now, will be unfavorable. It is ruled by the jaguar god, who does not wish the goddess to return to power. You must give to the goddess to make her stronger so that she can help you against her enemies."

"What can I give?"

"Something you value." Zuhuy-kak was looking at the coin and I closed my hand around it. My mind suddenly held a picture of the coin arcing high in the air, catching the moonlight as it tumbled toward the black waters.

"You hesitate," she said.

"Yes," I said. "I was thinking that you have never told me what we will find when we finish digging."

She frowned at me. "You were wondering whether the result would be worth the sacrifice. You cannot bargain with the gods."

I shrugged. "I think about these things differently than you."

"What do you want to find, Ix Zacbeliz?"

I thought for a moment. Tony and I joked about jade masks and gold, but that was just joking. What did I want? A tomb that added to our knowledge of religious ritual? Murals like the ones in the caves at Bonampak?

"I know what you want," Zuhuy-kak said softly. "I can tell you. You want power. That is what you will find when you reach the end. You will find the power of the goddess."

I was turning the coin over and over in my hand.

"You must sacrifice to the goddess to gain her favor. You must give to her willingly."

I held the coin, unwilling to let it go. It caught the moonlight and gleamed in my hand. A sound on the path distracted me. My daughter's voice calling, "Hello?" I turned toward her, slipped on the rock, started to fall and flailed my arms to regain my balance. My hand opened and the coin slipped away from me, through my fingers. I heard it hit the rock, slide. I heard a splash in the water below. Gone.

"Hello? Who's that?" Diane called. My daughter had stopped in the shadows where the trail reached the pool's edge. She was alone. "Who's there?"

I walked around the pool to stand beside her. "What are you doing here?" My voice sounded strained and I fought to control it. "It's late to be wandering around."

She shrugged. "I thought I might go for a swim," she said. "I thought it might help me sleep."

"The water should be cool." I stood with my hands in my empty pockets, looking at the cenote.

"What are you doing out here?" Diane asked hesitantly.

"Thinking," I said. "It's cooler here. And quieter."

"Sorry to interrupt," she said quickly. "I didn't know—"

"It's all right," I said. "It's fine." Her eyes were large in the moonlight, like the eyes of a little girl. "I was just heading back to camp."

"All right," she said with a trace of relief. She turned away, kneeling by the pool to test the water with her hand.

And suddenly, I don't know why, I was afraid to leave her there by herself. "I'll wait for you," I said. "I'll walk you back to camp."

She frowned at me, puzzled. "That's all right. I'm fine by myself."

"No, I'll stay. I'd like to just sit here for a while anyway," I said.

She shrugged. "If you want."

When she dove in, she shattered the silver moon that floated on the surface of the pool. The moonlight rippled around her. I think she shortened her swim because I was there. She ducked beneath the dark surface once or twice, did a slow breaststroke to the far end of the pool and back.

Walking along the dark path to camp with my daughter at my side, I realized that she frightened me. I am not used to caring. The breeze blew and I thought I heard laughter in the branches overhead.

That night, I dreamed of the city of Dzibilchaltún before the coming of the ah-nunob.

In the dream, I walked north along the sacbe that led from the outskirts to the city center. The city was quiet and still. Most houses were empty, but the desertion seemed temporary. I could see through the open doorways into the huts. In one, an old woman tended a fire and stirred a pot of atole. In another, a child cried, a sound as thin and lonely as a fingernail scraping on a classroom chalkboard an hour after school was out. In one solar, I saw tall water jars, elegantly painted with black on red. A woman hurried along the sacbe, glancing warily over her shoulder. I saw a man lying in a hammock, while a woman sat beside him, her head bowed, rocking his hammock as if he were a child. I guessed the date of the dream to be sometime near A.D. 900, sometime before the Toltec invasion.

The huts I passed grew more affluent as I approached the city center. First, the huts of well-to-do peasants; then, those of rich merchants. An effigy of Ek Chuah, the black-eyed guardian deity of the merchants, pouted at me from one yard. He was an ugly god, and the cedar carving portrayed him accurately, showing his misshapen lower lip, the black markings on his face, the burdens on his back. Finally, the huts of the nobility and priests. The solars around these huts were well tended and filled with flowers. But something was wrong. An evil smell hung in the air. The horizon was clouded with smoke.

I left the huts behind and entered the first ceremonial plaza. As I approached the far end of the court, three ravens flew up, shrieking and cursing. The black birds had been perching on a heap of sun-bleached coconuts, and that seemed odd, since coconuts did not grow in this part of the Yucatán.

The coconuts grinned at me and watched with hollow eyes.

The round objects were not coconuts, but the skulls of men. I suddenly realized what was happening: Dzibilchaltún was at war. These were the skulls of enemy warriors killed in battle. Scraps of dried flesh clung to the topmost skulls, the most recent additions. The other skulls had been there longer; they had been picked clean by birds, insects, and night-wandering rats. The faint aroma of dead meat hung in the warm air.

I was surrounded by the heavy scent of death. The sky was cloaked in clouds and the air was thick. From somewhere far away, I heard the slow beat of drums, growing louder with each beat.

When I woke, I was drenched in sweat. The hut was filled with darkness. I lit a candle, but that only pushed the shadows back; it did not chase them away. It was strange to walk through the dark camp and fear the shadows. They pressed too close, these shades of darkness. Something was wrong here. The smell of death clung to me.

I stood by the open door to Diane's hut. I remembered a long distant evening, buried deeper than any jade mask, when I watched my four-year-old daughter sleep. She was covered by a quilt, surrounded by stuffed toys. Her red-gold hair fanned out over the pillow; her thumb had found her mouth under cover of darkness. The next day, I packed my bags and left for New Mexico the first time.

Now I listened to soft breathing in four voices: Diane's breath was a husky whisper in the chorus. She was quiet in her hammock, at peace. I turned away from my sleeping daughter.

Zuhuy-kak stood in the shadows by the water barrel. She walked beside me as I strolled toward my hut. "You and I have much in common," she said to me. "I had a daughter once." She walked in the shadows and I could not read the expression on her face.

"What became of your daughter?"

"The ah-nunob came and she died. Many died." Her voice was very soft.

The uneasy residue of my dream lingered. "I dreamed of the time before the ah-nunob came," I said.

"You dreamed of bad luck," she said flatly. "Bad luck is coming. You did not make a willing sacrifice to the goddess."

I walked in silence for a moment, imagining what Tony would say if I suggested we take a holiday in the middle of the week because I feared bad luck. When I entered my hut, I was alone. I returned to my hammock, but it was a long time before I fell asleep.

The week began badly and got worse. On Monday, John spotted a rattlesnake on the trail to the tomb; Robin was afflicted with heat rash; Pich was bitten by a centipede, a nasty sting that quickly began to swell.

The students were growing restless. At breakfast and dinner, I heard talk of what they would do after the dig was over. They were as nervous as birds just before a storm, fluttering here and there with little purpose other than the movement itself. I think they felt the tension in the air, but they blamed it on isolation, on hot days and lonely nights.

On Tuesday, two workmen did not come to work and two others arrived late. I was in a bad temper when I drove the jeep to Mérida and tried to track down the chain hoist and winch that we needed to raise the stela. After much searching, I located a man who would rent us the equipment on Thursday of that week, later than I had hoped but better than nothing. On the way back, I had a flat tire, discovered the jack was broken, and finally put out my thumb and hitched a ride with a farmer. I arrived at camp crouched in the bed of a pickup truck with a mournful pig. I spent the evening with Tony, drinking aguardiente and calling curses down on the workmen who had not come.

And on Wednesday, the day Ix, our luck turned bad, very bad. Philippe, Maria's younger brother, was working in the passageway when a large rock rolled down onto his right foot.

Philippe was young: a basketball player, a boxer, a university athlete who was earning a little cash doing work that he considered beneath him. Salvador had hired him, I believe, partly because Maria had asked him to do so. Certainly, the young man was strong, but he lacked the traits that make a good worker for a dig.

Older men make the best workers: they appreciate the virtue of a slow steady pace; they take advantage of delays to stand in the shade and smoke; they are wiry and enduring but not overly muscular. They know how to conserve their energy.

Hot-blooded and restless, eager to see signs of progress, Philippe had grown impatient with the work, annoyed at the frequent delays while John photographed the site. In the moist warm passageway, he had shoved too hard on a crowbar, using muscles built through long hours in the gym. A boulder, suddenly loosened, tumbled down so quickly that Philippe had no time to dodge. The rock pinned the young man's foot beneath it.

Working in the narrow passageway, squeezed between unyielding masonry walls, was difficult. It took half an hour for the other workmen to lever the rock off the wounded foot. When Salvador and Pich carried the young man from the passageway, his bravado and impatience were gone. He was pale; his jaw was set; and his face was covered with sweat. Salvador and Tony took him to the hospital emergency room in the pickup truck.

Dinner that evening was not good. I believe that Maria was punishing us for indirectly causing, by our existence, her younger brother's injury. The chicken was smothered in a sauce that left the tongue scalded and numb. Beneath the sauce the chicken was scorched. The salad was limp and the tortillas were cold.

I was lingering in the plaza over a cup of bitter coffee when I heard the coughing roar of Salvador's pickup truck. After a time, Tony came to find me and report. Philippe's ankle was broken and the foot was badly bruised. With his ankle in a cast, he had returned. Now that the ordeal was over, his bravado was restored.

At Maria's insistence, Philippe would be staying with

Salvador's family until he was better. Maria was determined to nurse him back to health.

"Tomorrow," Tony said, "she wants Tony to bring the *curandera* from Chicxulub to come and see him. Apparently she thinks this is more than a medical problem."

I offered Tony a cigarette and lit one myself. "Of course," I said. "She wants a specialist in matters of bad luck, evil winds, and sorcery."

"I don't suppose there's much we can do to talk her out of it," he said.

"I don't suppose so." I leaned back in my chair and watched the red-hot coal on the end of my cigarette. "That leaves us short another man and marked as unlucky in the bargain." I shrugged. "Nothing we can do about it. Nothing at all."

"Do you suppose there's a chance that she'll give us a clean bill of health? No bad spirits here."

I shook my head. "I doubt that. At best, she'll blame the Aluxob." The Aluxob were mischievous gremlins that haunted the old ruins and occasionally harassed people who disturbed the ancient places. "At worst, we'll need an exorcism. For that, we'd lose a few days' work."

"That's not so bad. We could weather that," Tony said.

I watched the shadows grow longer and I hoped he was right.

On Thursday, the day Men, we dragged the winch and other equipment out along the sacbe to raise the stela. Salvador and five of the men from his crew constructed a wooden tripod and rigged an arrangement of pulleys that culminated in the small gas-powered winch. Salvador politely ignored most of my advice on how to rig the pulleys, quietly setting them up his way, and in the end I sat with Tony by the mound and picked thorns and burrs from my clothing while listening to the workmen. In digging to slide a rope beneath the stela, they had disturbed a nest of stinging ants and they were cursing steadily, colorfully, with many anatomically impossible suggestions.

Not far away in space but very much removed in time, two

young men, h'menob or apprentices studying to be h'menob,
were playing what looked like a gambling game with the red
fortune-telling beans. I tried to listen to their conversation,
but Tony kept interrupting with comments about the weather,
the dig, the stela.

Throughout the morning, the sky rumbled with thunder
and the sun hid behind a solid gray expanse of clouds.
Salvador sniffed the air and said that it would not rain before
afternoon, but I had my doubts.

Just before noon, as Salvador's crew was digging a depression in which the stela could rest once it was upright, the
survey crew came tromping through the monte. The end
point of their latest transect was about a mile away, so they
had decided to join us for the raising of the stela. Diane
looked cheerful enough, smiling even though her legs were
covered with insect bites and scratches.

When Salvador started the winch, it made a horrible sput-
tering noise, then died immediately. He swore, made various
adjustments, and tried again. It caught this time and began to
turn. One man on each corner of the stela held a guy wire,
steadying the great stone slab as it shuddered, then began to
tilt, lifting slowly from its bed in the dirt and leaves. At first,
it moved smoothly.

The wind blew, fluttering the leaves of the trees around us.
Birds flew here and there, calling their displeasure. The sky
cleared its throat. The rain began when the upper end of the
slab was a foot off the ground and rising steadily. In minutes
we were drenched. The stela's steady ascent faltered as the
workmen holding the guy ropes slid in the mud. I ran to help
the workman who was guiding the northwest corner of the
stela, clinging to the guy rope and planting my heels in the
mud in a vain effort to stop sliding. Tony was on another
rope, shouting encouragement. Diane and Barbara were dragging on another rope, helping a thin old man who was calling
loudly to the saints for assistance.

The rain whipped us, stinging on my bare skin, soaking
through my thin shirt. The flashes of lightning shattered the
world into fragmentary blue-white images: Tony's face, his

mouth open to shout; Diane's hands, knuckles white as she tried to grip the rope harder; black exhaust rising from the coughing winch; wet metal glistening in the rain. Thunder crashed as if the sky were tumbling down around us, overwhelming Tony's shouts, Salvador's instructions, and the old man's prayers.

The slab was nearly erect, sliding slowly into the hole that had been dug for it, when the thunder crashed with a cataclysmic rumble and the lightning struck the end of the stone, filling the air with the crackling smell of ozone. I could hear a man's voice, shouting in Spanish to the Virgin Mary for mercy and another calling to Saint Michael and the Chaacob. The winch coughed once, a petty imitation of the thunder, then roared with a sudden surge of power, jerking on the stela. We gripped the guy ropes, our hands wet and slippery, our feet sliding in the mud, and the great stone slab kept moving, tumbling with majestic grace, its momentum overcoming our puny efforts to stop it, continuing on its slow inevitable path. It fell.

The thunder mocked us with deep demonic laughter, and I scrambled through the mud to see the stela, ducking involuntarily whenever the lightning flashed. The limestone had broken when it fell. An irregular diagonal crack—bright white but darkening already in the falling rain—cut through the relief carving, separating the slab into two parts.

The leaves and dirt that clung to the surface made the relief carving stand out. On the top section, a Toltec warrior stared down, resplendent in an eagle headdress, a jaguar-skin cloak, and full military garb. His eye was a dark clot of mud, and angry ants ran over his robes, his spear, his round shield.

The crack separated him from the Mayan woman who crouched at his feet. Her head was lowered and her hands held out an offering—a bowl of something. I recognized her face as that of Ix Chebel Yax, the fickle Mayan moon goddess who sometimes brought healing and sometimes death.

The lightning flashed again and the thunder rolled more softly, as if it were moving away, having finished its work. I looked up and saw Zuhuy-kak watching me from the far side of the stela, smiling in the rain. Angrily, I called to her in Maya, asking why this had happened. She did not reply.

The thunder rumbled again, distant now, and I became aware once again of the people around me. The Mayan workmen stood in the shelter of the trees, far away from the stela. The rain was still falling, though it was gradually letting up. Diane stood beside me, drenched as a drowned cat. Barbara, Tony, and Salvador stood at the winch, all shouting at once in voices intended to carry over the thunder, which no longer rolled overhead.

Diane was looking out where Zuhuy-kak had been standing, as if trying to figure out who I had been shouting at. I put my hand on her shoulder to distract her. "Are you all right?" I asked. She nodded. "Welcome to the romance of archaeology," I said.

——— Chapter Fourteen: Diane ———

"There is nothing wrong with being afraid.
When you fear, you see things in a different way."

—Carlos Castaneda,
The Teachings of Don Juan

MY mother was chain-smoking again. She had been in a
bad mood since the beginning of the week, but it had grown
worse since the stela fell. Tony was drinking. Maggie and
Carlos were trying to persuade John and Robin to join them in
a game of cards. The air was hot and heavy and slow-moving.

"Want to go for a swim?" Barbara asked. I shrugged and
followed her to the hut to get our swimsuits, then down the
path to the cenote.

As soon as we were out of sight of the plaza, she grinned
at me. "I have a treat," she said. "A present from Emilio."
She pulled a joint from her pocket, waved it delicately under
my nose, and tucked it back in her pocket. "I think we need
a little relaxation."

"I think you're right."

On the edge of the pool, she stopped. "Swim first or
smoke?"

"Smoke."

We left the path and scrambled around the pool to the high
rock from which Carlos liked to dive. If anyone from camp

wandered down to the cenote, we could sneak away, follow-ing the path to the tomb site. Barbara lit up and took the first hit, closing her eyes and drawing the smoke in deep. I took the joint and drew on it, fighting the urge to cough out the smoke, drawing it in deep and holding it in my lungs.

"Emilio said to think of him when we smoked it," Bar-bara said, holding the joint. "I'm thinking of him quite fondly."

I nodded. With the second hit, the world around me began losing its hard edges. The air was cooler here, and bats skimmed low over the water. "He's a fine man, Emilio. He has risen immensely in my estimation." I accepted the joint and glanced at Barbara. "Are you going to sleep with him?"

She shrugged, leaning back on her hands and staring out over the water. "Don't know. Wouldn't mind it, but I get the feeling that he's playing some variation on the game I'm used to. I think he would like me better if I didn't sleep with him." She shrugged again. "I'll play it by ear. What about you? You like that young basketball player?"

"Sometimes. But I know what you mean about the game. The rules are different."

For a moment, we sat in companionable silence, trading hits. Long shadows stretched across the cenote. The surface was still, disturbed only by spreading ripples when an insect landed on the water or when a fish rose. Barbara took a paper clip from her pocket and bent the wire to make a primitive roach clip. We finished the joint.

"Let's go for a swim," Barbara suggested.

The water was cool and I swam several slow laps, watch-ing the last of the sunlight play on the rippled water. I floated on my back, looking up at the deepening blue of the sky. I relaxed and my thoughts drifted. There was a rock ledge a few feet beneath the water's surface at one edge of the pool. I rested there for a moment, sitting on the submerged ledge with my head above water, my knees pulled close to my body. The last sunlight shone on the mound beyond the path. I could see the traces of relief carving on the stones, here and there. I wondered idly what the temple had looked like before the stones had tumbled and the trees had overgrown it. I studied the hill and drew a picture in my mind: three doorways, side by side in a rectangular building.

Barbara glided to a stop beside me. "What are you looking at?"

I jerked my head toward the hill. "That pile of rocks. Liz told me, one time last week, that you can choose to see the past. I'm trying it out."

"Liz can be a very strange lady," Barbara said. She sat on the ledge, let her toes rise to the surface of the water, and regarded them solemnly.

"Yeah."

"I'm going to head back to camp before my toes turn to prunes. I've still got to write up today's field report," she said.

"In your condition?"

"It'll probably be better than all the ones I've written straight. I feel inspired."

"I'll stay here a while," I said. "I'll meet you back there."

She swam languidly to the rocks on the far side and dressed. "If you don't come back soon, I'll send out a search party," she called.

I waved and she headed back to camp. I returned to my consideration of the rock-strewn hillside, and the picture in my mind came into sharper focus. Above the doors, the wall was an intricate lattice of stone, which rose high above the pool. The stones around the doors were carved with hieroglyphics, a jumble of shapes and faces and strange symbols, painted in bright red and blue. A curving stone jutted out just above the central door; a little higher on the wall, two dark recesses in the carvings flanked the stone, making the doorway appear to be a cavernous mouth in an enormous long-nosed face. A steep stairway led from the mouth to the edge of the pool, and the stones of the stairway were carved and painted, a riot of unreadable symbols.

I leaned back in the water, squinting at the slope and holding the picture in my mind. I was still tired, a lingering weariness from all the sleepless nights in Los Angeles. and the pot had relaxed me. I listened to the beating of my own heart, steady as a drum. I relaxed, half asleep though I could still feel the ledge beneath me, the water around me. I listened to the crickets in the monte, and their trilling seemed to come and go, keeping time with the beating of my heart. The tone of the cricket's song seemed to change as I listened, growing harsher, a sharp buzzing like beans in a rattle.

Suddenly I was afraid. I smelled smoke in the air, an acrid scent like burning pitch. My eyes were closed and I was afraid to open them, afraid of what I might see.

I shivered suddenly and opened my eyes. For an instant, I saw a temple at the end of the pool, as detailed as I had imagined it. On the steps, a blue-robed figure stood watching me. Then there was nothing but rocks, sunlight, and shadows. The temple was gone.

The sun was nearly down. A bat flew overhead, dipping and dodging in erratic flight. I shivered again, climbed out of the pool, and dressed. I returned to camp through the darkness where the trees shaded the path. I knew the path from each afternoon's visit to the pool, but things seemed different now: the trees seemed closer to the path; the path seemed rougher; the noises of the monte seemed louder, and it bothered me that I did not know what animals were rustling in the bushes. Something moved at the edge of my field of vision, and I turned toward it. Nothing there. Maybe a bird flying overhead. Again, I caught a flickering movement in the corner of my eye. Again, nothing. Maybe the shadow of a swaying branch. I hurried along the path to Salvador's hut, where the lantern light would chase back the shadows. I hurried from the trees by Salvador's hut and almost tripped over Teresa.

The little girl crouched in the deep shadow by the garden wall, playing with a scrawny black kitten. The kitten came to greet me, mewing piteously, and I knelt to stroke it. Teresa stood by the garden wall, one hand at her mouth, the other clutching the hem of her dress. The air was hot and heavy. Already, I felt sweaty and dusty again. My mouth was dry.

"What's the cat's name?" I asked Teresa. At least, that's what I intended to ask. I think I said something like that in Spanish.

She did not answer. She watched me with round brown eyes, as if I were dangerous yet fascinating.

"Cat got your tongue?" I asked in English.

Still she didn't speak. The kitten was purring, a steady desperate throbbing under my hand. I smiled at Teresa, seeing in her expression a reflection of my panic down by the cenote. I think she wanted to run back into her yard, but she found me intriguing. "*Qué tal?*" I asked her. "How's it going?"

The creak of an opening door sent her scurrying away through the gate and into the foliage of the yard. An old woman was stepping through the doorway of Salvador's house; Maria was just behind her. Maria was speaking quickly in Maya, and her hands were clasped together in supplication. Salvador followed the two women, saying nothing. I remained where I was, petting the kitten and listening to it purr.

The gate was right beside me. The old woman stopped in the middle of the path and said something sharp in Maya. I looked up at her and smiled, but she did not smile back. She said something to me in Spanish and scowled when I did not reply. Maria murmured something, and the old woman shook her head. She thumped her walking cane on the ground angrily and repeated herself.

"I don't understand," I said. "I'm sorry. *No comprendo.*"

Maria quickly made the sign of the cross, still staring at me. The old woman leaned forward. She took hold of my arm and peered into my face as if she wanted to remember it later. Her breath smelled of chili peppers. I drew back, startled, but her hand stopped me. I tried to smile. "What do you want?" I asked in English.

She shook her head, released my arm, and started down the path to the plaza. Salvador glanced at me and followed the old woman. Maria retreated into the house. I stood and watched Salvador and the old woman walk away. The kitten rubbed against my legs, gazing up at me expectantly. I found that I was holding my arm where the old woman had touched me as if I were stanching the blood flow from a wound. I let my breath out in a rush.

For a moment, I stood where I was, unwilling to follow the old woman and Salvador along the path to the plaza. The hair on my neck prickled, and I glanced toward Salvador's hut. Maria stood in the doorway, her arms crossed, watching me. I turned away, stumbling a little, following another path, one I had noticed but never followed, away from Salvador's hut.

I felt strange and unsettled. Nothing had happened—I reminded myself of that. Drug-induced paranoia, that's all. A dream, an old Mayan woman—nothing really. But the shadows around me seemed darker and my hand kept touching my arm where the old woman had held me. I wished that I had understood what she had said.

The path led through the monte to a dirt road that ran along the edge of the henequen field. To my left, the henequen field stretched away, mile after mile of spiky brutal plants. The sun had set and the moon was rising. In the moonlight, the henequen plants cast distorted shadows. Each plant made a tangle of darkness beside it, a black net of shadows that could trap anyone foolish enough to stroll among them. The dirt road was clear of plants and I walked in the center between the wheel ruts.

On my right grew the monte. Near the road, the scrubby mass of brush was no taller than I. Beyond that, maybe fifty feet from the road, larger trees reached for the sky with dry branches. The wind made the leaves rustle, but it was not strong enough to stir the branches.

When I was in junior high school, my father sent me to summer camp for a month. I remember walking through the woods at night from the campfire to my tent. I was always very careful to stay on the path. The path was safe; it was marked ground. The woods beyond the path were unknown, filled with strange sounds. But at the same time, the woods fascinated me. I found excuses to walk along the path at night, and each time that I passed through the woods un-harmed I felt that I had accomplished something noteworthy.

I was never sure what the danger was. Nothing concrete: I did not fear mad killers or wild animals. I never thought it out completely, but I think I felt that if I stepped off the path I might vanish, blend with the darkness and be gone. The darkness drew me and repelled me, and I walked the thin line, never straying from the path.

My footsteps seemed loud. I could hear an owl hooting in the trees. I walked with my hands in my pockets, knowing that I was walking along a thin line once again.

The old woman stepped from the shadow of the monte. For a moment, I thought it was the same old woman who had touched my arm. No, not the same. She was dressed in blue and she grinned at me, displaying crooked teeth. Her head seemed misshapen, though perhaps it was just the way her hair was arranged. I recognized her face: the face I had seen on the stone head, the face of the Madonna in the Mérida cathedral. I backed away.

Her grin grew wider and she held out her hand as if to welcome me. I took another step away from her, back toward camp.

She said something in a language that I did not understand, and she laughed. The sound was like dry leaves rustling against one another. My hands, still in my pockets, were trembling. I took them from my pockets and made fists to stop them from shaking. Then I turned and hurried back toward camp, pursued by the sound of her laughter.

What was it that my mother had said in one of our morning walks? At twilight and dawn, the shadows show you se-crets. I don't know why I ran. She was probably just a woman from the hacienda or maybe a companion to Maria's visitor. She would probably tell Maria that she had met this gringa wandering in the bush and scared her to death. I must have imagined that her face was familiar. The dim light played tricks.

I had reached Salvador's hut when I saw a flashlight beam

bobbing down the path to the cenote. "Hello," I called out, my voice a little shaky.

"Hey," Barbara called back. "I wondered what happened to you." She came up beside me and shone her light on me. She laid a hand on my shoulder and said, "What's up? You don't look good."

"Nothing. Just went for a walk and got caught in the dark, that's all." I shrugged. "It gets creepy alone at night. That's all." I didn't mention the old woman. I didn't want to feel any more foolish. "Let's go back to camp."

Chapter Fifteen: Elizabeth

The Fates guide those who will; those who
won't they drag.
—Joseph Campbell,
The Hero with a Thousand Faces

THURSDAY night, after another burned dinner, I sat in my
hut, checking my notes on the Mayan calendar. I had caught a
chill on the way back from our attempt to raise the stela.
Though the evening was warm, occasionally I would be
taken by a violent spell of shivering and chills. I considered
asking Maria to prepare me a pot of hot tea. Boiling-hot tea
laced with rum might head off a cold, but in the end I
decided against asking anything of Maria. I had heard Salvador's truck roaring back to camp, returning from the village
of Chicxulub with the curandera, and I did not want to
blunder into a touchy situation.

I checked my calculations, and rechecked them. Today
was Men, a day governed by the old goddess of the moon. It
should have been a favorable day, yet the stela had fallen, an
outcome I would not consider favorable. I had not seen
Zuhuy-kak since that afternoon.

The camp was quiet; the students were either writing up
field notes or swimming in the cenote. Camp had been quiet
ever since Philippe's accident. The sun had set and the moon
was just rising when I saw Salvador walking toward my hut.

The old woman who walked beside him took two small steps for every one of his. Tucked under one arm, she carried an orange-and-red plastic shopping bag, the kind that Yucatecan housewives use to carry groceries. She walked slowly, leaning on a cane.

Salvador stopped in the doorway to my hut and removed his broad-brimmed straw hat. "Senora," he said in Spanish. "I am sorry to interrupt you. This is Doña Lucinda Calderón, the *curandera* from Chicxulub. She wanted to meet you."

Doña Lucinda was examining my hut and myself with great interest. She was a thin old woman with eyes like a predatory bird. Her huipil was elaborately embroidered around the neck and hem with a pattern of twisting green vines and flowers. A rebozo was draped casually over her gray hair and her shoulders; leather sandals were strapped to her feet. Her cane was rosewood; the face of an owl watched me from its carven head.

"Welcome, Doña Lucinda," I said in Maya, rising from my chair. I took my other folding chair from the corner and put it in the open doorway. The old woman placed her bag on the ground by the chair and sat down, leaning forward on her cane—the tip set on the ground, the owl's head locked between her hands.

"Thank you," she said in Maya. Her voice was strong. "Performing the cleansing ritual leaves me weary. I have grown old."

I nodded in sympathy. "How can I help you?"

For a moment, she continued her scrutiny of my hut. Her nostrils flared, as if she were trying to place an elusive scent. She studied my hands, my face, the papers on my desk top. The sleeves of my shirt were rolled to the elbow.

She lifted her cane from the ground and pointed the tip to the scars on my wrists. "How did you come by this?"

I glanced at the scars and made a cutting gesture with one hand on the wrist of the other. "By my own hand," I said. "Many years ago."

"Ah." She glanced again at the papers on my desk. "And what is it you are doing now?"

"Writing," I said. "A book about this place."

Salvador, standing in the doorway, was holding the brim of his hat in both hands and turning the hat around and around restlessly. I offered cigarettes. Salvador accepted; the old woman declined. I lit one for myself and for a moment we filled the silence with smoke.

"How is Philippe?" I asked at last.

"The doctors at Hospital Juárez have set his broken bones," she said. "They will heal."

"Yes," I said. "I understand that."

"I respect the doctors at the hospital," she said. Her eyes were dark and shrewd. "You must understand that. My grandson, a clever young man, is studying to be a doctor. The hospital is very good for treating natural illness." She was leaning forward as she tried to impress me with her progressive attitude toward medicine. "But you must understand that Philippe has more than broken bones. As you know, he has bad luck."

"That is true," I said. "Salvador said that we are digging in a place of bad luck."

She glanced at Salvador then frowned at me. "The place that you are digging does not matter so much. But the gods are strong now. And Philippe was digging on the day Ix, a day of ill fortune."

I glanced at Salvador, but he was looking at the burning tip of his cigarette. He did not meet my eyes. Strange, to have my calculations confirmed so directly. "The bad luck is past then," I said. "That is good to hear."

She rolled the rosewood cane between her hands and the eyes of the carved wooden owl stared in a new direction. Doña Lucinda scowled and continued staring at my face. "Do not be a fool," she said crossly. "You know better. Tell me, what day is today?"

"On the Mayan calendar?" I shrugged. "I don't know."

She narrowed her eyes as if she expected better of me. "Today is the day Men," she said. She jerked her head toward the rising moon, but did not look away from my face.

"She is a fickle old woman, Men. Contrary. Always turning a new face. She is not to be trusted."

I was uncomfortable under her gaze. I shrugged.

"Today is the eighth day in Cumku, the last month of the year," she said. "This is not a safe time. The gods are strong now." Her voice had dropped. I could barely make out her words. "You must be careful." Salvador was not watching us; he was smoking his cigarette and looking away, gazing out into the open plaza. "The year is almost over."

I shook my head, took a drag on my cigarette, and stubbed it out in the ashtray. My hands were shaking and I folded them in my lap.

"Why do you look at me as if you do not understand? You know these things," she said. "I can see that you have the second soul." The second soul is what gives power to a witch—a *bruja* in Spanish, a *wai* in Maya. The second soul is a source of power.

What did I say before? The mad recognize their own. Her head was cocked to one side, and she was watching me carefully. "You are a strong woman, and that is a danger to you. You seek to stand alone in the evil times, and that cannot be. Unlucky days are coming."

She stopped and waited for me to speak. "How can I be careful?" I asked. "I cannot change the time of year."

"Leave this place," she said.

"Impossible," I said.

"It is not safe here. Not for you, not for the rest."

I shrugged.

She frowned and thumped her cane on the ground. "I want to help you, Señora Butler, you must understand that. You are a clever woman. Now you must listen. This is a serious business." Her hands gripped her cane more tightly. "Send away the young one, the redheaded woman, your daughter."

I was shaking my head slowly. "My daughter has nothing to do with this," I said in English.

The old woman shrugged. She did not understand the words, but she seemed to understand my tone. "It is your choice. You may choose to be a fool. You speak our language well, but you do not understand this place. You do not belong here.''

My hands were in fists. Who was this old woman to tell me that I did not belong? I belonged. I spoke with the dead; I knew the day of the year. My hands were trembling and I shivered with a sudden chill. "That may be so," I said to her. "But I cannot leave now."

"I tell you to leave this place," she said. "If you choose not to . . ." She shrugged. "I will pray for you and your daughter."

I wondered what gods she would pray to. "Thank you for telling me this, Doña Lucinda. I will think about it." I stood up.

The old woman remained seated, staring up at me with beady black eyes. "Listen to me, señora."

"Thank you for your advice, Doña Lucinda."

She stood reluctantly with the aid of her cane, bent slowly to pick up her shopping bag, and turned away. In the doorway, she stopped and turned back to make the sign of the cross and mutter a blessing.

Salvador put on his hat. "I am sorry, señora," he said, but whether he was sorry for bringing the old woman to me or sorry that I was a witch, I did not know. He turned away to follow the old woman across the plaza. Whatever he was sorry about, I knew he was embarrassed.

I could see a lantern burning in Tony's hut, but I did not want to speak with him, not now, not yet. I walked alone to the tomb site. Zuhuy-kak was there, sitting on a stone beside the picks, sifting trays, and buckets. The moon was rising and she cast a shadow in the dim light.

As I approached, she looked up and nodded in greeting. "What do you want from me, Ix Zacbeliz?" she asked.

"Answers," I said. "Why did the stela fall when we tried to raise it? This day was governed by the goddess. We should have had good fortune."

She squinted at me, her eyes as shrewd as the eyes of the curandera. I realized that she was more solid than any other shadow had ever become. Even in the moonlight, I could see the fine lines etched on her jade beads, the stitches in the embroidery on her robe. She spread her hands on her lap. "That was good fortune, Ix Zacbeliz. When the stela fell, the warrior lost his place. His strength is gone and the strength of the goddess is returning. Today was governed by the goddess and you helped her gain strength."

"Not good fortune," I said irritably. My joints ached and I knew that the chill that I had caught was creeping into my bones. "We wanted that stela intact, not in two pieces."

The old woman was staring at me in surprise. "Do you only care for things, Ix Zacbeliz? Did you want to find only old pots and bits of jewelry? I am giving you secrets greater than that. You and your daughter."

"Leave my daughter out of this," I said. "She has no part in this." I wanted to take hold of the embroidered garment and shake the old woman, make her listen. I was alternately hot and chilled, and I felt dizzy. I wondered, gazing into her shrewd dark eyes, whether I could catch hold of her. Would it be like trying to catch a wisp of fog? My hands—clenched in fists at my sides—were shaking.

"Your daughter chooses her own way." The woman was frowning at me. "You and I do not determine it. The cycle is turning and she is here."

"If I send her away, she will be safe," I said. "She will be out of all this."

"Send her away? Where will you send her? The cycle is turning. When the world changes, everything will change. And why will you send her away? She belongs here, just as you belong here."

"The turning of the cycle doesn't matter," I said, suddenly angry. "This is not . . ." I stopped short of voicing my thoughts.

"This is not real?" Zuhuy-kak calmly finished the sentence. Her voice was very soft.

I did not look at her. I took my cigarettes from my pocket and lit one, cupping my hand to shield the match from the wind. When I looked at Zuhuy-kak, she was smiling at me. "I am real," she said.

"No. This is a game that I play with myself. I have played it for years. I can stop playing it. I can return to a world where you do not exist, where there is no danger, where there are no jaguars in the shadows." I looked into the distance, drawing in the smoke and feeling my heart beat faster. The smoke was real; the cigarette in my hand was real; the rock beneath me was real. Zuhuy-kak was a dream in which I chose to believe. I could stop believing.

I blew out a stream of smoke and watched it swirl, catching the moonlight. Just a game. I looked at Zuhuy-kak and she was watching me, holding her conch shell in her hands and smiling.

"It is not as easy as that," she said. "Not nearly so easy. You cannot stop the cycles of time by turning your back."

"I can send you away."

She shrugged. "You can try."

"You shrug like a Californian," I said suddenly. "That gesture could not have been part of Mayan culture."

"I learn from you just as you learn from me," she said. She grinned, showing me her inlaid teeth. "You think that you can control the world. You are wrong."

"I made you up," I said. "You're my invention. I can make you go away."

"Why would you want to do that?" she asked easily. "We are friends, Ix Zacbeliz. I am helping you."

I shook my head slowly, fighting the dizziness. "I am not so sure of that."

"You are my friend," she said with quiet dignity. "I consider your daughter as my own."

I shook my head again. "I can make you go away," I repeated. I did not like the tremor in my voice, but I could not stop it.

"It is not so easy," Zuhuy-kak said. "You choose your gods, but you do not invent them."

I closed my eyes. In the distance, an owl hooted softly— once, twice, three times. I imagined myself alone by the tomb site. I listened to the wind rustle through the grasses and I knew that I was alone, I had always been alone.

When I opened my eyes, Zuhuy-kak was still there. "You want the power of the goddess," she said. "Then sacrifices must be made. You belong here—you understand that."

I walked away from her, feeling old and fragile as I crossed the open plaza. At the far side of the open area, I looked back. Zuhuy-kak lifted a hand and waved.

Chapter Sixteen: Diane

THE door to my mother's hut was halfway open when we reached the plaza. I hesitated. "I think I'll see how Liz is doing."

"Fine," Barbara said grumpily. "I still have to finish that report."

"I thought you were inspired."

"My inspiration expired when I got back. So far, I've written the date at the top of a page and read half that rotten romance novel you bought in Mérida. I'll see you later." She left me by my mother's door and I watched her flashlight bob toward our hut.

I knocked on the door, then peered inside. The only light was a candle burning in a small chimney. The card table that served as my mother's desk was strewn with books and papers.

"Sorry to interrupt," I mumbled. I felt awkward and embarrassed. Already, the thought of talking to her about the old woman I had seen in the monte was fading, like Barbara's inspiration.

"No problem," she said, closing the book on the table before her. The candlelight etched shadows on her face, making her look old and weary. She looked pale, though that could have been a trick of the light. "I'm glad you came. I understand you met the local curandera."

I shook my head. "I don't think so."

"The old woman," my mother said patiently.

For a moment, I was confused, then I realized she meant the old woman by Salvador's hut. "Oh, yeah. I guess so." I couldn't read her face in the candlelight. Her right hand was on her desk, fidgeting with a pencil, tapping it on one end so that it lay parallel with the edge of the desk, then tapping it out of line. She was watching the pencil very carefully.

"The curandera remembered you better than you remembered her," she said lightly. She tapped the pencil again, a little too hard, and it rolled off the edge of the table, bounced on her knees, and fell into the shadows. Lost. She looked at my face then. "I haven't asked you—what do you think of the dig so far?"

"I like going on survey," I said cautiously.

"You like hiking through the jungle and battling the bugs?"

I shrugged. "Barbara and I get along. I'm glad to be able to help her."

"Perhaps you should leave the dig for a while," she said softly, almost as if she were talking to herself. "Rent a car and go out to the Caribbean coast—out to Isla Mujeres, Playa del Carmen. Beautiful beaches, wonderful snorkeling. I'll meet you there when we're through here." She was gazing thoughtfully at the ground, where the pencil had disappeared. Her face was still, masklike.

"I like it here," I said.

"You shouldn't waste your entire vacation out here in the sticks," she said. She did not look at me.

"I don't understand."

She took a cigarette from the pack on her desk and lifted the glass chimney to light it from the candle. The hand that held the cigarette was trembling. The light of the candle reflected in her eyes.

"Have I done something wrong?" My voice was shaking.

She turned from the desk to face me, leaning forward on the metal folding chair and resting her elbows on her knees. The hut was very quiet. The crying of the crickets was very far away, on the other side of the moon. My mother wanted to leave me again.

"The curandera, the old woman you met, thinks that you are a witch," she said. "You're in good company: she thinks that I'm a witch too. She has more reason to suspect me. I mutter to myself and talk to people who aren't there. I wander around at dusk and dawn, when the spirits are out." She was watching me, her face fixed in a strange smile. "Surely you've noticed these things."

I hunched my shoulders forward. "I didn't think anything of it. I just figured you were working on your book."

"In the United States, people interpret these things as eccentricity or—if taken to an extreme—madness," my mother said mildly. "Here, they are the mark of a witch. Of the two interpretations, I have to admit I prefer the second. A witch has some power. A madwoman is just a nut." She tilted her head to one side, considering me. "What do you think?"

I shrugged, unable to speak.

"Suppose I told you that I get up early to chat with the spirits. I see the past—I described it to you, remember? What would you think then? Would you go to the Caribbean coast and meet me there?"

"You think that I should leave because an old woman thinks I'm a witch?"

"I think you should leave because I want you to leave. I want you to go away—to Isla Mujeres, to Los Angeles, anywhere you want."

I found myself standing, my hands in fists. "You can't tell me what to do."

My mother remained as she was, holding the cigarette loosely in one hand, the other hand relaxed in her lap. "That's true. I gave up that right long ago. I am only saying what I want. What you choose to do is your responsibility." She stubbed the cigarette out in the ashtray, glancing at my face as she did so, a sidelong considering look.

"I won't let you run away again," I said, looking down on the strange woman who was my mother.

She wet her lips and shook her head slowly. "I just want you to be careful."

I left, slipping through the door without saying good-bye. I never did tell her about the old woman in the monte.

The lantern burned dimly in front of Tony's hut. Tony sat in a lawn chair, smoking his pipe and sipping a gin and tonic with no ice. He was dressed in a bathrobe and slippers.

"I'd offer you a cold drink," he said when I sat down in the other chair, "but the gin is warm and we packed all the ice around Philippe's foot yesterday, then forgot to buy more. Want a warm one?"

I shook my head. I could feel tears stinging behind my eyes and I did not want to let them go.

"What's wrong?" He put his hand on my arm. "Are you all right?"

"Nothing's wrong." I managed a very weak smile. "Nothing. I just . . ." I shrugged. I had no idea what to say.

He kept his hand on my arm and he watched me with concern. I had to say something.

"Have you ever . . ." I began shakily, "have you ever had your life fall apart underneath you? Where suddenly everything and everyone that you trusted went away? It's as if the ground moved out from under you, as if the world shifted and you didn't belong anymore." My voice was shaking and I crossed my arms as if to keep warm. My thoughts weren't clear—I grasped at fleeting images: Brian's blue eyes studying my face when he told me our affair was over; my father's coffin being lowered into the ground; the family portrait on the desk of my boss—to avoid meeting his eyes, I kept glancing at that picture when I told him I was quitting. And from some other time, I could hear my father's voice saying that my mother was gone. She had left us. Bits and pieces, scraps and tatters. A jumble and a mess. I closed my eyes and said, "You get through it and you think that everything's fine again. But you keep thinking that it will happen again. You watch. You see little signs that suggest that things are going on under the surface of things. And you don't know what they are. Someone is angry, and you know that they will vanish forever. Everything is too close to the surface."

I shook my head. The words had come out suddenly. I had not intended to say all this. "I don't know how to make it all right again," I said. "I don't know how I can stop feeling like this. It's crazy, crazy. . . ." That was the other part of it. Normal people did not feel like this. I kept a barrier between myself and the darkness; that was what kept me sane. If that barrier were breached, I knew the world would be swept away in a great bloody flood of emotions. I knew it. Normal people are not like that.

My breathing was coming back under my control. I was bottling up the feelings, pushing them back behind the barrier. I made myself unclench my fists, use my open hands to push back my hair. I almost smiled at him. "Sometimes, you get more of an answer than you bargain for."

"That's all right," he said. "Sounds like you'd better have that drink." He went into his hut and I heard the sound of liquid pouring from a bottle. He gave me a glass of warm gin and flat tonic water, then returned to his seat. "Can you tell me what set this off?"

I took a deep breath. "Liz wants me to leave the dig. She told me to go away." I could feel my face reddening and I stopped for a moment. "I don't want to go."

He frowned. "That's strange. I thought you were getting along."

"I thought so."

"What did she say?"

"She said she thought I shouldn't waste my vacation here."

"I can see her point, I suppose. Many people would agree."

"She said . . ." I hesitated. Somehow, I did not want to tell Tony what my mother had said about being a witch. "The curandera, that old woman, told her that I should go."

Tony leaned back in his chair, shaking his head. "I'll talk to her. Until then, don't push her. It doesn't pay to push Liz. If you try, she shuts up like a clam. I just wait and sometimes she tells me. Sometimes she doesn't.'' He shrugged. ''You and your mother are both very stubborn women.''

"Leave me out of this.''

"If you aren't stubborn, then why aren't you packing your bags and heading out of this place? If she doesn't want you here, why stay?'' He took his pipe from his mouth and inspected the ashes in the bowl. He held a match to them and puffed until they lit. Then he looked at me. ''Stubborn.''

"I'm worried about Liz,'' I said then.

"Why's that?''

"She talks to herself.''

"She's been doing that for years.''

"She's always up at dawn. I don't think she sleeps well.''

"She's been doing that for years too. Tell me something new.'' He waited, puffing on his pipe.

I didn't like the way my voice sounded, kind of thin and stretched out and weak. ''I think . . . Do you think she's crazy?''

"I think we're all crazy, living out here with the bugs and the dirt, drinking warm gin, and digging up things that most people don't give a damn about. Normal is what most people do. None of us is normal, so we must be crazy.''

"I mean really crazy.''

He poked at the ashes in the pipe bowl with a small stick. ''I would hesitate to call anyone really crazy.'' There was a slight edge in his voice now. ''I'd say your mother was no crazier than she has been for years.'' He studied my face. ''What do you want to do about it? Put her under a doctor's care? That's what your father tried.''

"Tony, I'm sorry. I'm just . . . I'm worried. I don't know what to do.''

"I told you what to do last week,'' he said. ''Give her time. Don't go rushing to conclusions. Take it slow. And I just told you again. Let me talk to her.''

"But she wants me to leave.''

"And you said you wouldn't. What else did she say?''

"She said to be careful.''

"Always good advice. So stay if you want, but be careful.

And admit that you're stubborn. It's not such a bad trait to have. I'll talk to her about this business of making you leave. See what she has to say.''

I was watching my hands. They were in fists in my lap. I heard Tony move and one of his hands closed over one of mine. "Take it slow," he rumbled. "I'm still your friend.''

I never did tell him about the old woman in the monte.

—— Chapter Seventeen: Elizabeth ——

AT the best of times, I mistrust students. They bring back memories of lecture halls filled with the dusty smell of chalk, rustling notebooks, and arrogant young men and women with the sleek and well-fed look of wolves in autumn after a long summer of abundant hunting.

I remember afternoon class in an overheated hall, and outside the rain is darkening the cement sidewalks, rattling the leaves, making Strawberry Creek, the campus's captive brook, rush and swirl in panicked eddies. The students drowse in the warmth of the lecture hall.

I know that I cannot let them see my true self—thin and hungry and draggled as an alley cat crouching beneath a parked car for a moment's shelter from the rain. The university is my temporary shelter; to keep this lecture post I must waken these somnolent beasts and teach them something, make them blink, shake their heavy heads, and grope for answers in their sluggish brains. I must breathe life into the dusty air.

I lecture like a shaman conjuring spirit forces to life. I work at it—throwing questions like rocks, whirling anecdotes over my head like bolos, calling up visions of burial customs, rites of passage, and ancient cities, dodging, pacing, always on the move. I am afraid, but I keep them at bay, alert but wary, a little confused, always on edge. No one sleeps. I keep my shelter.

*   *   *

Friday, the day Cib, is portrayed in the glyphs by a conch shell, a symbol of rebirth, of passage through the underworld and return to the light. I do not know what god governs this day.

On Friday, tension hung in the air, ran with the lizards over the rocks, hissed with the grasses in the wind. My body ached, and the chills and shivering had continued through the night. The mild fever made me irritable and restless. When I smoked, I felt a trembling in my chest, and my heart seemed to beat too fast.

Throughout the day, the wind carried the sound of chanting. Somewhere in the past, men and women raised their voices to the beat of a drum, the murmur of rattles, the wailing of conch shell trumpets and pipes. I could not make out the words. I searched, but I could not find the source of the sound.

I stayed in camp, drinking hot tea laced with aguardiente and trying to rest. I lit cigarettes one after another, drawing the smoke deep into my lungs as if the nicotine would soothe me and make the shivering stop. But the trembling remained. It seemed a part of the place, like the scrub of the monte, the dust on the stones. In the afternoon, I wandered out to the Temple of the Seven Dolls. In the plaza near the temple, a group of young men were decorating their shields with the richly colored feathers of jungle birds. They did not talk, but worked in grim silence, preparing for war.

Late in the afternoon, Carlos, Maggie, Barbara, and Diane left for Mérida to seek the dubious pleasures of the city. Only Tony, John, and Robin remained in camp. We made our own dinner over a camp stove and for the first time in days the food was not burned, not overspiced. I had tea with aguardiente, then aguardiente without the tea. The aguardiente warmed me but did not ease the trembling. Tony and Robin talked about pottery.

For the past week, Robin had been helping Tony with basic pottery analysis. The young woman seemed to share Tony's interest in the topic: she talked with muted enthusiasm about color on the Munsell chart and hardness on Mohs' scale, about burnishing and paint composition, about rim stance and spout attachment.

John was listening with an intensity that seemed unwarranted by the subject. At one point, he reached over, brushed a strand of hair out of Robin's eyes, and gently touched her shoulder. She smiled and took his hand. I realized that they were lovers and wondered how long this romance had been going on.

After dinner, before the fading of the daylight forced us to resort to lanterns, John brought out his spiral-bound notebook to show us his site drawings: partial floor plans and on-site sketches of the structures immediately surrounding the tomb site. Though I had glanced over his shoulder at the site, noting his progress on each sketch, this was the first time I had seen his work gathered together.

John had studied architecture and his sketches reflected that training: meticulously executed in India ink with sharp black lines and careful shading. The lines were, if anything, too precise, too straight, too crisp. His sketch of the mound to the northwest of the tomb site failed to capture the air of abandonment and decay, the softness of the weather-beaten and eroding limestone blocks. Even so, his work was beautiful.

He flipped through the pages slowly, stopping at the site drawings and passing quickly the work that he judged inappropriate for our attention: quick pencil sketches, a detailed drawing showing exactly how the lintel rested on a particular doorway, a portrait of Pich's sagging features, a profile of Robin examining a potsherd. He stopped at a sketch of the opening to the tomb that showed the placement of each masonry block, then he set the notebook on the wooden crate beside him.

While Tony and Robin praised the work, I took the notebook and flipped back through the pages, stopping at one that had caught my eye earlier: a pencil sketch of the plaza near the tomb. For once, John had relaxed and allowed himself to imagine the structures as they might have looked. The piece combined meticulous detail with softness, in a style reminiscent of the work of Frederick Catherwood, the nineteenth-century artist who had been the first to sketch the ruins.

The facade of the palace on the left was decorated with stucco Chaac masks and serpents; the low steps that fronted on it were carved with indecipherable glyphs. I recognized the place from my dream. The pile of skulls had rested before these steps; I stood on the edge of the plaza and the ravens flew up, shrieking their warnings.

That's not right, I thought, looking at the temple facade, and remembering how Zuhuy-kak had described it to me and how I had dreamed it. This was the temple of the moon goddess, and the Chaac masks and serpents had no business there. No business at all.

"What's wrong?" John asked, and for a moment I thought I had spoken aloud. He leaned close to me, looking over my shoulder at the sketch. "You were frowning. Is something wrong?"

I shook my head to clear it. "The facade's wrong. It should be more like the facade over the temple at Tulúm. Seashells and fishes."

He took the sketchbook from my hands. "Why do you say that?"

Why did I say that? Because I had been drinking and remembering a dream. Because the aguardiente hummed in my head. The past and present had momentarily crossed. I tried to smile, but my face was frozen. "Just a feeling."

He gave me a strange look. John did not like statements based on vague feelings. "I don't really have enough information to do a reconstruction drawing. I was just fooling around a bit."

"Nothing wrong with that," I said. "Nothing wrong with using your imagination."

An awkward pause. John held the sketchbook as if he did not know what to do with it and frowned at me. Finally Robin leaned over to him and gently took it, asking if she could look. Tony got up to light the lantern and pour me another cup of tea. And the conversation went on.

I sat at the edge of the circle of light, listening and

watching the three of them. John relaxed again, after a moment. They were comfortable together: Tony and Robin joked about studying pots; John's arm rested lightly on the back of Robin's chair; now and then, she smiled at him or touched his hand lightly. I watched them, much as I watched shades of the past, an observer but not a participant. But somehow, I could not leave.

Much later, Robin and John left the circle of light, walking hand in hand toward the cenote. Tony poured me another glass of aguardiente. Sitting together in the circle of lantern light, watching the moths circle and tasting the bite of the aguardiente at the back of my throat, it seemed that there was something new between Tony and me, or else something very old that was stirring once again. Something was shifting uneasily beneath the surface.

I had another glass of aguardiente, leaned back, and closed my eyes against the lantern light. The brown liquor comforted me, slowing the beating of my heart, blurring the cries of insects and birds in the monte.

Tony's lawn chair creaked as he leaned forward to take his pipe from the crate. I heard the rustle of his tobacco pouch as he began the endless process of packing the pipe with tobacco and lighting it. The sweet scent of unburned tobacco hung in the warm air. I heard the scratch of a wooden match and smelled the sulfur when it caught, then the first smoke of the tobacco. Tony's voice was as rough and warm as a block of granite in the sun. "I've been drinking too much lately," he said softly. "I wanted to let you know that I'm cutting back."

I opened my eyes. The glass at his elbow was empty and his hands were busy with his pipe. I had noticed that he had not been sharing the aguardiente, but had thought little of it.

He glanced at me. "I know that you've been worried about it, about my drinking. It just got to be a habit after Hilde died."

I nodded, not knowing what to say. "I guessed that."

"It's a habit I'm breaking. I wanted to let you know that."

"Good."

His pipe had gone out and he began poking in the bowl with a burned-out wooden match. He was avoiding my eyes and I knew that he was edging around a difficult topic.

I waited for a moment, then asked, "What is it, Tony?"

"Diane told me that you asked her to leave," he said abruptly.

"That's so." I leaned back in my chair, feigning a relaxation I did not feel.

"Why?"

"It doesn't much matter, does it? She refuses to go."

He sat on the edge of the chair, his hands clasped before him, drooping between his knees. Behind him, the open doorway was a blaze of light. He stared down at his hands. "Diane said that the curandera told you to send her away."

"Does that sound like something I would do? Listen to the advice of a Mayan shaman?" I shook my head.

"Then why do you want her to go?"

"I thought she might want to see something of the Yucatán besides one little dig. Just a suggestion."

"She was pretty upset. She seemed to think that you really wanted her to go."

I shrugged angrily. "Yes, there are times that I would like her to go. She seems to expect something from me that I can't give her." I rubbed my hand across my forehead, wishing I could clear away the liquor and the fever and think straight. "She's trying to learn who she is and she seems to think I can tell her. I can't tell her anything."

"I think that sending Diane away would be a mistake," Tony said quietly. "I think that you want to run from a situation that you're afraid you can't handle. You're afraid of getting to know your daughter, afraid you will be hurt. But you can't go on being afraid forever."

"Tony," I said, leaning forward. "Tony, listen to me." I stopped. What could I tell him? Nothing. An ancient priestess of a long-dead moon cult is showing an unhealthy interest in my daughter. "I just have a bad feeling about this place. I think somehow it's dangerous for Diane, maybe dangerous for all of us. I can't control what's happening here."

"What is happening here?" he asked. "What do you see that I don't?"

I leaned back in my chair and looked down at my hands with their broken nails and old scars. "Can't you feel the danger?" I asked him. "I know you don't see things as I do, but you must realize that what you see is not all that there is to the world. There are always things just beyond your gaze when you walk alone in the darkness, or in the dim light just after sunset or just before dawn." I studied his face. "I guess you don't walk alone, not often. You keep people around you. Even when you are by yourself, you think about your friends, worry about them, keep them wrapped around you like a blanket that keeps you warm." I shook my head. "I live in a more solitary place."

"You don't have to," he said. He looked up at me and held out his open hands. "You don't have to be alone."

I shook my head.

"I think it was hard enough for Diane to find you once. If you send her away, you shouldn't expect her to try again."

"I don't expect anything from her."

"And from me?"

"Nothing, Tony. There's nothing you can do." His open hands were in his lap and I wanted to reach out to him, put my hands in his. But I was a danger to him. I would hurt him by being near. I clasped my hands in my lap and shook my head.

He looked up and hesitated. "Liz, we've known each other a long time. I've known . . . ." He stopped and started again. "Ever since I have known you, you've been watching things that aren't there. I accept that. It doesn't bother me. I have never mentioned this to you because I thought that if I did you would back away from me. I've always been afraid to talk about this." He was watching me steadily; he held his pipe, but his hands were still. "Do you believe that?"

I nodded, not trusting my voice. In the monte, the crickets shrilled. Above us, the palm thatch hissed like a roof full of snakes. I could feel the touch of a breeze stirring the hairs on my arms, tickling my neck with loose strands of hair. The camp was very quiet.

"But lately I have heard you talking in Maya when you are alone—in your hut, out at the site. I wondered who you were talking to." His voice was very gentle.

The aguardiente had slowed my mind and body. I leaned toward him, cradling my cup in both hands. "You don't have to worry about this, Tony. Like you said, I've been seeing people who aren't there for years. Why start worrying now?"

"Diane is worried about you," he said.

The sudden rush of anger was a product of the aguardiente; I knew that. "She told you that she was worried about my sanity, right?"

"She did mention that."

I leaned back in my chair, realized that one of my hands was gripping the other tightly, forced them to relax. "And what did you say?"

"I told her that you were no crazier than you had always been." He shrugged. "I think that's true."

"And how crazy is that?"

He looked at me steadily. "Depends on one's definition," he said. "I don't worry when you see people who aren't here. I only start to worry when you ignore people who are. I don't think that you should send Diane away."

I sat silent. The moon was up. I remembered my view of the moon from the ward. I could see it only if I stood on the back of one of the toilets and peered through a tiny grill-covered window. Clinging to the dusty ledge, I could watch the moon reluctantly lift her battered face over the horizon and gaze down on the earth. With the flowers that Robert brought me, I bribed another woman to keep watch at the door while I watched the moon rise. I could watch until I tired of the scent of urine and disinfectant, or until an orderly caught me and escorted me roughly to bed. I remembered.

Tony reached across the space between us to touch my hand, but I stood up and moved to the edge of the circle of light. I stumbled a little and put one hand on the chair back for support. The aguardiente had left my body heavy and my head light. When I turned my head, the world moved too quickly around me. "I don't mind being told I'm crazy," I said, looking out into the plaza. "I don't care what you think about that. But I won't be locked up."

"What are you talking about, Liz? I didn't say anything about—"

"No, you didn't say anything." He was starting to stand, to move toward me, but I glared at him and he sat down again. "You think I've been crazy for years."

"You know better than that."

My hand was in a fist and my fingernails were etching painful crescents in my palm. The tension was all around me. I was afraid. No words came. When I groped for words, I thought of the great silence that surrounded the mounds at dawn, the scrabbling of the lizards on the rocks, the crying of birds in the monte, the hissing of grasses in a light breeze. No words.

"I'll stay," he said. "I've been battling shadows of my own for years. Fighting yours might do me good."

I felt empty. I heard my own words slurred by alcohol, remembered too vividly the stench of the ward. I looked at Tony, leaning back in his chair, and remembered Robert and the way he had comforted me when I was upset. "Don't worry about it," I said to Tony then. "I won't send Diane away. Don't concern yourself."

"Now wait," he said, holding out a hand. "Relax. Don't—"

"I said it's all right. Don't worry." I left him and returned to the safety of my hut.

Chapter Eighteen: Diane

AT Barbara's suggestion, we left camp before dinner on Friday. We dined at Los Balcónes, a small restaurant on a terrace that overlooked Parque Hidalgo. From this vantage point, Barbara amused herself by watching the men who were watching the women in the square below. The men loitered on the benches and corners, discussing important things, gesturing and laughing. When a woman strolled past— especially a young woman—the discussion was disrupted. One man stared at her. Another man, noticing that his friend had been distracted, turned his head to see the source of the distraction. A third man saw the second man turn to look and followed suit. By that time, the first man had returned to the discussion, but a fourth man was just beginning to look. Whenever a woman, any woman, walked by, a ripple of turning heads followed her.

"Look," Barbara said. "Why don't you go down and walk through the square, and I'll check out the reaction? Then I'll go down, and—"

"I don't really feel like it."

"Yeah?" She stopped watching the men in the square for a moment. "You feeling sick?"

"No."

"Then what's wrong?"

I shrugged. "I'm just pissed at Liz."

"Yeah? Why?"

"She wants me to leave the dig."

"Yeah? Where does she want you to go?"

"The Caribbean coast. Back to Los Angeles. Anywhere, she said."

"Why?"

I watched the men in the square. They had returned to an animated discussion. "She said . . . this is weird, but she said that the curandera said that I should leave."

"Liz said that?"

"Yeah."

Barbara tapped her fingers restlessly on the table.

"Do you think . . ." I hesitated, uncertain.

"What?"

"Sometimes she watches things that aren't there. Her eyes follow them, and when you look there's nothing there at all."

"I've noticed that. She has always done that."

"Sometimes, she talks to herself. I keep meeting her wandering around early in the morning and half the time she is talking to herself."

"That's so."

"Do you think she's crazy?"

Barbara looked down at the square. The two flower-selling children were pestering a retired American couple in matching leisure suits. "She's not normal, but that doesn't mean she's crazy." She shrugged. "I mean . . . who is normal? Those people?" She pointed at the retired couple. "I like your mother. She acts a little odd sometimes, but that's all right with me. I act a little odd sometimes. What did you tell her when she asked you to go?"

"Told her I wouldn't."

"And what did she say?"

"She said it was my responsibility."

"Sounds fair enough. So you're not going."

"I guess not."

For a moment we sat in silence. The bronze statue in the square caught the last rays of sunlight. A hammock vendor strolled through the square and hailed the retired couple without success.

"You know the night that we had a smoke down by the cenote," I said suddenly. "I met the curandera over by Salvador's hut. I wish I had understood what she said to me. She was pretty excited about something."

"You hang around this place long enough, and eventually you realize that you won't ever understand half the stuff that goes on around you. Even when you understand the words, you can't catch all the nuances." Barbara shrugged. "I wouldn't worry about it." She glanced at my face and reached across the table to pat my hand. "Why don't you just relax and enjoy your vacation. Don't worry about Liz. Things will sort themselves out."

We slept that night in real beds. Of course, we had breakfast at Cafetería Mesón, and of course Emilio and Marcos—"the boys" as Barbara had taken to calling them—showed up as we were drinking our coffee. Emilio bought a round of coffee and I tried to forget camp.

"So what are you going to do today?" Emilio asked, spooning sugar into his coffee.

"We were talking about going to Chichén Itzá," Barbara said.

Emilio looked up. "You want me to come and drive?"

"Depends," said Barbara. "Do we get a cut of the profits for providing transportation?"

Emilio's grin widened. "Sure. I'll pay for gas."

Barbara glanced at me and laughed. "Don't look so shocked, Diane. This bandit makes a hell of a good profit on his sales. Even on a bad day, he makes more money than a graduate student."

"What does that mean—bandit?" Emilio asked, stirring his coffee.

Barbara grinned and shook her head.

He looked up at her, pouring more sugar into the pale brown coffee. "I think you like this bandit," he said. He set down the sugar and grinned at Marcos. "We will have good luck today."

In the end, we all went to Chichén Itzá: Barbara, Emilio, Emilio's hammocks, Marcos and I. Emilio hailed a German couple on the steep stone steps of an ancient pyramid and sold them two hammocks on the spot. He dickered with an elderly couple in the shade of the feathered serpent columns that topped the Temple of the Warriors. He haggled over a hundred pesos on the steps to a platform carved with jaguars clutching human hearts. He offered a man a good price, a very good price, on the steps that led to a crumbling stone dome. Grass grew between the stones of the steps.

Barbara took to hailing the young male tourists herself. "Hey," she called happily to two blond college students. "Want to buy a hammock?" They stopped to talk in the shade of a massive structure that was little more than a tumble of stones. A dark passage that led to the inner recesses of the structure smelled faintly of rot and urine. The blond man in the University of California T-shirt bought a matrimonial hammock at twice Emilio's usual rate.

Emilio led us into Old Chichén, the older portion of the site where the monte had been cut back but the buildings were unrestored. In a secluded corner beyond the main ruins, out where the only sounds were the rustling of leaves in the monte, we smoked a joint and listened to the birds call in the trees. Then Barbara insisted that we had to go see the Sacred Well.

Marcos led the way. Emilio had his arm around Barbara and they strolled slowly, stopping to look at carved stones and buildings. We passed a stone wall where each limestone block had a relief carving of a skull. The blocks were carefully stacked so that row upon row of grinning skulls watched us as we bought soft drinks at a refrescos stand and walked to the Sacred Well to drink them.

We sat at the edge of the precipice, where we could look down on the green water, a small pond far below. Emilio rested his head on Barbara's lap. Blue-green birds with long tail feathers—Marcos called them motmots—skimmed over the water's surface and perched in the trees that clung to the crumbling limestone cliffs on the far wall of the well. The drop to the water looked like more than a hundred feet. Marcos pointed out the platform from which the Mayan priests threw gifts into the well, a small ledge of limestone on the south side.

"They threw people in, didn't they?" I asked lazily, leaning back against a boulder.

Marcos nodded. I squinted at the ledge. I wouldn't want to dive from that height, let alone be thrown. Marcos offered me a cigarette, then lit one for himself. The cliffs shimmered in the sunlight and the dope made the world brighter. "Beautiful, isn't it?" Marcos said.

I nodded, my eyes still half closed, still watching the ledge. I saw something move there: a flash of blue the color of the Virgin Mary's robes, something falling. Then Marcos took my hand, leaned over, and kissed me gently, blocking my view.

Back at the hotel that evening, Barbara and I compared notes. On the drive back, Marcos had asked me if I wanted to go to the beach at Progreso with him on Sunday. Barbara said that Emilio had asked her if she wanted to go swimming at the village well at Tixkokob. "Sounds like the theme is 'divide and conquer,'" Barbara commented.

"Looks that way."

She shrugged. "I said I'd go. It's a chance to see a Mayan village with a native guide. And the village well sounds safe enough. Happy children playing in the water. Village women washing their clothes against the rocks."

"Ah, yes." I lay back on the bed and tucked my hands behind my head. "A rare anthropological opportunity." The ceiling fan rattled rhythmically, like a boy running a popsicle stick along a picket fence.

"That's right." She kicked off her sandals and sat on the edge of the other bed. "Look for trouble and sometimes you find it. Let's go for it. What trouble can you get into at a well in the heart of a rural village? Or at a public beach?''

"I'm sure we'll find out."

The bus to Progreso was of the same vintage as the crosstown bus. It stopped a block from the beach.

Beneath an overcast sky, an endless line of palms marched alongside the white sand. Coconut hulls and broken seashells washed in the surf with the crowds of laughing brown children. Young men were courting teenage girls by chasing them into the water. An older woman was splashing herself while standing in thigh-deep water. The little skirt on her one-piece swimsuit lifted when the waves hit and hung limply around her thighs when the water retreated. Each time the water reached her, she called to her husband in excited Spanish.

The sun was hiding, and the colors seemed muted and dull: an amateurish watercolor where paints had become muddy. Near the shore, the water of the gulf was the color of turquoise, an opaque milky blue. Farther out, it darkened to green. I could not see beneath the surface.

My mother would see this beach in a different way. What would she see? Mayan women collecting shells to be carved into jewelry. Mayan men drying salt for trade. Would she have seen the woman falling from the platform at the sacred well?

"Qué piensas?" asked Marcos. He was walking beside me.

I shrugged.

"You don't know what you are thinking?"

"I can't explain."

We kept walking. As we walked farther from the bus stop, we left the families behind. There were only a few couples strolling along the beach. Marcos put his arm around my waist. He stopped beside a palm tree that leaned away from the ocean, reaching toward Mérida with grasping fronds. "Want to sit in the sun?" he asked.

"Sure."

He rubbed suntan lotion on my back, his hands lingering longer than necessary, carefully stroking the lotion into the skin along the edge of my bikini. He began rubbing lotion on the backs of my legs and his hand dipped between my legs and pressed against me with a gentle insistent caress. The other hand stroked my back.

"Hey," I said, rolling away from him.

He smiled. "I like you very much. You make me a little crazy." He looked around us. The nearest family was a few hundred yards down the beach. "No one saw. It's all right."

"No it's not."

"Yes it is." He reached out and ran a hand along my shoulder and arm until he reached my hand. "I like you very much. We could have a good time together." He smiled at me brilliantly and squeezed my hand. "What do you think?"

"Not likely."

"*Porqué no?* Why not?"

"It doesn't seem like a good idea."

"It's a good idea," he said. "You don't know what you think." He released my hand and lay back on the sand, tucking one hand behind his head. "You make me a little crazy."

I lay on my back and closed my eyes. The surf washed in a steady rhythm.

"What have you found, out where you are digging?" he asked.

I told him about the stone head, the manos and metates, the tomb site.

"When I was a little boy, I found a very old pot in the fields near my grandmother's house. A very old pot, with paintings on the sides. I took it home to my grandmother, and she said that I must take it back to the fields. She said it was very bad luck to take it from the old ones, very bad. I went back to the field and buried the pot." I could tell from his voice that he was smiling. "If I found that pot now, I'd sell it to someone like your mother for lots of money. I wouldn't worry about bad luck."

I lay on my back, listened to the surf, and worried about bad luck.

"Your friend Barbara will have a good time at Tixkokob," Marcos said. "You and I could have a good time too. Why not?"

"Because I don't want to," I said.

"You want to."

I shook my head and listened to the surf wash the beach clean.

"Qué piensas?" he asked.

"I'm thinking about my mother."

"Why are you thinking of your mother?" I believe that Marcos was growing impatient with me. He wanted me to be thinking about him, not about my mother.

"She doesn't want me to come back to the dig."

"Why not?"

The sunlight was warm on my eyelids. "She is afraid of something. She won't say what. I think she's like your grandmother. She's afraid of the old ones."

"Your mother is afraid of the old ones? She's crazy."

I opened my eyes to protest and saw the old woman standing by the surf. She was dressed in blue and in her hand she held a conch shell. I turned to Marcos to ask him if he saw her too. He leaned toward me, forcing me back down on the sand. I felt a warm strong hand on my breast and another between my thighs and he leaned on me, kissing me hard on the mouth. "You're crazy too," he said. I pushed him away and he laughed. The woman was gone.

"Later," he said. "At your hotel, we will have a good time. I like you very much."

I left him on the beach and went swimming in the warm murky water of the gulf, swimming far away from the beach and looking back at the line of palms, the strip of white sand. Floating on my back in the blood-warm water, I admitted to myself that I was afraid of the strange apparition in blue. I was afraid. I was haunted by a Mayan ghost and I felt very much alone.

As a child, I had played tag with other neighborhood kids on summer nights. As the sunlight faded to darkness, we would go on playing, but the nature of the game changed. The kid who was It would not chase the rest of us—he would slip into the shadows and sneak up on people, appearing out of the darkness like a ghost. I remember jumping at shadows, thinking that each one was going to tag me. I felt like I was playing night tag now, fighting with shadows that appeared and disappeared.

Eventually, I had to swim back to the beach. Marcos smiled when I came back, and said that he was sorry, that he would not try to kiss me again. I lay in the sun for a time, but I felt nervous, on edge. I kept glancing toward the water, expecting to see the woman. She did not reappear, but I could not relax.

We ate dinner at a small restaurant by the beach and took the bus back to Mérida.

Of course Marcos was playing a game. The name of the game was get the gringa into bed. I told him so on the bus back to Mérida. "I don't know the rules to this game you're playing. And I don't play games when I don't know the rules."

"You think I'm playing games? I'm sorry you think that." He sat in silence for a while, staring out the window. When we stopped in Mérida, he stood abruptly and headed for the door. "Come on. I will take you to your hotel. No games." I followed him, saying nothing.

Early evening and the shadows were thick in Parque Hidalgo. "Why won't you sleep with me? What are you afraid of?" he asked me as we walked.

I shrugged. I looked in the shadows for the old woman, but I did not see her. But I could not stop looking.

"Maybe I won't see you again," Marcos said. "You don't know what you want, so maybe I won't see you anymore."

"As you like." I was watching the shadows. It seemed to me that there were too many of them, more than other evenings. The lights of the Cine Fantastico sign scarcely penetrated the gloom. A beggar woman in the square called out to me and I jumped, startled. When I gave her a coin, my hand was shaking. I did not know why I was afraid. Nothing had happened. The woman had not threatened me. No reason.

Marcos followed me into the lobby of the hotel and up the stairs to my room. The shadows were darker here, gathering in the corners like dust. The hallway was stuffy, and the shadows crept like rats along the baseboards.

The room was dark. Barbara was not back yet. I unlocked the door but did not step inside, reluctant to venture into the shadows.

"You see," he said, "Barbara is not home yet. She is having a good time at Tixkokob. We can have a good time too." He put his hands on my shoulders and pulled me close to him. I saw the shadows moving and I let him hold me and kiss me on the neck. I wanted protection; I wanted comfort.

Through his jeans and my thin dress, I could feel his cock pressing against me. "Marcos," I said, "wait."

His hand pressed against my ass, rubbing me against him. "You want it," he said. "We'll have a good time." He half lifted me through the open door and pushed it closed behind him with one foot. The shadows were all around us and I clung to him for protection.

"Wait," I said. "Barbara will be back."

"No," he said. "Not yet. Don't be afraid. It'll be all right."

His hand left my back and undid the top buttons of my dress. He fumbled inside, pushing aside the top of my bikini and cupping my breast, rubbing his thumb over the nipple until it hardened under the pressure. My breath came faster and the shadows seemed far away.

"Yes, I like you very much," he said, bringing one hand under me and pushing me down on the bed, taking my breast into his mouth and sucking gently, then harder. I moved against him. I felt warm and the shadows were very far away. He teased the nipple with his teeth. He ran his other hand up my thigh and under my dress, reaching inside my bikini. He had unbuttoned my dress to the waist and pushed my bikini top up around my neck. Both nipples were erect, and he pinched them between his fingers. The fingers of his other hand were inside me, urgently rubbing, stroking.

He lifted the bikini top over my head and pulled the dress down over my shoulders, dragging it under me and stripping away my bikini. The bed creaked when he stood and turned on the ceiling fan. He left his clothing in a heap on the floor and lay on top of me. My hips rose to meet him when he cupped my breasts and thrust deep inside me. The rattle of the ceiling fan drowned out the squeaking of the bed and the sound of my breath coming faster and faster.

I woke up when Barbara came back. The ceiling fan still turned. "Hey," she said softly. "It's time to go back."

I lay still for a moment, pretending that I was still asleep and thinking about the Caribbean coast, the place my mother wanted me to go. Pure white beaches where there were no shadows. Then I sat up and shook my head. "How was the village well?"

She shook her head and flicked on the light switch. "The village well is tucked away in a secluded limestone cave. No laughing children. No village women. I had to throw Emilio in to cool him down." She turned her head and I saw two bright red hickeys on her neck. "But not until after he had made his mark."

"You decided you weren't going to sleep with him?"

"I actually think he likes it better this way," she said. "It's a power game, and sleeping with him would end the game. I think."

"We'll find out." I stretched beneath the covers. "I slept with Marcos, so the game may be over." The shadows in the room were just ordinary shadows, nothing more.

"Yeah?" Barbara perched on the edge of the bed. "So how was it?"

I frowned. My memories were a jumble of shadows and urgency. "A bit quick for my taste."

"Ah, those hot-blooded Mexican men," she said.

I got out of bed. I showered and dressed while Barbara camouflaged her hickeys beneath a layer of calamine lotion. We drove back to camp through the evening gloom.

Chapter Nineteen: Elizabeth

SUNDAY was Etz'nab, a day of pain and sacrifice. I woke up
feeling dizzy and aching, with no appetite for breakfast. I
lingered in my hut, avoiding Tony, until late morning, when
I went for a walk to the tomb site. En route, I saw an old
man stirring a ceramic pot that was warming over a small
fire. The resinous scent of sap filled the air. The woven cloth
bag that lay on the ground beside him was dusted with dark
blue clay; the carved wooden stick with which he stirred the
pot was tinted a vivid blue.

Blue is the color that the ancient Maya painted the cakes of
incense that they burned in ceremonies. Blue is the color they
paint the victims that are sacrificed to honor the gods.

I did not like the look of the old man and his pot of paint. I
walked past quickly and did not look back.

The students dragged into camp that evening, battered by
civilization. On every dig there are times like this. People are
weary from the rigors of field camp and dissatisfied with the
limited civilization within reach. Relationships grow strained.
Maggie and Carlos were squabbling because a casual fling
had gone on too long; Robin and John were clinging together
because departure and separation were approaching too fast.
Field school had only three weeks to run.

Diane and Barbara came in late. I was sitting in the plaza
when they returned, drinking still another pot of hot tea.

Diane said hello, then headed for the hut. She seemed quiet, dispirited, but I did not pursue her. I did not know what to say to her.

Monday was Cauac, governed by the celestial dragon who brings tempests, thunder, and wild rains. I woke before breakfast and went walking. On the way to the cenote I saw a stoneworker chipping thin blades of obsidian, ceremonial blades of amazing sharpness. He smiled as he worked and I did not stop to watch him.

At breakfast on Monday there was little talk, but that little was stormy. Barbara had misplaced the rope she used for site mapping on survey and there was no peace until she found it, coiled in a corner of Tony's hut where she had dropped it on Friday. The survey crew stumbled out of camp half an hour late.

John and Robin had apparently disagreed over something—I could not guess what—and they ate in silence. John left early for the tomb site; Robin strode off to the lab. Tempers were short and people were itchy and restless.

I went to the tomb site at nine and found John shaking the sifter. He wore a red bandanna tied over his nose and mouth to block the clouds of dust that rose as he shook the rectangular screen, sifting potsherds and stone chips from the dirt. When I hailed him, he laid the sifter down, waited a moment for the dust to clear, then pulled down the bandanna, exposing clean skin. "We're finding chips of flint," he said. "And a few large potsherds. And we have something that looks a hell of a lot like a wall."

The flint was a good sign. Generally, the fill that led to Mayan burials and tombs contained flint chips.

The workman who was carrying a bucket of dirt up the eight stone steps from the lower level grinned when he saw me, recognizing the opportunity for a break. He asked if I wanted to take a look at the work so far. His grin widened when I said yes, and he called down to the other two workmen. Their jeans were stiff with dirt; their bare chests were powdered with white limestone dust. I offered each one a cigarette and they retired to the shade to smoke.

I stepped down into the tunnel and blinked for a moment in the sudden darkness. The air was humid and smelled of sweat. The passageway ran about six feet beyond the last step, dark and narrow enough to be oppressive. A pickax, a trowel, a whisk broom, and a bucket lay on the stone floor where the men had abandoned them.

John was right: the stones at the end of the passageway did look like a hastily constructed wall. The stones were not as neatly aligned as the stones of the side walls, but they were not as jumbled as the ones that the workmen had extracted from the passageway.

"What do you think?" John asked. He had stopped on the bottommost step. "A dead end?"

"Have them clean it up a bit," I said, pointing to the side walls. The corner where the walls met the floor was filled with dirt. "They're getting careless. Document this, then go on through."

I took the larger sherds back to Tony for analysis. I left the sherds, described briefly the situation at the tomb site, and retreated to my hut to rest. The fever made me weary, light-headed.

That evening, I sat in the plaza after dinner, drinking gin and listening to Robin and Tony discuss the sherds. Tony had dated a large gray sherd to the late Pure Florescent Period, at about the time that construction of new buildings at Dzibilchaltún had ceased. He speculated that the largest sherd was a piece of water jar. The clay was coarse-grained and tempered with calcite sand; the jar had been burnished slightly when leather-dry and coated with a layer of wet clay, the slip that gave the jar its gray finish. I did not care about the particulars as much as I did about the conclusion. "No earlier than A.D. 900," Tony said. That fit with my estimates and with the date we had deciphered on the capstone of the tomb. Whatever was beyond the wall dated from about the time that the Mayan cities had been abandoned, sometime after the Toltecs had invaded this region.

Tony and Robin went on about the sherd for a long time, but I stopped listening. Maggie sat at a nearby table, writing a letter. Probably a note to a boyfriend back home. Diane shared her lantern light, reading a paperback novel. I watched her, but she never turned a page. Occasionally, she looked up, stared out into the darkness beyond the lantern light, then returned to the same page. She started when I sat down beside her.

"How was survey?" I asked her.

"OK."

"The book any good?"

She shrugged and showed me the cover. A romance novel by the look of it. "Not much choice in Mérida," she said. "It was this or a western."

"Are you finding archaeology a little dull?"

She shook her head with a quick jerk. "Not really " She sat with her hands in her lap, clutching the book. She did not look at me. The darkness was all around us. Tony and Robin were absorbed in their discussion; Maggie had left for her hut.

"What did you and Barbara do this weekend?" I asked.

"We visited Chichén Itzá on Saturday."

"What did you think of it?"

She bit her lip, staring out into the darkness. "I don't know. I thought . . . I didn't like some of the carvings. Skulls. Jaguars holding human hearts. It seemed pretty harsh."

"That's the influence of the Toltecs," I said. "A group from the Valley of Mexico that invaded this area and took Chichén Itzá as their capital city. Most of the Mayan sites show the Toltec influence in later years. The warrior on the stela you found is a Toltec. The woman at his feet is a Mayan goddess. The original Mayan work is buried beneath the work of their conquerors."

"What happened to the Maya?"

I shrugged uncomfortably. "They worked the fields and went on living their lives, I suppose. Added the new gods to their pantheon. People who were unwilling to accept the new ways kept quiet or died, I would guess." I stopped talking. "You must be getting bored with all this."

"Not bored."

I waited, but she did not continue. She gazed off into the shadows, and I could not read the expression on her face. The muscles in her neck were tense. "What, then?" I asked.

She glanced at me. One hand tapped the book restlessly into the palm of her other hand. "I feel like I'm waiting for something to happen. Sometimes I'm afraid."

"Afraid of what?" My voice was low.

She shrugged, a quick jerk of the shoulders, as if she were shaking off an insect. "I don't know. If I knew, maybe I could do something." She shook her head. "Or maybe not."

"You could go to Cancún," I said urgently. "I will meet you there after the dig is over. The Caribbean coast is—"

"No," she said. "I'll stay."

She went to bed shortly after that. I returned to the table with Tony and Barbara and listened to them talk. Tony, I noticed, was not drinking. After a time, I went to bed myself.

The week passed. We were short on workers. The incident with the stela had frightened a number of the older men away. But our luck improved.

I did not see Zuhuy-kak. I looked for her, but I did not see her. When I went walking in the morning to look for her, I met Diane by the cenote. When I went walking in the evening, I met Diane by the Temple of the Dolls. When we met, we returned to camp together in silence. I had little to say to her. I felt I had already said too much, drawn her in too close.

Wednesday was Ahau, the day of the sun, a favorable day. No equipment broke down; no men fell sick. I could not quite shake the fever, and it made me restless and irritable. I was content only when I was sitting at the tomb site, watching the men work. But even there I was plagued by chills and shivering.

I dreamed that night, strange vivid feverish dreams. I remember dancing in the rain, holding an obsidian blade. The moon shone down, almost full, and I was young again. My robes swirled about me. A feeling of power that surged through me, a great ancient power that stemmed from the moon.

Thursday was Imix, the day of the earth monster, a dragon-like creature with a protuberant nose. A good day for digging, for taking things to their roots. Late in the afternoon, Pich finally worked one stone of the wall free, pulling it from the place where it had rested for a thousand years.

I was on site—I spent most of the working day on site—and I went down into the tunnel. Cool moist air blew through the gap in the wall. With a flashlight, I peered through the opening, trying with little success to see what lay beyond the wall. A large open space, a low platform, vague pale shapes that could be pots or skulls—I could see little. The wall was about a yard thick.

The workmen stayed late on Thursday, but at five o'clock it was clear that we would not remove another stone that day. We stopped then, covered the opening with a tarp, and reluctantly left the site.

I went to the cenote that night after dinner and I sat by the pool, listening to the sound of the crickets and watching the shadows of peasant women come to fetch water. Zuhuy-kak did not come to join me. My daughter did not come. I was alone, and when the moon rose, I went to bed.

Friday was Akbal, a day of darkness. It is governed by the jaguar in its night aspect, lord of the underworld.

On Friday, Tony went with me to the site. By noon, the workmen had loosened and removed another stone, making an opening large enough for me to slide through on my belly, pushing my flashlight before me.

The skeleton lay on a stone slab, flat on her back with her legs stretched out. Her rib cage had collapsed; the flashlight beam shone on a jumble of pale crescent-shaped bones and glinted from the smooth jade beads scattered among the ribs and vertebrae. One arm lay over her ribs and across the pelvic girdle; the small bones of her hand were strewn between her thighbones. The other arm was crossed over her chest and the finger bones were lost in the confusion of ribs and vertebrae. The bones of her feet and toes had been scattered, perhaps by mice scavenging for food. Not far from the arm that was crossed over her chest, an obsidian blade lay on the stone platform. Nearby, the stone was stained by a splash of red: cinnabar spilled from the scallop shell that lay beside her.

Her skull was deformed, flattened at a steep angle to make an elongated expanse of forehead. Her mouth had fallen open and the teeth were intact. I recognized Zuhuy-kak by the jade inlays in her front teeth. A white shape lay by her pelvis and I played the light on it: the conch shell that had dangled from her belt. One thighbone had a knot in its center: a break that had not healed properly.

I heard Tony slide through the narrow gap behind me. His flashlight beam played over the pots that surrounded the skeleton: a jug in the shape of a turkey, a cream-colored three-legged bowl painted with glyphs, a squat vase in the shape of a spiraling shell, an incense burner in the shape of a jaguar, an assortment of bowls, jars, jugs, and vessels.

Tony's flashlight stopped, spotlighting a large bowl at the skeleton's feet, a vessel as big around as the circle I could make with my arms. It was elaborately decorated with glyphs and pictures. The ceramic lid had been knocked askew. Tony stepped closer, peering into the bowl, then gently lifted the lid aside.

A skull the size of a large grapefruit smiled out at us—a dark-eyed child whose teeth had long since left the jaws. Smooth and pale, the skull nestled among the curving ribs and long bones like an egg among twigs. Here and there, the bones were touched with cinnabar. By the look of things, the skeleton of the child had been disinterred, cleaned, dusted with cinnabar, packed neatly in the bowl, and buried again. I stepped closer, and the dark sockets of the eyes, set low beneath the flattened forehead, followed me. So frail: I could easily snap these ancient ribs in my hands. So young. The bones had been arranged with care, gently placed in the bowl, and I wondered who had tended to them.

In the end, the grand movements of civilizations matter little. What matters is the skull of a child beside the skeleton of its mother. I glanced up at Zuhuy-kak's skeleton and the

obsidian blade beside her. What mattered was how this child
had died. A cool damp breeze touched me and I shivered.

"It goes on," Tony said, and for a moment I did not
understand. Then I followed his flashlight beam with my
gaze and realized that the darkness was a sloping passage,
the beginning of a limestone cavern extending down beneath the
earth. The limestone walls were studded with fossil seashells.
The hairs on my arms prickled and my skin rose in goose
bumps. I could smell water somewhere far away. No sound
but Tony's breathing and mine. He stepped toward the opening.

"No," I said sharply. "Don't go in there."

It was not until he looked back at me that I realized I had
spoken too loudly.

"Is something wrong?" he said, stepping toward me.

"No," I said, "nothing."

"We have our work cut out for us," he said. "I hadn't
counted on spelunking."

"We aren't equipped for it," I said. I played my flashlight
over the walls and knew that there were shadows just beyond
the reach of the beam. I did not want Tony to go into the
cave. I did not want anyone to go into the cave.

"That's never stopped us from doing anything before," he
said. "I'll see if John wants to organize an expedition
tomorrow."

We began excavation of the burial that day, setting John
and Robin to work with trowels and whisks while the men
continued bringing down the wall. When the survey crew
returned, they all trooped down to the site and exclaimed
over the skeleton. We finally quit working when the sun went
down.

—— Chapter Twenty: Diane ——

ON Friday night, I woke to the sound of stealthy footsteps on the path. The hut was dark. Barbara breathed in a steady rhythm. Maggie mumbled something in her sleep and shifted uneasily in her hammock. Robin breathed softly, like a small animal curled in a burrow.

I don't know what woke me—a change in the song of the crickets, the hooting of an owl, something. I don't know. But I sat up in my hammock and stared out through the open door, then left my hammock and stood by the opening. The dirt floor was cool beneath my bare feet.

The lights were out; the moon was down. The sky was immense, endless blackness dotted with too many stars. Even Tony was asleep—the light by his hut was out. A bat flew overhead, briefly blocking out the stars and chittering in a high-pitched excited voice.

I saw something move in the shadows near the water barrel. I watched carefully, and it moved again, a darker shadow within the shadows. "Is someone there?" I said softly, not wanting to wake the others. "Who is it?"

No answer. I thought I knew the answer: waiting in the shadows was an old woman dressed in blue.

In the starlight, the world was black-and-white, a late feature on a black-and-white TV. In late-night movies, monsters live in the shadows. The heroine always goes to investigate and the monsters always get her. Always. When I

watched late-night horror movies, I never knew why the
heroine didn't just go back to bed and pull the covers over
her head and sleep until morning, when the sun would come
out and the birds would sing and the vampires and were-
wolves would go back into hiding. I was no late-night-feature
heroine; I could go back to bed and sleep until morning.

Except for the uncertainty. The lingering doubt that had
been nagging at me since I saw the old woman in the monte.
The suspicion, faint but growing stronger, that I was going to
be as crazy as my mother someday soon. I was afraid of
things that were not there. I saw shadows by day; I heard
noises at night. When I was not aware of them, my hands
formed fists—they were doing it now.

I snatched my flashlight from the table, slipped through the
door, and hurried along the path toward the shadow, hurrying
because if I did not hurry I might go back to bed and lie
awake all night, listening for the sound of footsteps coming
nearer.

The figure beside the water barrel did not move as I
approached. I shone my flashlight beam into the shadows,
and my mother blinked in the sudden light. Tousle-headed,
clad in blue pajamas, barefoot, and blinking like an owl. Her
eyes were large and her face was haggard. I touched her
shoulder and felt the frail bones beneath the thin layers of
cloth and flesh. She was trembling. "What are you doing
here?" I asked. "What's going on?"

"I'm watching over the child," she said. Her eyes had
turned away from the light, but they focused on nothing.

"You scared me," I said. "You didn't answer when I
called." She was not listening.

"Someone must watch over the child," she insisted. "She's
too young to be left alone." She was looking at my face, but
I didn't think she saw me. "I can't run away again."

I put my arm around her shoulder and tried to turn her
away from the hut. She would not move. I could feel her
trembling.

"I'll watch her," I said. "I'll keep her safe."

"You must be very careful," she said to me owlishly.

"She is stubborn and she doesn't want to leave. But it isn't safe here."

"I'll be careful."

"How do I know I can trust you?"

"I'm a friend of hers. A very good friend." I hesitated, then said softly, "Tell me—what must I watch for?"

"The old woman," she said, blinking into the shadows. "Watch out for the old woman."

She let me lead her through the silent camp to her hut. In her hut, I lit the candle on the desk. The big stone head watched from the corner as I helped my mother to bed. I used the sheet that had been bunched at one end of the hammock to cover her. Her skin was hot and dry, and I wondered if she were running a fever. She tossed and turned in her sleep. When she spoke in Maya to people I could not see, I told her that everything would be all right. I hoped that I was not lying. I sat beside her, listening to the sounds outside and holding her hand.

When the faint gray light of dawn shone through the open door, my mother was sleeping quietly. I blew out the candle and returned to my hut. I had just finished dressing when Barbara woke.

"Come on," I told her. "Let's get out of here."

She blinked at me sleepily. "Hey, give me a minute to wake up."

I waited for her to roll out of bed and dress, and we walked out into the plaza. "I was thinking of sticking around here to see what Liz turns up in the tomb today," she said. "After all, this is our first big find."

"Whatever's in the tomb now will still be there on Monday," I said. "Are you willing to go without a hot shower to see it one day sooner?"

"You've got a point there." She stopped at the water barrel and splashed water onto her face. "You sure are eager to go to town all of a sudden. Did Marcos steal your heart?"

I shook my head, wondering how much I could tell Barbara. "I just need to get out of here."

"More troubles with Liz?"

I nodded.

She studied my face, then shrugged. "I suppose you're right. The secrets of the ancient Maya can't really compete with a hot shower. Let's go."

We arrived in town early in the morning and had breakfast at the usual table beneath the trees that shed yellow flowers like a cat sheds fur. Emilio arrived with his hammocks at the usual hour, bought the customary round of coffee.

It was Barbara, not I, who asked about Marcos. Marcos, it seemed, was busy that day; he had business that took him elsewhere. Emilio was evasive; he would not look at me. Barbara frowned and asked him a few questions in Spanish, then shook her head. We finished our coffee in silence, then Emilio said that he would be selling hammocks in the zocalo. He would meet us at lunchtime, he said.

After Emilio left, Barbara ordered more coffee. "It seems we were right about the game," she said. "You all right?"

"I'm fine. If he's busy, he's busy." I shrugged. "I don't care."

"You can stop being polite," she said. "Emilio's gone."

"I really don't care. It doesn't make any difference."

She looked at my hands. "You're shredding that napkin," she said quietly.

I put the pieces of paper napkin down on the checkered tablecloth. "It shouldn't make a difference," I said. "He doesn't mean anything to me. It doesn't matter."

"What a stupid asshole," she said.

I shrugged again. "No big deal."

"Look," she said, leaning forward and putting her hand on mine. "I know it's not a big deal. I know your heart isn't broken or anything like that. But it's still no good. You can get mad about it if you want."

I sipped my coffee, watching a blind beggar trying to sell a badly carved wooden animal to the couple at the next table.

"Think I should tell Emilio to buzz off?"

"Why? It's not his fault."

"Whatever you want." She leaned back in her chair and

spooned more sugar into her coffee. "Maybe we should get out of town today. Go tour the ruins at Uxmal. Something different."

"I'm all right," I told her. "I don't care."

She studied my face, then nodded. "Have it your way. What do you want to do? Go swimming?"

"Fine."

We went swimming in the hotel pool, a tiny patch of water in a turquoise concrete basin. I lay on the cement by the side of the pool and tried to read the paperback romance, a stupid story about beautiful people who always wore the right clothes. The world of the heroine was filled with vague anxieties, overblown fears. I felt right at home.

Barbara swam and periodically tried to get me to talk. After an hour of this, I told Barbara that I wasn't hungry; she and Emilio should eat without me. "I think I'll wander around in the market. Maybe buy a dress. I'll meet you back here."

I walked. I didn't go to the market; I wasn't up for the crowds. I wandered around the zocalo, bought a lemon ice from a sidewalk vendor, and sat down on a bench near the cathedral to eat it. The clock on the Municipal Palace said it was one-thirty, but it seemed much later. The air was heavy with the promise of rain.

I didn't miss Marcos. I had expected little of him. He was a person to cling to when the shadows came, no more. But now, I didn't even have that.

Two withered women wrapped in dark red shawls sat on the pavement before the cathedral, begging coins from passing strangers. The two middle-aged women who sold gilt-framed pictures of saints at the cathedral door were closing up shop, wrapping the garish frames in newspaper and stacking them in a cardboard box. Above their heads, pigeons trudged up and down on the stone lintel.

On the sidewalk, tourists strolled up and down. A neatly dressed woman with a sunburned nose was exclaiming over postcards. A man in a new panama hat was taking a picture of the Municipal Palace. All strangers. None of them would understand if I told them I was afraid that my mother was crazy, afraid that I might be crazy. They would not understand that I was being haunted by an old woman who looked like the stone head in my mother's hut.

I thought about calling my former lover, Brian. I hadn't spoken to him since I quit my job. What could I tell him? I'm seeing ghosts and I think my mother is crazy. No, I could tell him nothing.

I was afraid. A friend of mine had a dog that would chase after the spot of light cast by a flashlight beam, unable to catch it and unable to leave it alone. The dog would run after the spot on the floor and bark when it ran up the walls, until he collapsed with exhaustion. Poor dog could never figure out that he could never catch the spot. I felt like the dog. I did not know the rules and there was no one to tell me. It was like chasing a spot of light. Or like trying to catch soap bubbles as they drifted on the breeze. You end up with handfuls of nothing.

I did not see the curandera approach. She sat beside me on the bench and took my hand, holding it tightly in her warm dry hands. She said something to me in a low urgent voice and I shook my head. I didn't understand. I tried to free my hand, but she would not let go. She called out to a passing hammock vendor and he came near. Still holding my hand, she spoke quickly to him. He glanced at me curiously, amused by the situation.

"Do you speak English?" I asked him. "Can you tell her to let me go?"

"A little," he said. He spoke to the woman and she shook her head and said something else.

"She wants me to tell you . . ." He hesitated, as if searching for the right words. "You got to go away," he said at last. "Don't go back to your mother."

"What are you talking about? Why shouldn't I go back?"

He shrugged. "She says that your luck is bad." He shrugged again. "That is what she says."

"Tell her that I understand," I said. I looked at the old woman and she stared back. *"Yo comprendo."* Her grip on my hand loosened and I freed myself. I stood then, backing away from her.

"Hey," the hammock vendor called after me. "You want to buy a hammock?"

I was stumbling away, almost running across the zocalo. Thunder rolled across the sky, bumping from cloud to cloud. I went back to the hotel to get my bag and found Barbara and Emilio at the usual table. I told Barbara that I was going to catch a cab back to camp. When she protested, I just shrugged. I knew that I had to go back. I did not know why the old woman wanted to chase me away from my mother, but I knew I had to go back.

The first fat drops of rain began falling as I ran from the hotel across the square to the taxi stand. The bronze man on the pillar glistened in a flash of lightning. He stared out over my head, ignoring my hurried negotiations with the cabby.

The road to the ruins seemed longer in the rain. The taxi driver tried to talk to me. I think he was complaining about driving in the storm, but I just shrugged, understanding only a few of the words. I watched the shapes in the moving rain, never clear but always present. Once, I almost called to the driver to tell him to stop—I saw an old woman crossing the road. But she vanished into the rain, a shadow, nothing more. Thunder rolled overhead like the crash of falling monuments.

—— Chapter Twenty-one: Elizabeth ——

I woke on Saturday, the day Kan, as stiff and sore as if I had been hiking through the monte in my sleep. The sky was overcast and the morning was half over. I stopped by the kitchen and Maria gave me—reluctantly, I thought—a breakfast of atole. Barbara and Diane had left for Mérida; Tony was nowhere to be seen.

This day is governed by the smooth-faced young god who makes the maize grow. It is a good day, by most accounts, favorable for beginning new projects and continuing old ones. I considered this as I sat in the plaza and ate my atole. Then I gathered my equipment and went to the tomb.

I was halfway there when Zuhuy-kak fell into step beside me. She limped slightly and I remembered seeing the knotted thighbone that caused her pain. I looked at her broad face and knew the smooth white surfaces beneath it. I glanced at her, but did not speak.

"Are you happy with the secrets you have found?" she asked. When she spoke, I remembered the skull's gaping mouth.

We had reached the mouth of the tomb. I did not acknowledge Zuhuy-kak's presence. I pulled aside the tarpaulin that covered the excavation, and descended the steps into the tomb. In the passageway, I lit the Coleman lantern, reached through the opening to set it on the floor of the tomb, and squirmed in after it.

In the tomb, it was still night, governed by the jaguar, the dark aspect of the sun. The lantern cast a circle of light that faded before it reached the ceiling. In the silent darkness, I could hear my heart beating quickly, as if I had run a long distance. I lifted the lantern high and looked toward the back of the tomb. The floor sloped away, ending in darkness. Caves are the entrance to Xibalba, the Mayan underworld inhabited by gods of death and sacrifice. Cold air from the underworld stirred the hairs on my arm and I shivered. On the mottled stone wall of the tomb my shadow shifted and changed, monstrous and strange. I saw Zuhuy-kak standing at the edge of the circle of lantern light, watching me.

On Friday, we had begun clearing the area, brushing away the loose dirt. Our initial work had uncovered a vase that lay on its side on the floor near the skeleton's head. I set the lantern on the stone dais, so that the vase fell within the pool of light.

I knelt by the vase. On Friday, I had started cleaning it, but the vessel was still half covered with soft dirt and bits of straw brought in by generations of rodents. I used my whisk broom to brush the upper surface clean.

"I made that vase," Zuhuy-kak said. "When I emerged from the well, while I lay on the pallet, I painted it."

I noticed that my hands were shaking and I stopped for a moment, waiting for the trembling to subside before I continued my work. I breathed deeply. I could still feel a trembling deep inside me, but my hands were still. I recognized one glyph—the place glyph for Chichén Itzá. On the side of the pot, just below the band of glyphs, I could make out a thin black outline on the cream-colored pottery. I continued brushing. The dirt brushed away easily now, revealing the elaborate headdress of a priest or nobleman. The black outline was his hand, which was raised above his head. He was looking down, at something beyond and below him.

I continued brushing the dirt from the pot. The half inch of rim that I had exposed was circled with a band of black marks on a red background: glyphs that were scratched and illegible in the dim lantern light. On the vase, a priest stood on a cliff with a group of other priests and nobles. All of them looked down. My whisk broom uncovered feet first, then her blue dress, fluttering around her as she fell. Her hair was streaming behind her. The falling woman. The priest's hands were raised because he had cast her off the cliff. Her arms were crossed on her breast; her eyes were open and staring. She saw something, but I did not know what it was. She was falling through empty space, just as she had been falling for many years.

The glaze at the base of the vase was scratched, but I could make out curling waves of turbulent water, black swirls on the cream-colored background. In the swirls, between the cracks and gaps in the glaze, I could see an upthrown arm and a weeping face, several small figures struggling against the serpentine coils of the water.

"I brought that vase with me when I came down here," she said. "I wanted it with me. I brought my daughter's bones."

I heard the rain begin to fall outside the tomb. The tarp flapped in the wind and the water trickled down the steps—I could hear the soft liquid sound, like a cat licking itself.

I used my trowel to remove the soil surrounding the vase, transferring the loosely packed dirt and detritus to a bucket. The vase was almost free of its cradle of soil. When I brushed it, it moved slightly, rocking in place. I stopped for a moment, waiting for the trembling in my hands to stop. Then, with care, I lifted the vase from the soil.

The glaze on the side that had faced the ground was pitted and cracked, but the picture was still intact. The woman in blue—the falling woman—lay on a platform. At her feet lay a conch—a symbol of the water from which she had emerged and of the underworld where the sun dies and is reborn. One hand held a leaf-shaped obsidian blade. Her other arm was extended to display a bloody gash from which blood flowed. She was smiling and her expression was triumphant.

"You killed yourself here," I said.

"There was no one else left to kill me," she said softly.

''The goddess had no power and I had sent the people away.''

Zuhuy-kak was sitting on the edge of the stone dais, and she seemed as solid as the bones that lay beside her. She sat with her shoulders hunched forward, staring at her folded hands. For a moment, I felt sympathy for this poor mad ghost, exiled by her own doing, lost and alone. Without thinking, I reached out toward her. She looked up and I stopped.

''How did your daughter die?'' I asked.

Zuhuy-kak met my gaze. Her hands were folded in her lap. For a moment, she said nothing. ''I gave her to the goddess,'' she said at last.

''You sacrificed your daughter,'' I said, staring at the woman's face.

Zuhuy-kak did not speak for a moment. ''The ah-nunob were coming and the battle was not going well,'' she said. ''We had captured their warriors. I killed them at the altar and we heaped their skulls in the courtyards, but that was not enough.''

Her hands were grasping each other tightly. She turned her gaze toward the darkness at the back of the cave and swayed forward and back almost as if she rocked a child in her arms. She spoke in a singsong tone. ''There had been much killing, so much killing on the battlefield and in the temple. My husband, a man of power and nobility, a good man, had died that week on the field. The scent of blood hung thick and heavy in the air, overflowing the temple, filling the courtyard, spilling out of the sacred places and flowing down the sacbe, a river of rich red scent laced with the smoke of burning incense. The sound of the drum and the rattle followed me everywhere, beating like my own heart, steady and strong. Like my own heart.''

She had drawn her folded hands up to her breast, and she was rocking back and forth, back and forth to a drumbeat that I could not hear. Her words came quickly now. ''The smoke, the smell of blood, the cries of the wounded tended by the healers—these seemed natural things.'' She had closed her eyes. "I gave my child to the gods to stop the coming of the ah-nunob. I meant it to be a willing sacrifice, a gift. I prepared her, dressed her, and perfumed her, gave her balche mixed with herbs to drink. I took her to the place of sacrifice, filled with the power of the goddess. She did not struggle. She smiled at me, because I had told her that Ixtab would come and take her to paradise. She was afraid, but she smiled up at me. And at the moment that I was bringing the blade down, when the power of the goddess should have been greatest, I doubted. My daughter looked up at me, and I doubted the power of the goddess." She opened her eyes and the strange light that filled them reminded me of the madwoman who claimed to be Jesus Christ. "I doubted and the ah-nunob took the city. The cycle turned and the goddess lost her power."

My stomach ached, a solid steady pain that reminded me of the aching in my gut that plagued me throughout my pregnancy. A sad and heavy feeling, as if I carried a burden that was too great. The doctor who attended me during pregnancy said it was nothing, it was psychosomatic. Many pregnant women felt unhappy, he said; it wasn't abnormal. He said that they felt unhappy—I remember that. It did not seem to cross his mind that maybe they had good reason to feel unhappy, maybe they were in pain, maybe they carried a weight that was too great to bear. I wondered what the doctor would say now.

"Now it is time for the cycle to turn again. You can bring the goddess back to power. Your daughter—"

"No," I said.

"You can," she said. I noticed then that she was holding the obsidian blade. "It will be easy. And then, once it is done, you can rest."

"No."

"You are like me," she said. "I know you. I knew you when I saw you by the well. You too made a sacrifice that was not good. You began falling just as I began falling when my daughter died and the power of the goddess died with

her. I began falling long before the priests threw me in the
well," she said.

"You can rest now," I said. "You can stop."

"I tried to stop. When the people were leaving and the city
was in confusion. I asked two masons to wall me in, and they
did it for me. They walled me in and I stopped here. I wanted
to rest. But there is no rest. The cycle is turning again. The
time is near for sacrifices to be made. Once they are made,
we can rest, you and I."

"You can rest," I said. "There is no need for you to be
here. There will be no sacrifices, no blood spilled."

She looked at me with eyes as dark as the darkness beyond
the tomb. "Why are you here?" She did not wait for my
answer. "You are here because you want to learn secrets.
You want them, and at the same time, you are afraid to learn
them. You want power, but you fear it. You fear that you
will learn what you are capable of doing." She ran her finger
along the obsidian blade. "There will be blood."

She held it out, and I took it. Held it in my hand and
drew it gently along the skin of my wrist, testing the blade,
just testing it. Blood beaded in its wake and I felt a new
warmth and strength travel up my arm and into my heart. The
touch of the cold obsidian recalled my suicide attempt. I
remembered the feeling of heated anticipation, the sense that
the pain I felt was insignificant beside the power I would
gain. I watched the blood trickle from the wound in my arm
and I felt warm and strong.

Chapter Twenty-two: Diane

I paid the cabby and ran out into the rain. Behind me, I heard him gun his engine and roar away.

My mother's hut was deserted. Both doors were open and the rain had swept in, dampening the dirt floor. A plastic poncho hung on a nail, and after a moment's hesitation I pulled it on over my dress and headed back into the rain. I didn't know exactly why I wanted to see my mother right away. I think I had some idea that I would tell her about the old woman that I had seen, and then we would discuss the whole thing like adults, separating phantasms from reality carefully, bit by bit.

I followed the path to the tomb, splashing recklessly through the puddles in my sandals. I was already soaked; a little more water made no difference. Once, I slipped and banged my knee on the ground, and after that I limped.

The mouth of the tomb was a dark spot on the plaza floor. As I stepped down into the passageway, I felt a faint breeze that carried the scent of newly turned earth. The rain was splashing down the stairs into the tomb. Over the sound of the rain I could hear my mother's voice. I could not make out the words.

On the last step, my leather sandals slipped on the wet stone. I lost my balance, stepped into the puddle that covered the floor of the passageway, and almost fell. A beam of white lantern light shone through the gap between the stones.

The light beam shifted as my mother lifted the lantern up to the gap in the stones.

"Hello," I called to her. "I thought you might be up here."

I could see only her head, silhouetted in the gap.

"I came back from Mérida early," I said. "There really isn't much to do there. Barbara stayed, but I came back." My words trailed off. I could hear the rain trickling down the steps behind me, a river feeding the cold lake that lapped around my ankles. "It's pouring out there." I stood awkwardly in the puddle, waiting for her to move aside, to invite me to look at what she was doing, to say something. Water dripped from my hair down my back. The poncho clung to my bare arms and legs. I lifted it over my head and draped it over the handle of a pickax that stood, head down, in the water. I kicked off my wet shoes and set them in the metal bucket beside the pickax. The bucket was not yet floating, though it was a near thing. Uninvited, I squeezed through the opening, and my mother stepped back to let me through.

The walls arched high over my head, and the light of the lantern did not reach the ceiling. Here and there, the light reflected from seashells, embedded in the rock long ago. A skeleton lay outstretched on a stone platform, staring up into the darkness with blank eyes. My mother's notebook, trowel, and whisk broom lay on the floor near the skeleton's head. She stood near the skeleton, staring at me fixedly. In one hand, she held the lantern, gripping the wire handle. In the other, she held an obsidian blade. Her right wrist was bleeding. "You cut yourself," I said.

"Why did you come back?" she asked. Her voice was rough, hoarse.

"There didn't seem to be any reason to stay in Mérida," I said.

She was shaking her head. "What brings you hiking through a downpour in sandals and a dress?"

I looked down at myself. My shins were marked with mud and a line of dark droplets oozed from a scratch where a thorny branch had raked across my skin. My dress was soaked despite the poncho. "I guess I should have stopped to change."

"You shouldn't be here. You should have stayed in Mérida." She sounded on the verge of tears.

"I'm sorry. I . . ." I didn't know what to say. I held out my hands in a gesture of resignation and tried to smile. "What can I do? Can you tell me what's wrong?"

She took a step back as if I had threatened her and stopped beside the stone platform. She shivered like a wet dog. She looked thin and tired. "Go away," she said. "Please. Get out of here."

"It's raining," I said, trying to sound reasonable. "I'll stay out of the way. I just—"

"Get out!" Her words echoed from the stone walls, and I stepped back, the smile dying on my face. She straightened her shoulders and stepped forward. Her face was suddenly hard. "Go away from here! Now!"

I backed away. "I'm sorry. I just—"

"Get out!" Her face was a mask, washed from below with lantern light. Her eyes were wild, touched with red and too large for her face. She threw back her head and cried out again, not a word, but a groan, a wail of desperation. The muscles of her neck stood out in ridges and her breath came in great gasps. I took a step toward her and she glared at me, shaking her head like an animal tormented by flies. She lifted one hand in a fist, and as I stepped back, she struck herself in the leg, once, twice, three times, each blow hard enough to make me wince. "Go!" she said. "Go! Go away." The last words were not shouted. The blow did not have the force of the ones preceding it.

I stood by the opening. I could hear the soft trickle of water flowing down the steps, but the pounding of the rain had ceased. "The rain has stopped," I said to her, as calmly as I could. "I can head back to camp. Why don't you come back with me?"

Her hand was clenched in a fist, resting against her thigh. "You have to go."

"I'll go if you come with me."

The breath left her in a sigh and she seemed to shrink, her shoulders relaxing, her grip on the lantern easing. "All right," she said. "You go out."

I slipped through the opening and stayed right on the other side, where I could look through the wall. Newly washed light shone down the stone stairs and made a faint rectangle on the floor. The puddle was already lower. Water had drained away into the earth. "I'm right here," I said. "Why don't you hand me the lantern and then come on through?"

"Yes," she said and handed me the lantern. I stepped back and let her come through after me.

"That's good," I said.

She stopped in the center of the passage and turned to look at me, frowning though her face was still wet with tears. "No need to talk to me as if I were a fool. You may think I'm crazy, but don't think I'm stupid." She took the lantern from my hands, extinguished the light, and led the way up the stone steps into the steaming afternoon. She did not look back.

—— Chapter Twenty-three: Elizabeth ——

SUNDAY was Chicchan, the day of the celestial serpent. Carlos, Maggie, John, and Robin returned to the dig for dinner in the late afternoon, clean and well rested. With a tomb to excavate, a cave to explore, and only two weeks of field school to go, they were cheerful. Over dinner, they chattered about what they planned to do before returning to school. Carlos and Maggie were planning to spend a week on Isla Mujeres. John and Robin were heading south; they planned to travel through Belize and visit Mayan ruins at Altun Ha and Xunantunich. They all seemed so light-hearted, like sparrows that land for a moment on a garden path, squabble over crumbs, then fly away. Diane was subdued, taking no part in the conversation. I caught her watching me surreptitiously, then looking away when I turned to meet her gaze. She and Tony both watched me and I wondered if they had talked to each other since Diane met me at the tomb.

Barbara came in late, well after dinner. I was in my hut trying to rest and shake the fever that still sang in my ears. I heard the distant rumble of Barbara's Volkswagen and wondered if Diane would talk to Barbara, tell her of our conversation in the tomb, where I had lost my temper. I did not leave my hut to greet her.

When I tried to sleep, the sounds in the night disturbed me: the crickets, the palm thatch in the breeze, the footsteps of someone—I think it was Carlos—heading to his hut. When I slept, I dreamed of the obsidian blade that lay beside the skeleton in the tomb.

In the dream, I stood in the kitchen of the apartment in Los Angeles, holding the obsidian blade in my hand. I ran a finger across the edge to test its sharpness. I liked the feel of it—cool and sharp, with just the right weight. It was thirsty for blood. Sitting across the kitchen table from me was a young woman who was drinking a beer and listening to the water heater rumble. She looked at me and said something that I could not make out. I offered her the obsidian blade and she stood up, backing away from me. Somewhere very far away, a child was crying.

The kitchen was gone, the young woman was gone, but I knew that the child was still crying. I was in a very dark place and I went to search for the child. I was very tired, bone-tired—all I wanted to do was lie down and rest—but I had to find the child. I wandered, disoriented and confused, carrying the obsidian blade in my hand.

I stood in the doorway to the hut, listening to a chorus of breathing and crickets. Barbara—I think it was Barbara—muttered something in her sleep and shifted position, making her hammock sway gently. She sighed deeply, then her breathing became regular again. I could see the dark copper glint of Diane's hair in the darkness. Her breath came and went softly and easily—so gentle, so easily stopped.

When Diane was four—a cherubic child with soft green eyes—she would wake in the night with bad dreams, come to the bedroom I shared with Robert, and stand silently in the doorway. Somehow, I always woke, always knew to look toward the door where a diminutive apparition stood, waiting patiently for recognition. On those nights, I would take her back to her room and lie beside her in a bed that was over-populated with stuffed toys. In the darkness, she would tell me garbled tales of faces that came to her at night, of shadows that moved in the closet. I never told her that the faces and shadows were not real; I only told her that they would not hurt her. She was safe.

I stood in the doorway and listened to her breathing,

wondering why she did not wake to find me standing there.
Something had to be done with the blade that I carried.
Something had to be done to complete the cycle of time. I
started to take a step toward her, into the hut, but a hand on
my shoulder stopped me.

Tony, still fully dressed, stood just behind me. "What's
going on?" he said softly. "What are you doing?"

I shrugged my shoulder, still adrift in memories. "Watching over the child," I said, and my voice was as soft as the
dust beneath my bare feet. I blinked and a few stray tears
completed their journey down my face and fell.

Tony wrapped an arm around my shoulders and steered me
toward my hut. His arm was warm and comforting; he smelled
of tobacco. He dried my face with a dusty bandanna.

"What's wrong, Liz?" he asked me. "What is it?"

I shook my head. Words were hard to find in the soft
darkness that surrounded me. "The old woman in the tomb
says that the cycle must be completed. The child must die,
just as her child died." The words were soft. My own voice
seemed distant. "I must be careful. You understand that,
don't you? I must keep the child safe."

"Who is the old woman in the tomb?" he asked.

"Her name is Zuhuy-kak. She's the one who made them
leave the cities, long ago. She's a strong woman, very stubborn. I talk to her, but I'm afraid of her."

"The woman in the tomb is dead, Liz."

"That is why she is so strong. She is stronger than I am.
And she's crazy, crazier than I am. She wants me to kill the
child."

"I'll take care of you, Liz," he said. "It'll be all right."

"Who will take care of the child?" I asked. "I'm so tired,
but who will take care of the child?"

His hand rubbed my shoulders gently. "I'll take care of
her too," he said. "You know that. But you've got to rest."
His hand felt cool on my forehead. "You have a fever." One
hand was on my shoulder; one hand took my hand. He
hesitated, feeling the new scratch on my wrist. "What's
this?"

I looked at the thin red scratch and muttered, "I was testing the blade. That's all."

He led me into the hut and helped me into my hammock. I noticed that I no longer carried the obsidian blade, and I knew that it had returned to the tomb.

I sat up in the hammock, clinging to the strings to keep from floating away. I was very light and my head was too large for my body. I had to cling to the hammock or I knew I would drift away. I swung my legs over the edge of the hammock, still holding onto its side. Then Tony was beside me again, his hand on my shoulder gently pushing me back. "I have to go to the tomb," I said. "I have to talk to the old woman."

"You're not going anywhere, Liz," Tony said. "You're staying right here."

"I have to find her. I have to tell her that she can't have the child. She can have me, but she can't have the child. I have to tell her."

"I'll go to the tomb," he said. "I'll tell her."

"You promise?" I said. "You will go to the tomb? You promise?"

"I promise."

I lay back in the hammock and closed my eyes. "Be careful," I said softly. "Be very careful." I heard the rattle of pills, the splash of water pouring from canteen into coffee cup. He gave me the small red pills that brought sleep, and I took them, holding his rough hand tightly. I drifted away into sleep, listening to him softly tell me that everything would be all right.

I woke at dawn on Monday, the day Cimi, the name day of the god of death. Not a lucky day. I woke with vague drug-hazed memories of the night before. My bare feet were dusty and my bottle of sleeping pills was on my desk beside my coffee cup.

I went to find Tony, but he was not in his hut. The chickens that scratched in the plaza and the little pig that slept in the shade stared at me as if I were the first person to stir. Tony was not at the cenote. I continued along the path toward the tomb.

I was almost to the tomb when I saw him. He lay motionless, sprawled halfway across the path as if he had fallen in the act of crawling toward camp. Flies rose when I ran to him and buzzed curiously around my head when I knelt beside him.

His red bandanna was knotted around his leg just above the knee. He had slashed the leg of his pants with his knife to expose the wound: a dark mass of blood surrounded by the swollen flesh of his calf. Through the blood I could make out two ragged slashes, separated by about half an inch, the distance between the fangs of a snake. Bright fresh blood still bubbled slowly from the wound.

His breathing was shallow and uneven. His pulse was rapid. His skin was the color of the limestone blocks around him, slightly cool and damp to the touch. I called to him, shook him lightly, but there was no response. I pulled back an eyelid: his eye was bloodshot and the pupil was a pinpoint.

I hooked his arm over my shoulder and tried to drag him to his feet, but I could not lift him. I tried again, the blood singing in my ears, the beat of my own heart loud in the stillness of the morning. I succeeded in walking three paces before we both fell.

I caught him as we went down, almost wrenching an ankle and catching most of my weight on one knee. "Tony," I said. "Goddamn you, Tony. You have to help."

His breathing caught in his throat, then started again. He did not move. I laid him on the barren path, irrationally put my hat under his head as a pillow, then moved it to shield his face from the sun. I pulled his shredded pants leg to cover the open wound, and ran for camp.

I did not run well. I was too old for running. The sun was a hot blur low in the sky. My lungs were useless for drawing air, though they made noisy ragged gasping sounds. I felt as if I were watching from a distance: an old woman, hobbled by the passage of years, ran slowly down a barren trail, fighting to draw air into lungs clogged with cigarette smoke, struggling to shout for help across the ruins where genera-

tions had lived and died. As I ran, I swore that if Tony lived,
I would give up cigarettes. I would give them up. I did not
know to what gods I swore, but I swore I would stop
smoking to save him. The ache in my side was as bright and
hot and sharp as the wound from an obsidian blade.

Once, in the shifting light that sparkled through tears, I
thought I saw an old woman dressed in blue on the path
ahead of me. If I had had the breath, I would have cursed her,
but I could not curse or call to her. I tried to run faster, but I
could not catch her. She was far away, just a figure in the
distance.

The camp was still silent. I tried to shout, but I had no
breath for it. I reached Salvador's truck, parked outside the
plaza, and reached in through the open window to lean on the
horn, holding it down and letting it blare as if the length of
the sound would somehow dictate the speed of Salvador's
response. I could see Salvador step from his hut, a tiny figure
in the distance, shirtless and hatless. I released the horn and
blew it again. He ran toward me.

"Tony," I said when he reached me. "Snakebite." I
jerked my head in the direction of the tomb. "Unconscious
by the trail." He began swearing under his breath in Spanish,
a steady stream of curses.

It took too long to get to Tony. Salvador drove the truck
over the old sacbe as far as he could. The truck lurched
unwillingly over gullies and bumps, and the frame creaked
and groaned. Once, after a particularly nasty bump, I heard
something crack sharply, but nothing gave. Salvador left me
behind when he ran up the trail to where Tony lay. I was
toiling toward the tomb when I met Salvador coming down the
path. He was carrying Tony, cradling the old man in his arms
as if he were a child. The muscles on Salvador's bare brown
shoulders glistened in the sun, and Tony looked even frailer,
smaller.

It took too long to get to the hospital. Salvador drove like a
madman, but it seemed slow. He skidded in the gravel on the
shoulder as he passed a tourist bus that was lumbering down
the center of the road. A man on a road-repair crew leapt

aside as Salvador's truck raced by, refusing to slow down. Tony was slumped on the seat beside me, his head in my lap. Over the rumble of the truck, I listened to his labored breathing. We had reached the outskirts of Mérida when his breathing faltered and stopped, and I began mouth-to-mouth resuscitation, a steadying task that made me feel like I was accomplishing something.

At Hospital Juárez, two young attendants took over, clapping a respirator over Tony's face and carting him away. I felt cold, listening to the soft babble of voices in the hospital waiting room. The walls were painted white and pastel green, marred by scuff marks near the floor. A young woman with classic Mayan features sat on an orange plastic chair. She held a baby that wailed steadily in constant complaint. The woman crooned soft comforting words in Maya; she told the infant the same tired lie over and over: it will be all right; it will be all right. An old woman in a wrinkled huipil spoke softly to an old man who wore a bandage over half his face; they leaned together like the stones of a corbeled arch. The old man watched us with his one good eye. A young man, wearing the straw hat and loose clothing of a worker on a hacienda, clutched a white cloth to his arm; I could see the bright red of blood seeping through the cloth. When we walked past him, I caught a whiff of aguardiente— late night in the bars. Salvador and I found two plastic chairs, sat, and waited.

The nurse who called my name wore a stiff blue-striped dress with a white apron. Her dark hair was tucked beneath her nurse's cap. I followed her, listening to the stiff rustling of her skirt. She took me to a tiny airless office, where an officious young doctor asked me questions about Tony. The doctor was thin-faced and he wore the scent of disinfectant like an aftershave. I disliked him immediately.

I recited Tony's full name, age, residence, and professional affiliation. Each question seemed to come to me from farther away, as if the doctor were fading in the distance.

"I don't know how long he was there," I said. "I hadn't seen him since the night before. I suppose he must have been out walking very early.'' My voice was dull. In my imagination, I could see the snake, still sluggish from the cool night air, basking in the sun. I imagined Tony, preoccupied with the necessity of locking up his friend and colleague in the nuthouse, stumbling up the trail. I guessed he had not slept after he left me: he sat alone, drinking and considering the shadows.

"Why would he have been walking so early?"

"I don't know."

I knew, but I did not care to say. Why would he stumble through the monte in the pale light of dawn? Because someone he cared for was crazy; she was talking about secrets in the shadows. He was thinking about me and he did not see the snake.

Tony died in the early afternoon without regaining consciousness. The doctor's English was very good, but I heard a note of disapproval under his professional tone of sympathy. "He had been drinking heavily," the young doctor said. "That's probably why he was unable to reach the camp and seek help." He knew so little of the world, this young doctor. He seemed to think that heavy drinking was unusual.

Salvador was there, standing just behind my chair. An orderly had loaned him a shirt that was much too small for him. The shirt was unbuttoned.

"Would you like the body prepared for transport to the States?" the young doctor asked.

He had pens in his pocket and a stethoscope around his neck. He knew nothing of rocks, ruins, herbs, and old bones. Yet his face, as he looked down at the form on his desk, was a match, feature for feature, for the face of the young maize god of the hieroglyphics. He belonged to the rocks and the ruins, this young doctor, but he did not know it.

He looked up from the form and repeated the question. Salvador laid a hand on my shoulder. "Yes," I said then. "Yes. Have the body prepared."

From a pay phone in the hallway, I contacted the university and spoke to the department secretary, a woman my age who knew everything about everyone. She was appropriately shocked, yet still willing to ask—tactfully and carefully—about the circumstances. I did not like this woman and under normal circumstances she did not like me. But now her voice flooded with sympathy and false warmth.

"How terrible," she kept saying. "How terrible."

I could only agree wearily. She was a tinny voice coming to me from far away. She was not real. As I stood in the white hall, listening to her reassurances and sympathy, an orderly walked by. I watched his shadow move on the white wall. Here in the hospital, shadows had edges. They did not blur, one into the other. Here, people were alive or dead, conscious or unconscious. No gray zones of uncertainty. After explaining to the secretary that I would make arrangements to ship the body, after promising that I would call her on the next day, I hung up.

"Perhaps you should stay here in town, señora," Salvador said. "I will go to camp."

I shook my head. "You know I have to go back."

Salvador shrugged, a tiny movement of his shoulders. He was a practical man. He did not argue. He drove back to camp with the careful dignity of a man in a funeral procession. We said little to each other. I had nothing to say.

Camp was quiet. A thin ribbon of smoke drifted up from the kitchen; Maria was burning dinner. Barbara, John, Robin, and Diane were sitting in the plaza; they came to the truck as we pulled up.

"Tony died at Hospital Juárez this afternoon," I said. "Snakebite." They were all looking at me, their faces blurring in the heat and the tears. I had one hand on the open door of the truck, leaning on it for support. "Snakebite and bad luck," I said. Barbara started toward me but I waved her back. It was Cimi, the day of death, and touching me was not a safe thing to do.

"Pack your things," I said to them. "Go to Mérida for the night. We will do no work tomorrow or the next day. Tomorrow is a holiday." I did not tell them that tomorrow would be the beginning of the end. The first of the last five days of the Mayan year. Bad-luck days.

They were watching me, uncertain and confused. I summoned the voice of authority from my distant past, from lecture halls where, fearing the hungry young faces that watched me, I made my voice like a whip and told them what to do. I spoke as a teacher, hard-edged and irascible, no lingering trace of softness. I told them to pack their bags. I told them to leave. Carlos and Maggie had come up from the cenote, summoned by the sound of the truck. They stood, still dripping, just behind the others. I looked at Diane and spoke to them all. "Leave this place," I said. "Come back later and pack up the camp, but leave now. Tony would want you to go."

They watched me blankly and I remembered countless dusty lecture halls where I fought to give blank faces pieces of my dreams, to describe for them the worlds of the past that they would never glimpse, carefully cloaking my thoughts in the words of the professor, the scholar, the archaeologist, careful lest someone think I believed too much in my own dreams, that I saw too well, lived in a different world. "Go," I said. "Go now."

I left them there. I went to my own hut, as if to pack, but I took a flashlight and headed along the path to the tomb. It was late afternoon. The air was heavy with moisture and the sky hung low with clouds. I found my hat in the dust where Salvador had left it. I picked it up, beat it against my knee to knock the dust free, straightened the brim, and carried it as I continued down the trail. I was not willing to wear it now.

A few hundred yards farther down the path, I passed the spot where Tony had dropped his gin bottle. The shards of clear glass glittered in the afternoon sun. He must have dropped the bottle when he fell. Beside the trail, the grass was crushed and the ground was marked with blood.

I kept walking along the path. I was halfway to the tomb when Zuhuy-kak joined me. She kept pace with me.

Beside the mound, near a stone that would have made a comfortable seat, I saw burnt leavings of tobacco, emptied from a pipe. Tony had rested here, thinking about me, an old friend who was in trouble. Considering how he could help.

He had rested here until sunrise, struggling with demons less visible than my own, then headed to camp, meeting the snake on his way down.

The old woman was still with me. I could hear her sandals scraping lightly against the sandy ground. I turned on her suddenly. "Why do you follow me?" I asked her.

"The time is coming," she said. Her voice was very soft, like the gentle hissing when the wind blows dust over temple stones. "The year is ending."

"Why did Tony die?" I said suddenly. In the bright sunlight of late afternoon she was as solid as the silent stones around us.

"Your enemies seek to stop you," she said. Her voice was even and devoid of any expression. "I told you that."

"My life is nothing like yours," I said. "I did not sacrifice my daughter, I will not be hurled into the well."

"The year grows old and things happen," she said. "Perhaps not the same things that happened in my time. Nevertheless, things happen."

"Leave me alone," I said to her.

"It will do you no good to ignore me," she said.

"It did me no good to speak to you," I said. I turned away from her. I climbed down into the pit without looking back.

It was cool and quiet in the inner chamber. I flashed the light on the skeleton. That lay quiet at least. Her daughter's skull peered out of the nest of bones.

"I used that. blade," Zuhuy-kak said, jerking her head toward the obsidian knife that lay on the stone platform. "It is very sharp. Her pain will be brief."

I picked up the blade and tested the edge. Still sharp: a bright bead of blood formed on my thumb. I inspected the old scars on my wrists. The skin was thin and vulnerable. But Tony would not approve if I bled on a valuable artifact. I could use my pocketknife instead.

"Not yet," Zuhuy-kak said. "First your daughter, then yourself."

"I sent my daughter away."

The woman was not listening to me. She lifted her head as if she heard something outside the tomb, and she smiled.

"Liz?" My daughter's voice came from the dark gap that led to the outside world. "Are you there? Are you all right?"

What do you do when you are falling? Do you reach out and try to grab for support? If you aren't careful, you will pull others down with you. Unless you are very careful.

A flashlight beam found the gap in the wall, filling it with yellow light. Diane's head followed the beam.

"You don't belong here," I said. "Go back."

The hand that held the flashlight was trembling. "You can't tell me what to do." She climbed through the opening into the tomb.

"No." I took a step back, away from her. Shadows nestled in her eyes, making them into dark hollows, like the eyes of a skull.

She stepped toward me, holding out a hand in supplication or threat—I could not tell which. I backed away, the blade in my hand, retreating into the cave. I was not afraid of these shadows. I wasn't afraid of death; dying was an easy way out. I could not name the thing I feared, but I saw it in the reaching hand of my daughter.

I broke and ran, scurrying away like a bewildered rat in an unfamiliar warren. Some dark instinct had overtaken me, driving me to escape, to dart down any tunnel that led away from the light, to crawl where I could not run, to squeeze through narrow passages, rushing just ahead of the pursuing flashlight beam, a nocturnal animal seeking the safety of darkness.

She was just behind me, always just behind me. "Liz?" I dropped my light and did not linger to retrieve it. I could hear her behind me as I blundered forward, hands out like a blind man, touching the cool walls and the rounded stalactites.

"Mother?" she said, and the voice was so near that I leapt forward. I did not land for a long time. I fell in the warm velvet darkness, knowing that this was what had to happen, this was the destiny of the katun that was to come.

*   *   *

I woke with a sharp pain in my leg and the chill of water around me. For a moment, I thought I floated in the Sacred Well, but I opened my eyes to darkness. I was resting in a puddle of chill water, cupped in a low basin of limestone. My hips were in the water; my shoulders, on the rock. My leg was twisted beneath me, stabbing with a pain that distracted me from the aching of my head. I drew a deep breath and lifted myself on my arms, trying to straighten the leg, an effort that made me cry out in pain.

In response to the cry, like an answer from the gods, a beam of light flashed down from above, blinding me and making me cry out again. I could not see the source of the light—it was a bright spot high above me—but I recognized my daughter's voice. Her voice was ragged. "Why did you run? You shouldn't have run."

I squinted up into the beam. "That's so." My voice was as rough as the limestone beneath me. I was calmer now. The instinct that had made me run was contained. I looked down at myself, and by the light of Diane's flashlight I could see the twisted leg. Broken, I thought. When I tried to shift my weight and support it on my hands, I felt the bones grind. For a moment the flashlight seemed to fade and my head filled with a dull red thundering darkness.

When I could hear again, my daughter's panicky voice stabbed me from above. "Are you all right? Say something. Are you all right?"

"My leg is broken," I told her, my voice rasping. "You've got to go back and get help."

"I can't." The light did not waver from my face. Her voice was thin and strained, on the edge of tears. "I don't know the way. I lost track. You were going too fast."

There was a moment of quiet in which I could hear water dripping, a sweet, high sound. I looked around me. Beside the pool, a stalagmite rose from the limestone floor to meet a stalactite that reached down from the ceiling. Beside this pillar was a rounded stone, an altar of sorts. Pots and clay figurines clustered around the base of the pillar. On the distant walls, I could see paintings: Ix Chebel Yax watched me from the wall, and the serpent coiled on her headdress grinned. In one hand, she held a thunderbolt; in her other hand, a scrap of the rainbow. Women danced before her, and a child, painted bright blue, lay across the altar, her chest arched back to receive the knife.

"Why did you run?" she asked. "Why did you run from me?"

The water dripped, a steady liquid music. My leg throbbed, but as long as I did not move, I was spared the shooting pains that made me cry out. I did not answer my daughter because I had no answers. What would satisfy her? I had been dreaming of blood. I held an obsidian blade in my hands and I feared that I was capable of much. I knew that soon I would die, and that death would spare me the necessity of providing answers.

"I'm crazy too," my daughter was saying softly. I shivered in the darkness. "Shadows follow me. The old woman follows me."

"Not crazy," I said, but the words were an effort. The chill of the water had filled my bones and my voice was stiff with the cold. I could not stop shivering.

"Call it what you like." The light moved, as if she had shifted position. "What difference does it make? I'm lost up here and you're lost down there. I can't get down. We're not going anywhere. It doesn't matter."

"Salvador will find you."

"I doubt that."

I closed my eyes against the light. Surely it would not be so hard to pull myself out of the water. The limestone sloped at a gentle angle. Not so hard. I would die, but I did not want to die in the water. I opened my eyes and planted my hands against the bottom of the pool. The first shove moved me two inches higher on the slope and made me cry out like a beaten dog. I took a breath and pushed again, gaining another inch. Again. I knew that if I stopped, I would not begin again, and so I did not stop. I lost count after the tenth time I pushed. By that time, the cries had given way to a constant whimpering that rose and fell with the pain.

I stopped when I was stretched out on dry land. My leg was more or less straight. It was easier to bear the pain when I was still than when I was moving. I rested, then realized that my daughter had been talking to me for some time now. Coming back from the faraway place that I had been visiting, I opened my eyes. "What?"

"Do you remember the Christmas that you gave me a quetzal shirt from Guatemala?"

I lay on my back, listening to the dripping water. "Yes."

"Why didn't you let me come with you when you left?"

There are questions that have no right answers. "I couldn't."

"That's not a good enough answer."

I closed my eyes and remembered that Christmas. Diane had followed me to the car and asked me if she could come. Her face had been open, vulnerable, filled with raw need. "I couldn't take care of you. I could barely take care of myself. I wanted you to be safe. I knew Robert would protect you."

"I would have taken care of myself. I wanted—"

"You wanted too much." The words came out as a shout. "You still want too much."

The shivering had returned and the pain was increasing. I kept my eyes open now—when I closed them I was alone with the pain. The cold water had numbed the leg, but that had worn off.

"I'm sorry," I said then. "I'm sorry. I shouldn't have been a mother. I—"

"Why did you leave?"

"I had to."

"Why didn't you take me?"

"I couldn't take care of you." I was tired, so tired I wanted to die. "I couldn't." The same questions, the same answers, over and over. The pain rose in me and I said softly, "I'm not sorry I left. I had to leave. I loved you and I wanted to stay, but I couldn't."

Her words drifted down like snowflakes on a winter day. "I hate you."

"All right," I said softly. "I understand that." Perhaps Zuhuy-kak was right. She and I did have much in common.

We had both made sacrifices that were unacceptable. We had both failed.

I closed my eyes and began to find my way back to the distant place where I could not feel the pain.

"Mother?" The cry called me back.

"I'm here."

"What are the shadows that follow me?"

"Shadows of the past," I muttered to the darkness. I tried to raise myself up on one elbow, but the movement shot a new pain through my leg and I sank back down, letting my cheek rest on the cool rough stone. "You'll get used to them."

There was more I wanted to tell her, but I could not remember what it was. She seemed far away, farther than she had ever been. I closed my eyes and went away.

Chapter Twenty-four: Diane

> When one hunts for man as I have done,
> even dead men and their ruins, one goes
> up, high into the mountains where they
> may have fled and built in some final ex-
> tremity, as at Machu Picchu, or down into
> deep arroyos where their bones may pro-
> trude from the walls, or their mineralized
> jaws gape in the gravel fans. Or one enters
> caves and with luck comes out again, but
> not necessarily with treasure.
>
> —Loren Eiseley,
> *All the Strange Hours*

MY mother lay broken at the base of the limestone wall and I did not know the way out of the cave. She did not respond when I shouted at her. "Liz? Mother? Goddamn you, you can't leave me here. You have to help. Liz?"

The cavern echoed back my words and the darkness was filled with curses. "Wake up. Get up. Just get up!" The words rolled like thunder from wall to wall to wall, crashing and repeating. I shone the flashlight down at her crumpled body.

"All right then—you can be dead. I don't care. You can be dead!" Then with a rush, words abandoned me and I was wailing in anger, a cry that began as a low moan, growing louder and rising to a shrill keening that hurt my ears, joining echoes on echoes on echoes. I tried to stop the sound, but it would not be contained; it spilled from me like water overflowing a dam. I beat my open hands against the ragged edge of the limestone cliff, feeling the pain and letting it feed the howling. My face was wet and hot, and I could not stop crying. It was my mother's fault, all of it—the anger, the howling, the blood on my hands, and the terrible pain. Most of all the pain.

Through the tears, I saw a shadow moving at the edge of the flashlight beam. The old woman stood watching me. I fumbled for a loose rock to throw, found nothing, and with a quick movement snatched my sandals off my feet and hurled them at her—right foot, then left. She faded back into the darkness and I laughed, a sound akin to the howl of pain.

My mother lay broken at the foot of the cliff. She would not wake up. She wanted to leave me here, alone in the dark. I would not let her. She had to wake up and talk to me. I looked about for something to throw at her to wake her, but there was nothing. My sandals were lost in the darkness behind me, and I did not want to throw the flashlight. I studied the limestone cliff and decided to climb down and stop her from leaving me alone again.

The wall was pockmarked and uneven, studded with fossil shells. I wedged the flashlight in the back pocket of my jeans and lowered myself carefully over the edge, feeling with my feet for holds. My breath came in short gasping sobs, like the panting of a dog after a hard run. The sharp edges of the limestone etched new cuts on my feet and stung the gashes on my hands. The flashlight in my pocket moved with the movements of my hips, and its beam chased shadows on the cavern ceiling.

About halfway down, a foothold gave way beneath me, leaving me dangling by my arms and scrambling for another hold. A little farther, a rock came loose in my hand and I clung to the sheer face, groping with my worn and bloody hand. I found a protruding rock, tested it by pulling gently, then tugging hard. Then I trusted my weight to it and continued down.

My arms and legs were trembling when I reached the bottom. I was breathing heavily and tears blurred my vision. I stood over my mother and looked down at her. She lay on her back, one arm crossed over her chest and one stretched down to rest on the thigh of her injured leg. Her face was very pale in the flashlight beam. I knelt beside her and laid my hand on her forehead. Her skin was cool and moist to the touch.

"It's not that easy," I muttered. "You can't get out of it that easy. I won't let you." I was talking to myself, a low continuous murmuring of curses and abuse. I knew that I was talking to myself, but decided that it was all right. No one would hear. I was not myself just now. "Goddamn it, you're not leaving me here. I won't let you die."

I could not remember what to do for shock victims: elevate the feet or the head or both? I left her as she was. She moaned softly and tried to move away when I used her pocketknife to slit her pants so that I could examine her leg. The flesh was purplish and swelling around a lump in the middle of her calf. She moaned again when I pulled on her ankle to straighten the leg. I had nothing to splint it with except for a metal folding rule from her pocket, but I tied that in place with strips of cloth cut from her pants leg. My hands were shaking, but I ignored that. It took me three tries to knot the last strip of cloth. All the while I muttered curses and wiped sweat out of my eyes.

Her face was still and calm. Her wet shirt clung to her and I could see how thin she was—frail and small-boned and weak. I swore at her as she lay on the limestone floor, telling her that she couldn't get away with this, she couldn't run from me this time.

The cloth strips that held the splint in place were marked with dark spots; my hands and feet were still bleeding. With cool water from the pool, I washed the blood from my hands. The water stung at first, but it seemed to numb the cuts. I washed my face and splashed water on my arms.

I turned off the flashlight for a moment and sat in the darkness, listening to my mother breathe. Shallow and rapid, but steady. She wasn't going anywhere just yet. I heard the sound of wings and flashed the light toward the ceiling in time to spotlight a bat as it flitted past. I switched the light off and heard the sound again, another bat hurrying toward some unknown destination.

I didn't mind the darkness so much. It was restful, sitting beside my mother. I held her hand for comfort and listened to the bats. I had grown used to the darkness by the time the lights came—faintly flickering points of yellow and orange in the distance, moving as erratically as fireflies or glowing spots before my eyes. I stood up and peered toward them. They did not come from the cliff I had climbed down, but rather from deeper in the cave, through a tunnel I had not noticed. The lights bobbed toward us, growing larger and brighter.

"Over here," I shouted. "We're here."

The cavern echoed my voice, and then was silent. No reply. The lights moved no faster. I flicked on the flashlight and waved it, but the lights continued on their steady course, bobbing toward us slowly.

I waited, watching the lights come closer. Torches, I could see now, dozens of them, each one burning with a yellow-orange flame that flared and wavered with the movement of the person carrying it. The light reflected from the walls, catching on the white seashells.

Shadows marched on the cavern walls. Enormous and distorted, like the shadows of hunchbacks and giants and fantastic animals dancing and swaying with the movement of the torches. The people carrying the torches seemed dwarfed by their own shadows.

Feathered robes caught the light and gave it back in pieces. Feathered headdresses swayed rhythmically. Torchlight gleamed on sharp teeth—a fox head stared open-mouthed at the ceiling from the headdress of a fur-clad man. Beneath the fox face, the man's eyes gleamed red. A fox tail swayed between his legs as he danced. Other animals danced beside him: a woman wore the soft brown fur of a deer; a man waved the claws of a jaguar.

I could hear them now: the sound of the drums echoed from the walls so that each beat was multiplied many times, each sharp note repeating over and over. The gourd rattles sang in time with the drum, a steady susurration like waves on the beach. The chanting rose above the rattle and drum, human voices rising and falling in words that I could not understand. There was a wildness to the voices, a passion and urgency. Now and again, the chant was punctuated with a great howl, like a wild animal in torment. The howling seemed to spread through the procession as different voices took up the cry, the animals' heads tipping back to the smoke-darkened roof, and wailing to the gods.

The woman who led them did not walk; she danced, stooping and leaping and spinning in the torchlight, her shadow first a hunchback, then a giant. She wore a blue tunic woven of a thin cloth that let the torchlight pass through, revealing the moving shadow of her body within. She was my age, no older—young and swift. Though her skin glistened with sweat, she danced as if she were fresh, tossing her head so that the feathers laced in her hair bobbed and swayed.

She was coming toward us. I crouched at my mother's side, switching off the flashlight and moving closer to her, putting one arm around her thin shoulders. I could see the leader clearly now. One of her cheeks was marked with dark spirals, and the delicate skin beneath her eyes was painted with red lines, radiating outward like the rays from a child's drawing of the sun. Her black hair was tied back with a braided leather thong, and quetzal feathers were woven into the braids. A black object that looked like the head of a monkey dangled from a leather strap around her waist. A jade bead strung on a leather thong dangled from her right ear.

I recognized her then. She was the old woman whose face was on the stone head. Younger now, graceful and filled with life.

In a wide place on the other side of the pool, she danced. The others formed a circle around her, a respectful gathering of dark tattooed faces and glistening bodies. The air was thick with the smell of incense and smoke. The sound of the drums and chanting filled the cavern until the trembling in my hands seemed like a response to the sound. When the dancing woman threw back her head and howled, I clenched my fists and groaned at sudden pain from the cuts and gashes.

She held something high over her head. The torchlight caught on it: an obsidian blade. For the first time I noticed the rock formation around which she danced: a raised platform that made a natural altar. The animal cry began in the back of the crowd and passed like a wave through the sea, gathering strength until the limestone seemed to shake with it. The crowd swayed with the dancing woman, and the torchlight flickered on the bright murals that decorated the walls.

At first, I did not notice the child who stood beside the altar. I was watching the dancing woman as she used the blade to slash at her own wrists, making shallow cuts that bled profusely. With the blood, she anointed the altar, leaving dark smears that shone in the torchlight.

The child was dressed in blue, and her face and hands were smeared with blue as well. The little girl was watching the woman, her eyes wide and fascinated. Her face had been painted bright blue, the color of the sky in the late afternoon. The paint had been brushed on carefully; only her lips and her dark brown eyes were free of it. She held her hands clasped just under her chin, and they too were bright blue. The child moved with the rhythm of the dancing woman, rocking to and fro. Around them, chanting voices were as deep and low as the rumble of the earth.

As I watched, the dancing woman accepted a gourd bowl from a young man and took it to the child. The woman knelt, lifted the child's hands so that she held the bowl, and guided the bowl to her lips. The child drank and the cavern echoed with another howl. The sound startled the child, and though she was finished drinking, she clung to the bowl, staring around her. The woman in blue tickled her hands with one of the feathers, and the little girl let go of the bowl, distracted.

The woman touched the child's head gently, then picked her up and carried her in her arms as she danced.

The beat of the drum was faster now, and the woman whirled with the child. The girl was laughing now and reaching for the bright fluttering feathers in the woman's hair. One small hand clutched a feather triumphantly. The woman danced faster, whirling, her eyes gleaming in the torchlight.

The dancer set the laughing child on the stone altar. She lay on her back, her arms stretched to either side like a child lying in the grass on a summer day. She was smeared with blood from the dancer's wrists and in one hand she clutched a blue feather. The dancer undid the child's belt and tenderly folded back the blue robe. I saw the child laugh when the woman tickled her chin with another feather, but I could not hear the sound over the chanting. The child's eyes were half closed, and she looked as if she were falling asleep.

Four men in white loincloths stepped from the waiting circle and each one took hold of an arm or a leg. The little girl smiled up at the dancer, waiting for the next game to begin. The dancer lifted the obsidian blade, hesitated for an instant, then plunged the blade into the child's chest. The howl of the crowd drowned out any sound she might have made.

I cried out and closed my eyes and I must have squeezed my mother's hand because she stirred, pulling weakly against my hand. She said something, but I could not hear her over the drums and rattles. I leaned closer and watched her lips. She was struggling for consciousness, but losing the fight. She lay still, her hand once again limp in mine.

The altar was bloody; the four men were spattered with dark spots. The dancer held something dark and small over her head. Though the beat of the drum continued, her dance faltered. There was a new hesitation in her step and the drumbeat slowed, the chanting grew softer.

I saw the runner coming before the crowd surrounding the altar noticed him. A single torch bobbed toward them, growing larger. I saw a shadow taking long strides, then saw the runner in the torchlight: a young boy clad only in a loincloth.

He held the torch in his left hand; his right arm bled from a wound in his shoulder. He stumbled as he came toward the crowd, and he must have cried out, for some of the men turned to look, then ran to help him.

The chant faltered. The drumbeat continued, but people crowded around the boy, pressing close to him. The drumbeat stopped. I noticed now, seeing the people gather around the boy, that the men in the crowd were gray-haired, limping, toothless.

The chant had given way to the babble of voices. The power was gone. The drum had stopped. The rattles ceased their hissing. The people turned and snatched up torches and surged back the way they had come, away from me, carrying the runner with them.

The woman, the dancer, remained where she was. She had lifted her head to listen to the clamor, but she did not move with the others. A single torch, wedged in a crack in the wall, still burned beside her. The echoing clamor of voices faded in the distance.

The woman crouched beside the altar. Her expression had stiffened. She picked up the blue feather that lay on the cavern floor where the child had dropped it, and smoothed it between her fingers. Then quickly, like someone coming out of a daze, she reached out and caressed the child's cheek. A shadow of doubt crossed her face. Then she hugged the body to her and hid her face in the blue cloth of the robe.

The thunderous power of the chant and the drum remained with me. Watching the woman, I felt that she mourned more than the death of a child. I wondered what news the boy had carried. Somehow, it seemed that his news had changed the value of the child's death. The cavern was dark; the temple had fallen.

She remained like this for a time. I watched her, not knowing whether to fear her or pity her. My head was burning and my heart still beat in the rhythm of the drum. I heard, as if from a great distance, the sound of a woman weeping. I went to her, my head on fire. When she looked up, her eyes

vague and unfocused in the torchlight, I think she saw me. I
don't know.

When she stood, I returned to my mother's side. While the
woman was arranging the blue robe around her daughter's
body, I checked my mother's splint. It was inadequate, but I
could see no way to improve it. I used another strip of cloth
to knot my mother's hands together. Kneeling, I ducked into
the circle of her arms and hoisted her piggyback, leaning
forward so that her body fell against mine, stumbling as I
clambered to my feet, but catching myself before I fell. The
woman was lifting her daughter's body, staggering a little
under the burden. She slung the awkward bundle partly over
one shoulder, so that the child's face, still painted blue and
smeared with blood, looked back at me. In her other hand, the
woman carried the torch. I followed the light of the bobbing
torch as she trudged away from the pool.

She walked slowly, stopping now and then to adjust her
burden, to rest, to get a better grip on her torch. The flickering light of her torch showed me the way. Occasionally, a bat
flew over us—a rustle of wings and a burst of high-pitched
chittering. I listened to our footsteps, to the faraway musical
tinkle of water falling into a pool, to my mother's shallow
breathing. My mother grew heavier, but the woman stopped
frequently, and whenever she did I rested by leaning against
the cavern wall. The girl's dead eyes watched me over the
woman's shoulder.

The smell of incense hung in the air. Sweat trickled down
my back and my jeans clung damply to my legs. The stone
beneath our feet was glossy, worn smooth by the passage of
many feet. Once, I slipped and smashed my knee against the
floor, a new throbbing ache to add to the pain in my feet and
hands. I tried to ignore the pain and watch where we were
going. Was this the second large room filled with stalactites
or the third? Had I been trudging through the darkness for
hours, days, weeks, or years? It didn't matter. My mother's
breath rasped past my ear and I could still walk. That was all
that mattered.

My mother was very heavy. I thought about laying her

down on the floor and lying beside her to rest for a while, but
the torch bobbed on ahead of me and I did not stop. My
footsteps had taken up the rhythm of the drum, a steady beat
that matched the pounding of my heart and the soft sighs of
my mother's breath passing in and out.

The barriers were down. The anger that had surged forth
to make me scream at my mother and pound my hands
bloody against the rocks was still with me, but it had changed.
The first wild surge had made me scream; now I felt a strong
steady current, more like the movement of the tide than like
a crashing wave, or maybe like a big slow river, strong and
smooth and winding as a serpent. It carried me along like a
boat on the tide. The water was dark and murky, and I could
not see beneath the surface. But I had to flow with the river;
I could not resist it.

The great river washed me along, washed me clean of sin,
washed me in the blood of my own hands, washed me
through dark tunnels and caverns into a dead end. Then the
torch winked out; the woman was gone. A dead end.

I lowered my mother to the floor and sat beside her. Her
hands were dark and swollen where the cloth strip had cut off
circulation. I loosened the strips and rubbed her hands to
warm them and make the blood flow. I closed my eyes,
grateful for the rest.

I heard a bat fly overhead, but I was not listening to that. I
was listening to the soft hooting of an owl somewhere in the
darkness outside the cave. I was smelling the cool dry scent
of the monte at night.

My flashlight beam found the opening, a narrow slit
high above me in the wall of the cave. I left my mother
on the cavern floor and started climbing. The wall was
sheer and the handholds were covered with the droppings
of generations of bats. I climbed about five feet, then threw
my arm over a ledge and pushed myself through the narrow
opening.

The monte was dark, but not as dark as the cave. I
lay on my back and listened to the sounds—strange bird-

calls and animal rustlings. It was all right now. I would get my mother out of the cave somehow. Everything would be all right. The owl hooted in the distance and I laughed out loud.

—— Chapter Twenty-five: Elizabeth ——

"Does this path have a heart? If it does, the path is good; if it doesn't, it is of no use. Both paths lead nowhere; but one has a heart, the other doesn't. One makes for a joyful journey; as long as you follow it, you are one with it. The other will make you curse your life. One makes you strong; the other weakens you."
—Carlos Castaneda,
The Teachings of Don Juan

I woke from dreams of falling. I was alone in a Mexican hospital room, with a cast on my leg, a tube in my arm, and a foolish white hospital gown wrapped around my battered old body. When I called out, the nurse came, and I asked her what day it was. She told me that it was Sunday, and I calculated that it was Ahau, the first day of the new year.

Eventually they let Barbara in to talk to me. It seems that my daughter dragged me out of the cave with a rope she found in a shelter that had been built for the convenience of hacienda workers. The cave opening was not far from the hacienda. The locals knew about it, but, like many caves in the Yucatán, it had never been fully explored.

My daughter had carried me out to the road and flagged down a car driven by a Mexican restaurateur, who took one

look at my daughter and another at me and rushed us both to
Hospital Juárez. My daughter was treated for multiple cuts and
bruises, none of them serious. After she was released, she contacted Barbara, waited long enough to be sure that I was in
stable condition, and then left for the States. Barbara gave me a
curious sidelong glance when she told me all this. I don't
believe that she was telling me all that my daughter had told her,
and I said as much. Barbara just shrugged. I did not have the
strength to persist, and I supposed that if my daughter wanted
to keep secrets, she had earned the right.

I slept again, and when I woke Zuhuy-kak had taken
Barbara's place. She was insubstantial here, barely the suggestion of a Mayan woman sitting in a padded plastic-covered
chair. Through her, I could see the electrical tape that had
been used to patch a tear in the plastic upholstery. "Is it
over?" I asked her.

She did not move.

"There are still things I want to know," I told her. "I still
plan to dig up your bones and take another look at that vase."

She shrugged.

"I can't talk to you here," I said to her irritably. "They
won't let me have cigarettes. I think that goddamn American
antismoking propaganda has spread even here."

She faded when the nurse opened the door and I realized
only then that I had been speaking in English the whole time.

I went home a week after Tony. He went home in a box; I
went on crutches. I was asked to speak at his memorial
service, but I begged off, pleading illness. The department
head delivered a fine impersonal eulogy that painted Tony
with a rosy hue, flawless and unnatural as the cherubs that
flanked the altar.

I went back to my apartment in Berkeley, taking my
notebooks. I sent Diane a note, telling her to get in touch
when she felt like it. I did not know what else to say.

My leg did not heal quite right. I limped, especially in wet
weather, and walked with a cane that Barbara had bought for
me in the Mérida market. The university welcomed me back
for the fall semester. In the wake of the publicity attending

the finds at Dzibilchaltún, three publishing houses were vying for the hardcover rights to my still-unfinished book, *City of Stones*. I had laid plans to return to Dzibilchaltún to complete the excavation of the tomb and the ceremonial area. Barbara would be assisting me on the project. I watched the shadows of the past, but none of them spoke to me.

On an overcast day, I had paused on a wooden bridge that spans Strawberry Creek to watch an Indian woman weave a basket from water-softened reeds. Someone leaned on the rail beside me, and I looked up, expecting to see one of my students.

Diane was looking down at the creek. For a moment, she did not look at me. When she did, something seemed different about her. She held herself with a new confidence, a certainty that she had lacked before. "I've come to the conclusion that I'm crazy too," she said. Her voice was steady; she did not seem particularly upset. "It took a while, but I've gotten used to it. In fact, I don't mind it."

She paused for a moment, and I could hear the song that the Indian woman was singing to herself, a wandering melody based on an unfamiliar scale.

"Barbara tells me that you're planning another expedition to Dzibilchaltún," she said. "I'd like to go."

I watched the woman weaving her basket, carefully lacing the reeds together to make an intricate pattern of light and dark. "I don't know what we'll find there," I said.

"You never do know what you'll find when you dig in the past," she said.

"That's true," I said.

"Can I come with you?"

"I think that could be arranged," I said. I turned away from the bridge and Diane offered me her arm. I hesitated a moment, then took her arm.

"Tell me," she said, "about the shadows of the past."

THE BEST IN FANTASY